THE ADVENTURES OF PYC

THE POLICY OF NO RETURNS

Joz Rhodes

©Joz Rhodes

varulv BOOKS

varulvbooks@yahoo.co.uk

© Joz Rhodes 2021

All rights reserved

The moral right of the author has been asserted

The stories contained within this volume are entirely fictitious and do not refer to or represent real persons or situations

This book is sold subject to the conditions that it shall not, by way of trade or otherwise, be lent, re-sold, hired out, or otherwise circulated without the publisher's prior consent in any form of binding or cover other than that in which it is published and without a similar condition including this condition being imposed on the subsequent purchaser

Chapter 1:
The Point of No Returns

"Okay, thankyou, goodbye. See you next time!" Pygott called after the last tentacle creeping out through the door, which folded in on itself and disappeared with a hasty plop the instant it cleared the gap.

Pygott descended the last few steps and headed for the shop counter, feet swishing through the lush carpet. *You're getting rather long again. I'll have to fish out the strimmer before the weekend's done,* he mused. Glad of the distraction from Crone's woebegone expression.

"Is something amiss, Mr. Crone? You look like a man who just lit a match behind a dyspeptic Shoggoth."

"Hmm? What?" He peered up myopically. "Oh, sorry, Mr. Pygott. I didn't see you there. Have you finished taking subscriptions from Mr. Hul'hu?"

"Yes. Another few months of Necronomicon Press titles sourced. He's polite as ever, but it's the Devil to get a returns note from him!"

"And there's all the slime and noxious gases he leaves behind. Is it your turn or mine? I swear I can't remember."

"Don't worry yourself, Mr. Crone. I'll get onto that as soon as I catch the imp that sneaked out of the safe while I sought nuggets for the dwarves this morning."

"Not again?" He gasped. "They're getting so slippery these days. I sometimes wonder why we stock them at all! And on top of all this too..."

Pygott started. It wasn't like Crone to be so sharp. And certainly not on a Friday night. At least that small mercy might give Pygott the chance to discover the root of the problem, before it grew to insoluble proportions. He didn't ask the obvious question though, concluding the answer might already be on its way.

"I told you we should never sold Him that book," Crone hissed as his last customer waddled out of earshot. "And now things are getting out of hand." He added, mysteriously.

"Which book?" mused Pygott, straining to see over Crone's round shoulder. Pretending to enquire after the buying habits of the departing warlock. Pygott actually had more than an inkling about the nature of Crone's real concern, but decided it may be better to goad some confirmation first. Just to be sure.

"*The* book! *You know?* The one we *really* shouldn't have in stock in the first place, let alone sell a copy. It's bad enough that mad Arab wrote it at all, without us letting any Old Nick, Dick or Larry get His hands on it."

"Ah, *that* one. He's hardly *any* Old Nick though, is He?"

"And that makes it better?"

"Well, if you put it like that, maybe not. But He does of course have the highest – or lowest – credentials. And He's a regular customer. A very good one. You can't say we weren't thorough."

"For a book we're not even supposed to have ourselves? A book that doesn't officially exist, for that matter?" muttered Crone.

"Point taken. But it's hardly the first forbidden tome we've sold, is it? Not even the first this week, as it happens..."

"Yes, yes, I know!" Crone shook his head before staring up balefully. "But I think He's *using* it."

Pygott scoffed. *"Using it?* But He can't read it, surely?"

"He must have. It's the only explanation."

"But how? Even *I* haven't read it. And you know how good I am with that sort of thing."

Crone bristled.

"I don't know! But He *is* Lord and Master of the Underworld, Defiler of Vegans, Father of Lies, God's opposite number, blah-de-blah, etc. I wouldn't be at all surprised if He's in charge of old Abdul himself and has him recite chapters while Lucifer's being tucked up in bed, sipping a warm virgin, erm, blood."

"Hmmm. Perhaps I ought to defer to your better judgement. But I must say, I'm not entirely convinced. At any rate, the more important question begs what you think we ought to do about it?"

"Well, we must get it back, mustn't we?"

"What? Break our refund policy? Never!" He whipped the air with a defiant pose. "Don't you recall what happened the last time we accepted a return like that?"

"Yes, yes, of course I do." Crone blanched, twitched, shrank minutely. "But that's not how we're going to reclaim this book, is it?"

Pygott's crest fell. Drooped, withered and dropped to the floor with a hefty sigh. The combined weariness of all the world gathered and settled its arse across his shoulders. And Pygott felt the pressure of every ounce.

"Oh, no. Not again. Didn't we do enough damage the last time we took off on one of your little jaunts?"

"Everything was paid for-"

"I meant to us! And myself in particular." Pygott sighed. "There's still the odd night I wake up to find my leg's gone off to raid the fridge. At such times it's difficult to see the humour in it. *Before* you start giggling, thankyou."

"Sorry, but it is rather funny. Apart from finding footprints in the butter, of course."

"And if you recite the 'hopping mad' joke, I swear I'll erect the gallows again."

Crone shivered like a naughty jelly as the giggles took hold, snorting a most embarrassing whistle through one nostril as he fought in vain to stem the onrushing tide.

"Oh, I suppose I'd best leave you to your childishness. Some of us have work to d-" Pygott stopped. Craned his neck and pierced the last shelf with a withering glare. "Hmmm..."

"What?" Crone's good humour scarpered in a flash. "What is it?"

Pygott lowered to a whisper, spewing gobbledegook and waving his hands in tiny, baroque patterns above the counter. He dribbled the last syllable and turned back to Crone, smiling.

"There. That should do it."

Suddenly, there was an almighty scream near the front entrance. Closely followed by a roar of bestial ferocity, tearing, wrenching sounds and splashing, slurping munching.

"Ah, shoplifter," confirmed Crone to himself. "I hope your conjuration hasn't got the book again though, Mr. Pygott?"

"Oh, those damned elementals! Can we never teach them properly? It's as though they don't want to learn. You'd think they'd at least be grateful for the work!"

"Perhaps they learn too well? They'll eat us out of business one of these days. Though at least they clean up most of their own mess once they've finished."

"Which is more than can be said for that damned dwarf you get to look after the shop when we're closed. Which we'll no doubt be forced to do in order to pursue your insane quest."

"Ah! So you're coming around to my way of thinking already. I knew you couldn't resist the sniff of adventure for long," Crone smirked.

"I think it might be more suicidal tendencies coming through..." Pygott surveyed the shop as though he might never walk among its shelves again. "Let's just try to get this affair cleared up before C. T. discovers we've sold a live copy of *The Necronomicon* without permission."

"C. T?"

"Mr. Hul'hu."

"Oh. Yes. I see what you mean. Wouldn't do to get *him* in a bad mood. He leaves such a swathe of destruction behind once he's roused."

"And we'll get no end of esoteric crap landing on our heads if we're found out. Customers only appreciate covert double-dealing when they think they're the only ones receiving special treatment. Our reputation would be ruined." Pygott sighed again. "No matter how deserved the stigma."

Crone, however, grinned uncontrollably. "You really are convinced, aren't you?"

"Well, I suppose I'm swayed more by those pictures of the oil tanker being devoured by that shadowy behemoth on the 6 o'clock news last night. I've been trying to explain it away in a rational fashion; but it seems about time to put two and two together and make glarg."

"Quite right! We'll close early."

"No, no. That won't do. We don't wish to arouse suspicion, do we? It's now the weekend and we're staying open till dawn, as usual. Then we'll close up and be ready to set off after lunch. It should be starting to get dark again by then."

"Right you are, Mr. Pygott. Sensible as ever."

"So I am, Mr. Crone. So I am."

If only you weren't the only one who actually believes it!

Chapter 2:
Business as Unusual

Crone busied himself tidying the sales counter, even though it was a task he performed so often, the desktop literally groaned if anything dared move out of place. "Tsk! Tsk!" he muttered, as he moved the receipt pile one finger to the left, then back again, picking off a speck of dust so minute it hadn't yet realised it was dirt.

Pygott wandered down to the front of the shop to survey the damage left in the shoplifter's wake (for which no one had turned up). Apart from a slightly singed shelf (thankfully, the books' flame-retardant spells remained effective) and a rather nasty stain on the doormat – built up to a nice crust over the years; so much so that Pygott felt he might need to erect a *Mind the Step* sign – there seemed little out of place.

Hmm, I see the elemental's consumed Wormwood's Poison Gazetteer again. If I was a suspicious man, I might begin to think she was aiming for it on purpose. Pygott tutted, sighed and turned on his heels once again. *I'd better go clear up after Mr. Hul'hu, I suppose. He's such a nice, erm, thing, but his aroma never quite dissipates and the slime oozes into every nook and cranny. It scares the Hell out of the guard-dragons.*

"Yes, of course, sir. We even have a couple of Crowley's books that *he* didn't know he'd written." Pygott overheard Crone over-enthuse as he slipped through the door into the back office. Mr Hul'hu's musty, foetid stench wiggled at the hairs in Pygott's nostrils like a playful, twenty-feet-tall puppy. He fished out a can of *Olde Shoppe Mildew Spraye* and set about trying to return the loft-space to its original, antique fustiness. His forefathers had to pay handsomely, even back then, to secure premises with *authentic* odour. There were plenty of charlatans doing the rounds these days hawking potions and spells to enchant bookshops, but nothing could properly recreate good, old-fashioned olfactory patina. The spray didn't do the shop justice, but until Pygott could properly air the space, it would have to do. The old place couldn't be expected to regenerate her unique flavour, after such a pungent intrusion, at the drop of a hat.

"Oh, bother!" growled Pygott, as he stepped in something slimy. It wriggled and squirmed and squeezed itself down through a crack between floorboards. "There goes another one. I do wish C. T. would be more careful with his minions. We've a collection of living mucus bigger than the whole world sneezing all their colds together into one room."

He reached for the mop and set to work, before settling down to review the new subscriptions. He prayed that none were biters: he still had a livid scar from the last list after taking his eye off the 23rd edition of *Practical Lycanthropy Attack Methods.* It was a good job the book wasn't infected. Although last full moon, Pygott's palms itched fit to drive him to distraction and he still couldn't quite get the taste of raw liver out of his mouth.

Chapter 3:
Speak of the Devil...

"I notice the human skin bound editions section is looking a little thin, Mr. Crone. I *do* hope you're not planning to discontinue the range?"

Lucifer wore the expression of an immortal super-being whose entire world seemed to be changing for the much-worse. With little or nothing He could do about the inevitable march of progress.

"Oh, no. That's one section that will *always* remain popular! Too popular, it seems. It's so difficult to keep up with demand."

"Not enough interest from the publishers, eh?"

"Well, not from the mainstream press, obviously." Crone tipped Lucifer a totally pointless wink. "But the more respectable ones are having such difficulty getting hold of the skins, what with all these damned new regulations. Not to mention Professor Van Hagens poaching so many of the better specimens for plastination. And then there's pollution and tattoos and ugh, Hell forbid, sunbeds damaging the product. There's precious few good pelts to harvest anymore."

"I flay people every day as a matter of routine! Why don't they ever come to me? I could provide a steady supply."

"But aren't you obliged to re-skin them again, so that they can be stripped *ad infinitum?*"

"Weeeell; strictly speaking, I suppose there *is* a modicum of truth there. But I *am* the Father of Lies, am I not? Sticking to the rules is hardly part of my make-up, wouldn't you agree, Mr. Crone?"

"Splendid, Your Disgrace!" Crone clapped like an excited schoolgirl. "But then, I have come across one or two of your smuggled pelts in my time. And as I remember, they were already so toasty, they were destined to be made into long-pork scratchings..."

"Ah. Yes. Well. I suppose anything mortal that sneaks out of my realm does tend to be a little, ah, *crispy.*" Lucifer leaned in to deliver a grin possessed of such deep, leering, malevolent beauty that Crone's sole reason for not wetting his pants was the impromptu retreat of his bladder and intestines into a large chest he kept in the attic for just such an embarrassing emergency. "At least anyone who doesn't come prepared, eh?" The resultant wink finally made Crone wet the box.

First time ever.

Where was Mr. Pygott? Surely he'd sensed Crone's utter panic by now? Lucifer never failed to scare the pants off him whenever He entered the shop (which is why he never left the counter to fetch Him a book personally – Crone was far too self-conscious of his stubbly, stubby legs). But today, of all days, His presence was nothing short of pure torture. It wouldn't be so bad if He just came in and bought something, but He always stayed so long and insisted on chatting away like an old woman hanging over her neighbour's fence.

I'm sure he doesn't actually enjoy my conversation. The evil old goat just likes to watch me squirm!

And squirm Crone did.

"So, where was I?" Lucifer boomed out of the corner of His face. His attention still lingering elsewhere in the shop.

Crone squeaked, startled.

"Erm, flaying?"

"*Flaying?* Good God, no! That wouldn't do much for your evening trade now, would it?"

"Erm, no. Not really. Of course not…"

"You're sweating: are you alright? Is it hot in here? Bit difficult for me to fathom, for obvious reasons." He gave Crone a playful nudge that nearly knocked him into the Romanian restaurant next door. "Seems to me you need to lose a little of what's *inside* your skin first, eh?" Lucifer roared a blast of spirited amusement. Three customers fainted and one troll suffered a hernia – even though trolls have no intestines to herniate. Sadly for them, none of these particulars were covered by the establishment's Esoteric Liability Insurance.

Crone patted his girth, as much to check whether it was round enough to attract comment as he was providing panicked self-sympathy. "Ah, well. I don't have much chance to get out these days. It's not all adventure and derring-do in the book trade anymore." His eyes clouded wistfully. "Not like the old days…"

"But you're still young, Mr. Crone! Bags of time to put yourself in mortal peril before you need to start thinking about side-stepping my eternal hospitality, eh?"

Crone blanched.

"He-he. Don't worry yourself, young man. I know how many safeguards my favourite booksellers have in place to avoid settling in my own retirement village. But you're *always* welcome a visit. You know that!"

"Er, yes. And we're always grateful…"

"Well, make it *soon*, dear boy. It's far too long since you graced the Lower Kingdoms. And The Sisters miss you so very much."

Crone had by now descended to the state of an uncomfortable, agitated worm-farm. "Erm, ah, indeed." *Change the subject, you fool!* "So, what was it you were looking for again? You perused all the new torture titles the last time you were here and there's been nothing of note since, I'm afraid."

"Pah! Sounds like work to me!" He slammed down a meaty palm on the counter, which shuddered with suitable respect. "What's the point of going on holiday if I take a customer service manual with me to read?"

Very, very suddenly, Mr. Crone's demeanour brightened fit to cause him alarm.

"Holiday? You're going away? Isn't it a little late for your annual sojourn?"

Calm down, Crone! Don't give the game away.

"Yes, well, it's been more than a little busy this summer, hasn't it? The old trickster upstairs has sent down plague after flood after famine after religious festival stampede this year. And there's no such thing as piety anymore! Even the hideously goody-goodies get sent straight down to me for a while first, just to put the fear of, erm, Satan in them, before they're allowed to ascend. And it's such a ghastly, sickly spectacle when they go – fair turns my stomach, I can tell you."

"Ugh," agreed Crone, with a grimace. "I'm sure it does."

"So I think it's way beyond time I took myself off to recharge the old brimstone somewhere. And of course, I'll be needing something to read while I'm stretched out on a glacier somewhere, won't I, Mr. Pygott?"

Crone jumped as though he'd been the one caught snooping.

Pygott on the other hand couldn't believe his luck. At least Lucifer could have waited just a little longer – time enough for Pygott to actually start eavesdropping, Damn Him! *Ah, no. A little too late for that, I suppose.*

"Good day, Your Empiric Darkness."

Lucifer grinned, razor-teeth glinting.

"Give it a rest, you smarmy git." A wink. "What were you doing back there? I know you've elevated skulking to an artform, but surely there's more exciting places to indulge your hobby?"

Pygott relaxed. Old Nick was in jocular mood, after all.

"Ah, if only. I'm much too busy apportioning elbow grease at the moment, I'm afraid. First, a visit from Mr. Hul'hu and all that entails…"

"Hmm, yes. I hope your mop's still in good order?"

"Indeed. And though I say it myself, I've done a fine job masking the wake of the shoplifter we dealt with shortly before you arrived."

"Ah, I should've recognised that smell, shouldn't I? Trusty elementals, eh? I suppose they ate another book…?"

Pygott flinched at Crone's startlement. He thought he'd got away with confirming poor Crone's fear they'd have to write off yet another volume. It distressed him so much to lose a book.

"Greedy little swines, the lot of them! Still, as long as they didn't snaffle something I could take on my hols, eh?"

"Actually, I think I may have the very thing." Crone jumped into uncharacteristic animation. He generally didn't dare get excited while Satan was stalking the aisles. "I'll have it for you in just a moment..."

And with that, he waddled off with an overdose of purpose to disappear in the corner that held the 'Sick' section.

"Does he often walk about the place with no pants on?" mused Lucifer.

"Not as a rule, no." Pygott stared after him agog. "But it is the weekend, I suppose..." *Splendid, Mr. Pygott! I'm sure that will be more than sufficient to explain such behaviour.* Pygott considered seeking some sentence – *any sentence* – that could serve as improvement, but his brain had already decided it didn't want to be associated with anyone who made such limp statements and left him alone to flounder.

Lucifer turned away from Crone's receding, jiggling, pink buttocks and Pygott shuffled beneath the weight of His intrigued eyebrow, rapidly deciding to specifise his small-talk, before his brain made its absence permanent. Pygott thought it appropriate to probe a little, at least, to see if he could gather some forward information about Lucifer's impending absence from Hell. The cause of himself and Crone's looming escapade wouldn't be standing right of front of him much longer, after all.

"Been doing anything interesting lately?" *Limp. But a tiny step in the right direction, Mr. Pygott.*

"Not really. It can all get a little samey: toasting, skewering, eviscerating... You know the routine? The lesser demons all enjoy it so much that I tend to leave them to get on with the day to day grind. I never tire of showing the Essex boys endless repeats of *Manchester United's Greatest Defeats* though. I don't know if it's the look of dreaded disbelief on their faces, or the glee on mine that pleases me more. Red Devils indeed, pah!"

"So, the holiday will be a bit of a departure then? Will you be touring, or just hanging around a fjord or two?"

"I'm not too sure, really. I'll certainly be doing my fair share of yomping: stay in one place too long and I'm liable to melt through the permafrost and end up back where I started!"

"We can't have that, can we?"

12

"Good God, no! I'm not cutting this holiday short for anything! I don't care if that hoary old sod up there starts Armageddon while I'm away. Let Him win, for all I care. I've been the *real* owner of this world for far too long now. It's about time He either sticks His nose back into human affairs, or wipes the whole thing clean and starts again, as far as I'm concerned."

"Too true. Too true. Either way, some of us are protected against such eventualities, are we not?"

"Deals have been done…" Lucifer chuckled and tipped Pygott a lusty wink. "Good job the Elder Gods are all asleep, eh?"

Pygott paled and suddenly felt quite ill. Was he being toyed with?

"Speaking of which," Lucifer whispered in a boom. "Mr. Hul'hu doesn't know about-?"

"Ahem! Hrrrumm! Hach!" Pygott very nearly coughed up his lungs and another pair that happened to be walking by. All the while jabbing his finger in the direction of the pulsing, green globule on his neck, that seemed to have decided sitting on top of his skin and nosing at the world was far preferable to burrowing into flesh and being constrained by all the slimy discomforts within. "Never too sure how connected they stay," he whispered. "At least until they become attached to a new host. It's usually at least a few days before they become fully absorbed."

Lucifer nodded in an exaggerated, "Got you" display and took the hint to change the subject. Only He couldn't think of a subject worth bringing up.

"Here we are!"

Crone to the rescue. Pygott was amazed. When had *that* ever happened?

"Ziplock rubber, with flanges and a little stain-free coating on the pages. Should stay in prime condition, no matter how excitable your reading."

"Maximum flame-proofing?" Lucifer's eye danced a merry jig.

"Erm, well. Try not to get *that* excited."

Chapter 4:
To the Study

"You don't think he suspects, do you?" chimed Crone as the door swished shut in Lucifer's wake, to the faint accompaniment of screams and searing testicles.

"No, don't worry. I'm sure we're in the clear, Mr. Crone. We generally act like a pair of frightened imbeciles whenever He comes to call, so He won't have noticed anything different. I just hope He likes the manuscript we sold Him. That Unkle Joz could be a little extreme even for His Infernal Majesty. In fact, some of his writing makes me think the lad might have already taken over the reins."

"Not to mention the cat-o-nine-tails, manacles and anal penetrating whirr-blasters."

"Very droll, Mr. Crone." Pygott's crumpled owlbrow wasn't quite sure whether to be amused or appalled. "Now, do you mind finishing the night and closing up, while I get on with a few necessary preparations for the trip? I'll be downstairs if you need anything. Just send a spider if you want me to come up."

"That will be fine, Mr. Pygott. I can't see there being much trade now. Lucifer's atmosphere tends to linger awhile and scare the life out of browsers. It should be relatively quiet from here on." Crone assumed his calm, *king of all I survey* demeanour and settled himself into the chair for a relaxed veg-sesh.

Sadly, when he did so, he tended not to rouse until closing time rolled around and any intervening customers remained invisible, silent shadows. Pygott palmed the nearest copy of *Sperm Whale Mating Song and Sex Sounds of the Sea* on his way to the trapdoor out the back. If Crone managed to get *that* ejaculating from the speakers, it'd take a week to bring him out of the resulting torpor. He pocketed and patted the disc, safe and snug in his pocket. It complained and squirmed a little, but knew there was no fight to win, so it quickly relented and collapsed into snoring before Pygott had even neared the bottom step. He squelched onto the earthen floor and made his way towards the furthest, darkest corner, whilst reminding himself for the umpteenth time that he really ought to reverse the swamp spell before it started to get out of control. The next time his nephew came to stay, Pygott would stop trying so hard to impress him and just drag him around *Terror Towers,* like every other sad, old git trying to be desperately cool for their kids.

Where in fiery Hell is that light switch? It still couldn't settle on a comfortable wall space and complained bitterly wherever it briefly stopped: "It's too light," "It's too dark," "I don't like the view from here," "Ooh, it's too cold," "Nope; too warm," "Ugh! Damp!"

Predictably, it was currently in a lapse of sullen silence and flatly refused to give Pygott the slightest clue to its current location. He blundered blindly towards (hopefully) his private study, thanking the stars there were no obstacles on the floor within the impenetrable darkness between himself and his secret door.

A thoroughly unsavoury expletive jumped out of his mouth as he tripped over the light switch.

Chapter 5:
To Hex and Damnation

Pygott stumbled out of the room in a blaze of dehydration and temper, eyes unable to adjust even to the dimness leaking down from the stairwell. His limbs felt as though someone had borrowed them during the day to run a marathon while he slept, before sneaking them back underneath the sheets just before he woke. There was a growling ball of magma pulsing in his oesophagus that leaked hydrothermal vents out through his body to pierce his lungs.

The invocations had not gone well.

The hexes worse still.

And the preservation rite didn't even bear thinking about.

At least he'd succeeded in pushing them through to a bitter conclusion. Complete, if not perfect. But it had taken every ounce of strength and cunning to remain intact and retrieve his aim. He'd chosen all the right words, taken every precaution, readied every prop. But somewhere along the way, the mood had shifted, darkened and made backhanded attempts to wrest control out of his hands and turn the rite back on himself. Did someone, *something,* out there know something already? They couldn't possibly, surely?

Satan Himself had stood before him only a few hours ago and betrayed not a single sign of suspicion. Mr. Hul'hu had made no mention of anything untoward and anyway, to be fair, he'd never been the most incisive character to traverse the vacuum voids. Even his left-over slime – never the most intelligent dribbles, at best – had come to grips with its new home remarkably quickly and sat on Pygott's shoulder, making no attempt to either burrow into his nervous system or re-establish contact with its old host. And the Elder Gods were still asleep: there could be no doubting that. The world was still in as many pieces as usual and not three weeks ago, a US survey vessel out in the middle of the Pacific Ocean had reported detecting mysterious sound echoes from the deepest, darkest, impenetrable, mid-ocean trench. Baffled, they'd appeared in front of insistent news cameras and giggled as they pronounced, "It's cool, dude. It sounds kinda like my Gran'ma when she snores!" A monumental shiver had run down Pygott's back, quelled only by the realisation that if they were snoring, then stretching their wings and raising to destroy the Earth was an event likely to remain a long way off.

If they'd rather heard something more resembling farting and ball scratching, he really *would* have worried.

So what the Hell just happened in there?

At the moment, his resolve was way below even attempting comprehension. His brains were jelly and he was too tired to stick in a spoon and stir the goo. He staggered towards the expanding pool of grey until he collided with something hard and wooden that seemed to indicate an upward flexure. They may have been stairs, but he couldn't be entirely certain.

If he could reach his bed and sleep for a year or two, he felt he might just survive to face the next disaster.

What in God's name do we think we're doing? He silently wailed to himself. *Another day like this and I may be forced to rely on Crone's useless amulets to protect us. Because right now, rank stupidity may be the only thing that'll get us through.*

Chapter 6:
Beckon Call

"Good day. My name is Jeremiah Arbuthnott Pygott and I co-own, along with my esteemed colleague and friend, Mr. Jedidiah Haggard Winklefry Crone, not only this phone number, but also the shop attached to it. *The Third Left Tentacle* has been trading for longer than you can remember and was left to me originally as a third-rate brothel, filled with hairy whores, by my Great Uncle Xerxes, who was forced to give up the noble trade when even *his* steadfast spare parts began to wither. I initially tried to continue in his footsteps and succeeded for some years, but not only did I find it tedious sweeping up endless swathes of tart hair every day, it became obvious that the customers were spending more time waiting in the parlour, reading volumes from my extendible library – what with the spare copies fitting nicely inside the iniquitous den - than tramping upstairs to do the horizontal fandango with the attendant shag-piles. And the legendary Mrs. Wilton.

"Upon a chance meeting with a young, enthusiastic, scatter-brained bookseller in need of relief, I put it to him, on more than one occasion, that we ought to consider forming a partnership. Eventually, we spat and shook hands and entered the book trade. The remaining prostitutes turned out to be excellent at stocking the shelves and grateful for the chance to remain upright at work for the first time. The new dress code – actually *being clothed* – meant that I could scale down hair-bundling duties to only a single stint per week!

"Unfortunately, we no longer do *extras* (unless of course, you get particularly friendly with our Penisian scrying expert), but you can be assured of finding the largest range of occult, esoteric, mystical, barking, dangerous, brain-scarring and gelastic books in the known universes. And yes, of course we stock the 'Harry Potter' books. Our service is second to none, though admittedly, less stimulating now that our last surviving Madame is beyond pyramid age and is no longer even required to look at our books, let alone pick them up and foist them on our customers.

"Neither myself nor Mr. Crone is able to reach the phone at the moment, but if you'd care to leave a message, please don't bother, as anyone still listening to this monologue is either very sad and lonely and desperate to hear the sound of anyone's voice – which is your cue to hang up – or urgently requires our services and is praying that we really *are* listening and might just pick up if you shout your message *really loud*. This answerphone is only here as an excuse not to take calls anyway, as the phone is an instrument of the Devil and shouldn't be used by *anyone.* Even this message was recorded for us by a kindly, fiendishly convincing mimic, so as to leave me unsullied by the evil that infests those dancing light beams and crackling copper wires.

"When we're open, we have a particularly noxious ghoul who actually enjoys using this infernal machine and will be overjoyed if you ring during our hours of business, which is something those who aren't too insane or lazy to get off their arses and come to the shop itself will already know.

"Opening hours are clearly displayed on the door and there are a multitude of security devices in place to ensure your safety whilst on the premises. Although we can accept no liability for loss or damage to limbs, heads, sanity, pets or property.

"We do not have a website!!!

"Thankyou for calling and if you're still there, please go away!"

"Dammit!" growled Satan and slammed down the handset. It cracked in two as it hit the cradle and He glared at it as though it was purposely trying to upset Him. "Gone already."

He glared at the broken phone a while longer, until it started to smoulder, wondering what Pygott had meant about his instruments. *Surely everybody knows I play the fiddle?* Confused, He snorted His way out of the booth.

Chapter 7:
A Nice Cold One

Gazing out onto scenery that was getting colder and cleaner, He began to relax a little.

Long gone were the fiery pits of tar and smegma, the whiff of sulphur and abandoned bowel control. Gone also were the increasingly bright and brash London streets. He still remembered the good, old days, when darkness held sway over the night. Even the advent of street-lighting (which He'd worked against tirelessly, to no avail), had done little initially to diminish the grip that the gloom exerted once the sun retreated below the horizon. In fact, in some cases, the move had positively boosted His influence: creating pools of shadow and vaguery amidst the well-lit comfort zones, that only served to heighten the populace's paranoia beyond the coddling bright-embrace. Lurking became a true art-form, practised by the keenest criminals, the basest perverts and the barmiest of booksellers.

But Lucifer knew better than to be lulled by such fleeting encouragement. He alone seemed able to envisage where the rising flood of illumination could lead and had machinated with all His guile and influence to resist the spread of any artificial light-source, beyond candles, bonfires and arson. Hell's hierarchy had embraced the notion that humankind should be encouraged to advance themselves in any and every technological field, unable to see beyond the glittering promise of increasingly powerful weaponry, pollution and greed. Beelzebub and Astaroth, Baal and Baphomet had garnered too much support for the endeavour and were able to run roughshod over all His attempts at sabotage.

As a result, the denizens of the Dark Domain were paying a hefty price: demons destroyed by lack of faith, more effectively than any paltry exorcism could achieve. Dark, dank habitats disappearing apace, driving sallow species into cramped hiding; into dangerous, harmful contact with humans, with one another. And diseases were being battled and mutations accelerated to the point where they had begun to infect even succubi, homunculi and sports teachers alike. And it was becoming increasingly difficult to walk around even the smallest village these days, what with flashing neon assaulting the eyes, drunken revellers spending all night in hedonistic carelessness, oblivious to threats or superstition. Microwave communication saturated the air, scrambling supernatural powers and radio waves intercepted and confused diabolic thought waves.

And noise. Lucifer so detested the noise. An overdose of unhealthy, scratchy, white-noise, electronic whines and hums, sub-sound, supersound and industrial rumbling. Never ceasing. Battering at sensitive membranes that were hypertuned to seek out timidity and terror along similar wavelengths.

Perhaps I'm just getting old. Lucifer mused morosely. *But I'm not wrong in thinking we had it better in Ye Olden Dayes. Even the concept of evil seems to have been usurped by corporate considerations. Nothing really happens due to our influence any more. No one perpetrates an evil act for the pure joy of it being, well, pure evil! It's all justified by profit and power and one-upmanship. Perhaps we're just really victims of our own success? We've been far too successful infecting the human race with our essence. So much so that all the lines between grace and excess have become impossibly blurred; every act melting into one, huge, ignorant mess, with neither us nor the Heavens dealing any of the cards anymore. The whole game has turned into a grand mêlée – an impromptu, wind-blown, 52-card-pick-up scramble. Humanity, divine light and diabolism trampled under the conscienceless heavy boots of 'progress'.*

Where are the artists? Too, too few and far between. There would always be the supreme adepts like Dahmer and Jack, Torquemada and Jean D'Arc. But for every one of those, there used to be another hundred beavering away in the hopes of promotion to the upper league. But nowadays violence and depravity had become a way of life for the stupid, a regression to barbarism. An end to brutality as a beautiful, unholy form of expression.

Lucifer sighed.

"Maybe it really is time to call the Elder Gods and let them have their way? Another bash at Creation's long overdue."

"Pardon, Sir?"

"Hmm?" Satan roused, stared blankly at His reflection in the glass a moment, before finally realising He'd actually spoken aloud. "What did you say?"

"Could I see your ticket, please? And if you could have your passport ready? We'll shortly be crossing into Sweden." The guard had long since plastered onto his face an approximation of attention, but it was painfully obvious that he'd just come across the umpteenth spaced-out passenger and patience was a novelty that had upped and legged it sometime shortly after the train entered Denmark.

"So sorry, I must have drifted off for a while. Sweden, did you say? My word! It doesn't seem half an hour since we were stuck in the middle of all that awful noise in Belgium. What was all that again?" Lucifer was desperately trying to straighten His fugue-filled head, but the fog seemed to have settled in for a good, long snooze.

"A rock festival, I believe. Hordes of sweaty youths from England and elsewhere invading the countryside and banging their instruments, apparently." The guard stopped short and looked his passenger square in the chest, seemingly unable to understand why he'd actually answered the question, rather than his true intent to harden his frown and become more belligerent in the quest for this traveller's ticket.

"Youths banging? Maybe it wasn't such an awful racket after all. I should have stopped off to join in for a while. There wouldn't be many virgins, I should wager? But no doubt I'd find the odd Devil worshipper and mound upon mound of young flesh." He looked up from finally completing the tortuous round of rummaging around the bottom of every pocket to find His elusive tickets. *Better let the poor lad get on with his work.* "Here you are..."

Eventually, the guard roused from his own fuddlement, clipped the ticket on autopilot, dribbled a flat, "Thankyou" and tottered off down the carriage, absently feeling himself, as though he thought some part had gone astray.

"Funny chap..."

Satan settled His face back to the window, reminding Himself to ensure He didn't melt any glass this time – as had happened too often in the past. It didn't present any real problem to Himself, but it did cause an awful amount of fuss amongst the humans when they came across His head smouldering through the pane. But even more consternation (and sometimes panic) when He waved a nonchalant finger and put everything back to normal. The poor saps never could get the hang of seeing that little trick.

"Orson? Wake me up again when we hit the Arctic Circle, will you?"

"Eek!" squeaked His trilby. Leaving the Dark Lord to ponder whether He really spoke in such terrible tones, or if possibly He should endeavour to be a little gentler when placing His trusty titfer onto His horns.

Chapter 8:
Stressed Foot Forward

"Come, come, Mr. Crone! It's not *so* long since you were out in daylight!"

Pygott tightened his grip on Crone's arm and 'encouraged' him forward.

"Yes, I know. But does it have to be *so* bright? Couldn't we go out a little later, when twilight's at least putting its pants on? It's burning my eyes."

"Do pull yourself together, Mr. Crone! It's practically dusk, for God's sake. Anyone would think I'd dragged you out into the midday desert sun! Now, please stop whining and get a move on! We've a long way to go before we're close to the gate." At times like this, Pygott despaired of his partner. "It's not as though you're even affected by sunlight, is it? If you were a vampire, I could put up with your bellyaching. But you're not, so get walking!"

Crone grumbled himself into a grudging shuffle and shut up, making no sound, but for the odd scraping sole, intermittent tuts and sighs, popping knee and ankle joints, theatrical breathlessness and the swish of his longcoat.

"If we need to sneak up on anyone, let's not, eh?" muttered Pygott.

"Huh?" ventured Crone. Forgetting that he'd resolved to keep a sullen silence for the next half-hour, at least.

"Nothing, dear boy." Crone always suspected he was in the bad books whenever Pygott used that particular blandishment. "Let's just get on, shall we? There's one Hell of a long way to go, before we get to, erm, Hell."

They skulked off through the gathering gloom, thankful for the shadows stretching long and low across their path. Pygott had no axe to grind with sunlight. In fact he positively sought out a good sunrise or sunset, and was more than partial to taking tours of cemeteries and ancient burial sites during the summer months, when nights were short and trade was slower. But this was early autumn, when the nights were fast closing in and the Hallowe'en rush was already starting to build to its frenzy. *We shouldn't really be out of the shop at this time of year for something so trivial as saving the world.* But he supposed that in truth, they were more interested in saving their own skins and all they contained. *But if the business goes up the spout and we lose it all to that idiot, Crowley Jr. IV, it'll all have been a waste of time, anyway.* Life wouldn't be worth living in such circumstances.

"Ooh, doesn't it feel *adventurous*, Mr. Pygott?" Crone had unexpectedly shrugged off the whine, a gleam creeping back into the corner of his eye and his footsteps assuming an unnerving air of bounce. "Won't it be wonderful to see the Styx again? Those putrid, black waters reaching up for us like old friends. And the gates? Oh, the gates, Mr. Pygott! To see them gleam and pulse with the blood of a billion tortures, bowing under the weight of a thousand and one plucked skulls. Do you think our secret nick in the fabric will still be there?"

Pygott wasn't sure whether he preferred the sullen, timid child who'd set out from the shop to this boisterous, cavalier alter-ego. "I hardly think that particular route would be safe, Mr. Crone. After all, we haven't seen, let alone talked to The Sisters for a very, *very* long time. They're bound to feel neglected."

"But that's hardly our fault, Mr. Pygott. It's such a terribly long way to their doorstep. And they'd never come to see *us!* Why, even their essence wouldn't fit in the shop."

"True. But nevertheless, I think the likelihood of such intimacy is, though grammatically unsatisfactory, highly unlikely. Especially after the way you left them on the last occasion..."

"Ah well, that definitely wasn't my fault! Well, not entirely. Perhaps they'll have forgiven us after a period of reflection...?" Crone looked entirely unconvinced by himself. "It might be nice to hear them boom one more time."

Bother! I knew I'd forget something! Pygott scratched around in the bottom of his unhelpful pockets and even managed a perfunctory stir through his knapsack. Though he already knew the box of super-dense earplugs he sought wouldn't be there. *Two stone deaf booksellers should do wonders for improving customer service.*

"Yes, Mr. Crone. If they catch up with us, you could well hear them boom like never before. I can promise you that."

Chapter 9:
Crisp 'n' Home 'n' Dry

Pygott started at a movement off to his left, alert enough not to jump and panic Crone unnecessarily. He saw no point in bumping up his blood pressure without even finding out what his partner was, or thought he was seeing. He peered into the mouth of the alleyway as they neared, getting a little extra distance along its gloomy gullet with each step. Nothing else stirred. Until a lonely crisp packet rustled forlorn around the mouth of a grate before sinking back to soggy capture.

Pygott wasn't fully convinced and kept his eyes employed peeling the edges of walls and downpipes until he could see every inch of space down, around and up and down.

Nothing. And they were past.

Chapter 10:
I-Spy With My Third Eye

Pygott had assured him there was nothing there - in fact seemed almost annoyed that he'd been asked. But Crone was certain that he'd seen movement. Not just shadow or litter or scuttling wildlife, but something (he was also certain that it was definitely a *something,* rather than a *someone*) living and breathing and full of intent and *following*. Down deep inside the alley, where it thought nobody could see it creeping. Slithering along the walls, in and out of the shadows along window ledges and swinging across eaves and lamp-posts.

Silent. Malevolent.

But keeping one pace behind. Never closer than the corner of an eye, tripping around the edge of the blindspot with flawless ease. Such a shame it didn't realise that Crone's blindspot was where he kept the essence of his twin; dead and absorbed in the womb, but unable to let go the bond with his exaction. And so he sat inside Crone's skull and soothed him when he was down, talked back and forth in never revealed secret and held vigil to keep his winsome brother safe as he could. Even Pygott didn't know about the life kept alive inside his head, happy to believe that Crone's moods and bursts of conversation to the air were nothing but another eccentricity manifesting in order. Another one of his personality traits breaking surface.

Crone's twin kept track with the slight *wrongness* that was flitting along at the whim of their every step and reported back every nuance that let slip every gleam of a hidden eye.

But what did it want?

What was it *waiting for?* Had it wanted to launch an attack, rip out their hearts and glut on the muscle, it had already let the best opportunities lay bare and slip past. But it didn't seem to be spying on them. It *was* tracking their every move and taking their lead wherever they might turn, but it hadn't the air of the snoop. Didn't make an impression like the average reconnaissance. It didn't seem to care where they were or what they were doing, or even where they were going. Just so long as it *knew* they were there. And in sight. And easy reach.

That made Crone more afraid than any implicit threat.

He chose to let the thing go about its business undetected, so it thought. And decided to keep the presence from Mr. Pygott. There was no need to worry him any further. Just so long as Crone knew when to react, if at all, that was all that need concern them.

Crone's renewed enthusiasm for the jaunt had finally begun to mute though. Maybe this wasn't such a good idea after all? He was certainly coming round to Mr. Pygott's view that though there were few, if any other options open to them, there was likely to be little fun and more than a portion of danger along the way.

But it had to be done. There were signs all around that time was beginning to shorten. It had, admittedly, been a very long time since Crone had ventured out into daylight, but his memory was faithful enough to tell him that clouds didn't have bright red outlines. And rain wasn't black and didn't smell like half-eaten entrails. The sun, he was certain, didn't live at the end of a black tunnel and there was supposed to be birdsong. That was one of the things he definitely remembered enjoying about daytime. He still heard it tinkling through the windows of the shop and loved the lilting, overlapping warbling, the competition, *jousting* and one-upmanship that went on as the avians squabbled for airspace, quarrelled over some old gnarled stump and puffed out their chests to impress the ladies.

But they were silent. Absent.

Silent as the two booksellers who marched with as little conspicuousness and as much bravado as possible.

"Oww!!!" *Clang.*

It took Pygott at least until the fourth step to rouse from his brow-furrowed train of thought and realise that Crone was no longer abreast of him. Steadily, it also dawned on him that someone had yelped.

"Where are you, old man? If we can't stick together, we may as well build a nice, new balcony back home and go sit on it to have a grandstand view of the Great Old Ones put on a show of consuming the world. Oh-"

He turned and started, face dropping into more than a little concern.

"What happened?" called Pygott, hustling back to his stricken comrade and kneeling to inspect him for damage. There was dust on his coat and a nasty graze across the bridge of his nose. But apart from the fact that he didn't seem to be entirely conscious, Crone appeared to have suffered little injury.

"Wh-whut hhppnd?" Crone burbled.

"I asked you first." Pygott sniffed.

"Your basket's a purse?"

"No! I said – oh, forget it."

"No heads on Frogatt?" Crone looked even more confused than any possible concussion.

"Shut up and please don't start bleeding. Here I am exhausting myself raising hexes to protect us from all manner of foulness and you're busy trying to beat yourself to death through sheer absent-mindedness!"

"I must say, that seems very unkind, coming from a man who says he doesn't even know what happened to me." Crone was crawling back inside his own head and wiping the glaze from his eyes.

"Ah, is your *compos* becoming a little more *mentis?*"

"Issue compost to Baltimore dentists? Really?"

Perhaps not. Pygott sighed.

"So what *did* happen? Have you any idea?" Pygott levered his friend back onto wobbly feet, praying that a rush of blood to the ankles may restore a little of Crone's awareness.

"I, erm, sort of, ah, beat myself up out of sheer absent-mindedness, if you must know," he puffed, indignant.

"And how do you know that I don't know?" Pygott's suspicions roused again.

Crone's brow furrowed. "Ouch," he whispered. "My, erm, subconscious is starting to bring me up to speed, sort of."

Pygott couldn't even raise a glare, so grinned in grudgement instead. *Shifty, evasive, inventive. That's more like the Crone we know and love.* "Well, if you're up to walking, we're not far from the station. We'd best get moving before anything else happens."

"As long as you can hold me steady for a moment. There seems to be a grapefruit stapled to my head." He gingerly waved a finger around to locate the extent of his swelling, then felt the apex of the bump on his head. "Ow!" He winced, jumped and hobbled forward. "Shan't do that again..." he mumbled.

Pygott took a good hold of Crone's elbow and guided him on down the street. "Soon be there, old boy."

"Smooth my hair with toys?"

"Oh, for Hell's sake! The sooner the better, I think."

Chapter 11:
By the Short and Scaleys

Mephistophonob glowered out of the alleyway in their wake and left them to argue over who should open the door for whom and enter the railway station first, in a fit of misplaced etiquette. The sliding, automatic doors became more than a little agitated by them not noticing they could both walk through together, without the slightest need to be polite.

Better report back, it thought. *There's nothing much else can happen to them here. Unless they abandon all common sense and buy a cup of tea.*

Mephistophonob slunk off to find a handy demon-hole in the middle of the nearest backstreet and slithered down into steamy, inky stink – such a relief to be back underground! Away from all those hideously sweet-smelling humans and their buzzing, glaring, artificial daylight (it wasn't actually switched on yet, but its very existence irked it anyway). Its skin was already starting to itch and flame and it hadn't even had a moment to collect its eczema cream on the way to the surface, the summons had been so sudden. Devil knew how it was going to bear flitting across the station concourse after the pair of…things. What with its enormous, night-piercing, *Welcome to Bramsworth* sign and the all-pervading flood of strip-lighting that formed a painful barrier between its dim hidey-hole and the gloomy platform ends. It didn't even have chance to rustle up any semblance of disguise to protect itself from detection by horrible humanity. All this skulking about! Had it stumbled back into an alternative Dark Age?

To think it'd come to this!

Even the furore that had erupted in the wake of the Jeffrey Archer debacle, so very long ago now, shouldn't mean it still deserved to be slapped by punishment such as nurse-maiding a pair of witless paper shovellers on their misguided – if not downright dangerous – fool's errand?

No doubt there'd be nothing but complaints when it became clear that all it had to report was that there was nothing to report. As though it was all *its* fault! *Blast and salvation!* It had remembered, thankfully, in good time, that its licence to curse was still revoked. Such indignity! It couldn't even blaspheme now and then to cheer itself up.

"WHAT DO YOU WANT?" boomed something deafening and loathsome.

Mephistophonob quivered and shrank back, at least as impressed as it was terrified. "Squeak!"

"WHAT??? DID YOU JUST SQUEAK?"

"Sorry, I have a touch of wind. I said there's nothing to report, Your Hideousness."

"NOTHING TO REPORT? ON WHAT? WHO THE F*** ARE YOU? YOU WOKE ME UP!"

It withered. *I knew this job was going to be the end of me.* "It's Mephistophonob, Your Dribblesomeness. I'm following Pygott and Crone, as you instructed, and I'm just checking in, as you requested."

"WHO? MIFF-WHAT? OH, YES, I REMEMBER YOU. IN CHARGE OF THE ARCHER FIASCO, WEREN'T YOU? HA-HA-HA! BEST LAUGH I HAD IN MILLENNIA! EVEN SO, WHAT THE BLOODY HEAVEN ARE YOU TELLING ME FOR?"

"You *were* alone down there, weren't you?"

"WHAT? WERE?? WHAT ARE YOU BLATHERING ABOUT, IRKSOME DEMON?"

"Sorry, I'm overcome by your maleficence. You *are* alone down there, aren't you?"

"OF *COURSE NOT,* FOOL! I'M SURROUNDED BY A MILLION SUFFERING SOULS! CAN'T YOU HEAR THEM SCREAMING?"

"Er, no, Your Pustulousness."

"INSOLENT IMP!"

"*Demon*, Your Sewageness."

"ONE MORE CRACK AND I GUARANTEE YOU'LL *NEVER* SCRAPE OFF THE STINK OF THE ARCHER FARRAGO! NOW, JUST TELL ME WHAT THE F****** S**** YOU WANT AND THEN GO F*** YOURSELF!"

"Yes, of course, Your Bowelcurdlingness: Pygott and Crone." Mephistophonob wondered how Baal managed to pronounce the stars in place of each utterance of profanity.

"NICE CHAPS! GOT AN EYE-OPENING BOOK ON RECTUM RECIPES FROM THEM NOT A MONTH AGO. BIT CLEAN FOR MY LIKING, BUT AT LEAST *THEY* KNOW THEIR PLACE! AND THEY DON'T WAKE ME UP AT AN UNREASONABLE HOUR TO TELL ME A BOOK I HAVEN'T ORDERED HASN'T ARRIVED! SO WHAT ABOUT THEM?"

"You told me to follow them and tell you, regularly, what they're doing."

"YES, OF COURSE I DID! SO WHAT *ARE* THEY DOING?"

"Well, nothing really, Your Unmentionableness."

"SPLENDID! SPLENDID!" Somehow that boom was even more Earth-shattering than all the rest. Perhaps Mephistophonob ought to think about sticking to annoying its master. It was slightly less head-splitting. "WELL? WHAT ARE YOU HANGING AROUND FOR? GET ON WITH YOUR JOB AND

DON'T WAIT SO LONG TO REPORT BACK NEXT TIME! HOW ARE WE SUPPOSED TO KNOW WHAT'S GOING ON IF YOU DON'T TELL US?"

"Indeed, Your erm, Boomingness." It bowed as it backed up into the street once again. This was turning out to be much harder – and slightly more annoying - than it had imagined.

Knowing my luck, they'll be under a train by now, the clumsy oafs. That should finish off my career in fitting fashion.

It grimaced and sloped off to face the pitiless attack of the concourse lighting, issuing a rueful sigh as it slithered away to relocate two ridiculously conspicuous men.

Chapter 12:
The Flies in Scotsmen

"Ah, Sanctuary at last!" breathed Crone, as he flopped back into the carriage seat, in a fit of apparent exhaustion.

"Yes, we must have been walking for at least twenty minutes," grumbled Pygott, as he eyed his partner with targeted suspicion. "Should the journey become any more arduous, my dear Mr. Crone, I fear I may have to sell you for meat to survive."

Crone prodded one of his fleshy thighs, then pinched a generous lust handle. "Just so long as they don't like lean cuts." And proceeded to fidget, immediately, as though he'd been stuck in his chair waiting for a film to begin for the last four hours and was only just beginning to realise that the blaring hot dog advert was stuck on a loop.

"Why is it that trains should be designated Sanctuary? I don't think I ever did find out." Crone's brow wrinkled in concentration, even though his brain knew there was nothing within to set work upon.

"Because God spends more time playing with His train set than He ever has mooning about in churches, listening to people constantly trying to emotionally blackmail Him."

But Crone had already followed his inattention to burbling something about the buffet car and why the counter was always too high for him to see the server's legs. He didn't trust anyone to give him food if he couldn't be sure they weren't floating.

A big, fat, greeny-blue fly wafted into the cabin and bumbled in a confused arc, sniffing the recycled air, then plopped like a pelleted pigeon onto the end of Pygott's nose. Where it commenced a solo chorus of contented buzzing.

"Turdly! Off!" boomed the loudest voice in the known spheres (considerately calibrated down to a level where it wouldn't cause avalanches several countries away). "Leave the man alone! He doesn't want your filthy feet trampling all over his nice, clean nose." He wagged an admonishing finger at the fly, which backed up, raised its wings and buzzed in youthful defiance. "I won't tell you again, young man. Off. Now!" And he started as though rising.

The fly leapt backward giddily, denting the bridge of Pygott's nose in a blaze of stars. It hovered as though ready to play a particularly one-sided game of catch. But soon sloped off in a sullen huff as it realised that Daddy really wasn't in any mood for horse-play.

"Thankyou," offered Mr. Pygott, blinking away the knock. "Such a nice, little fellow, but *so* heavy!"

"I know," answered Beelzebub. "I suppose I do spoil them a little bit. But they're so adorable when they're young. It seems like only yesterday little Turdly was crawling around inside a rotting corpse and look at him now! All those legs and wings! The trouble is, he still acts like a three-day-old." He partially rose again, hand in swatting position. "Now leave Mr. Crone alone, you silly boy!"

Turdly thought hard about navigating a short course of defiance, before deciding it really was time to pack it in. Before *the can* appeared. He fizzled off in an "Up yours. I'll go find someone who isn't so boring, then!" kind of way and disappeared beyond the carriage door.

Turdly's other few thousand siblings continued to doze in a contented, gently humming mushroom above their master's head, as though he were off to Ascot, toting a particularly odious hat.

"Wrong sex, dear boy! That's ladies' day!" he boomed with a chuckle.

Pygott gaped. Began a word, stopped, gaped again. Then remembered.

"Just how much do you pick up on in that fashion, if you don't mind me asking?"

"Not at all, old chap! It's funny, but I only snag the odd thought here and there. And usually only anything I can make a quip about. It not such a useful skill, really. I *can* see through 360° though. At least I have one useful talent, eh?"

Pygott barricaded his next thought with some stern effort. "Where are you off to at this time of day? It seems a little funny seeing you out and about in daylight. I swear I can't remember you looking so, erm, illuminated."

"You too, Mr. Pygott. Must be something pretty important to coax the two of you out into the waking world?"

"Ah, that's exactly it: we don't get out enough and feel like we're becoming stuffy, old stiffs. We're taking a little time off to do some rambling. Have a little adventure."

"Adventure? A little old for a mid-life crisis, aren't we? Not jumping off any cliffs or boinging off bridges in the hope your pretty, young instructor won't notice the spare tyre, I hope?"

"My word! Nothing so grand," Pygott mouthed, cutting off at the knee the truth that leapt to mind, eager to be heard. "Just poking around in a few places we shouldn't. You know the kind of thing?"

"Splendid!" Beelzebub clapped and stomped a foot, practically shaking the train off the tracks. "I'm doing the same myself. The boss is away, so I'm out amongst the mortals to, er, shall we say, have a little fun? Raise a little mischief." He winked the most lascivious, loathsome innuendo the universe could contain without collapsing under the weight of pure filth and nudged Pygott in the ribs like Eric Idle's homicidal cousin.

I most certainly do, thought Pygott, as plainly as he possibly could. He would've said the words out loud, but it would be at least Birmingham before his ribs unfolded enough to let him reclaim hold of enough breath.

"Speaking of which; do you want anything from the buffet car?"

"No, thankyou," he winced.

"Good job too! 'Cause that's where I'm off to. It won't be pretty. I ought to prise Turdly off whatever mess he's no doubt created by now too. I'll no doubt see you later?"

And with that, The Lord of the Flies became the absent Lord of the Flies. Taking his flies with him.

Pygott sighed and returned his energies to attempts to suck in enough air to realistically describe the action as *breathing.*

"What's all the noise about? Are you going to the buffet car?" Crone's rousing was gratifyingly shallow and brief. "Close the window. I can't hear myself dream," he mumbled, and climbed onto another level of slumber.

Chapter 13:
The Demon Vandal

Aristophonob finished jamming all the toilet roll down the pan and proceeded to smear something unmentionable across the little window at the back of the cubicle, squirted a few splashes of stickiness either side of the porcelain and concluded by releasing a relief-fuelled, yellow stream all over the black, plastic (cracked) seat. It stood back, wrinkling its noses at the funk with great satisfaction. *Sanctuary stretches only so far. And if something's got to do this sh- er, I mean stuff, then it may as well be done by a pro.*

Slipping open the door, it flicked a blob of chewing gum just close enough to the pedestal to stick to the pants of the next unsuspecting crapper and waddled off down the train, rocking from side to side as it went. It wasn't quite sure why trains held such power over its contemporaries: nasty, horrible, noisy, smelly, draughty things. But in such a distinctly *human* fashion. It fair made its skin still. And these contraptions had such a terrible effect on its balance: making it walk like someone was constantly pulling the carpet from beneath it.

Boats. Now there's a way to travel! Nice, damp air, full of salt and decay and a biospheresworth of excreta. And a proper breeze – stiff and flapping at its calmest; screaming, pounding and flaying at its best. Mmmm – nothing like a good storm at sea to get my pecker up. And my labia tingling, for that matter. There's none of this stupid stumbling either! I can walk just fine on top of a natural yaw. It's all this synthetic atmosphere I can't handle, ugh. Still, at least the air conditioning never works on one of these things. Though the heating's always on full flaming blast! It's almost like being back in the pit...

'Nob (as it was known to its friends, as though it had any – Heaven knows what names its enemies spewed) halted; practically bumping into itself and thanking chaos it didn't have any toes to stub. Tuning out for a mental rant had dulled its faithful internal radar, and 'Nob suddenly realised it had wandered right past its quarry. But that never happened – ever. Having said that, the twitch was so faint. Masked by something else: something huge and black and evil and arrogant. *More than* arrogant. Right there in the compartment with Pygott and Crone. Aristophonob's bowels turned to jelly and tried desperately to sneak out to hide somewhere dank and safe.

So much power! No idea what I can do if anything kicks off in there. If there is *anything I can do. Better keep an eye on this from a safe distance,* it thought and screwed itself into an anonymous corner within close – but not too close – range. After all, it might have to react a bit sharpish before the journey was over.

It patted its pouches and furrowed a brow – the only one it had immediately to hand. *Now, where did I put my wits? I know they're about me somewhere.*

Chapter 14:
Midland Madness

A few more blank-faced, harassed travellers struggled past the empty seats littered around Pygott, Crone and Beelzebub, in a stressful, fruitless search for somewhere to drop their bags, sit down and cease spilling sun-hot coffee. "I *know* we have reserved seats, Tricia, but they're *not there!*" howled one particularly fractious character, his eyes wildly darting between the accusing eyes of his tight-lipped wife and the total absence of his promised reservation.

Trains were so obliging whenever practitioners of *The Arts* requested an old-fashioned, steam carriage glamour to preserve comfort and privacy. Otherwise, a trip up the East Coast Mainline would prove a most troublesome chore. Especially for the more unusual passenger, like Beelzebub and his retinue of swarming insects. Each fly weighed a good half-ton for a start. And one of them, like Turdly, deciding to alight on someone or something, free of the spell, caused a regrettable problem or two. Or squish.

Pygott wondered how many crushed fingers Turdly had sniggered on and off during his hunt for mischief?

Crone finally began to resurface within sight of life again within spitting distance (if the actions of the pair of children thundering up and down the aisle were anything to go by) of their proposed change.

"Where are we?" Crone mumbled a crack of the fuzziest croaks.

"Just coming up on the fringes of Hell, I think," offered Pygott, squinting at the onrushing scenery.

"Doncaster already? My word! Have I been asleep that long?" He yawned, rubbed his eyes, scrutinised the tipful of grit dug out of each corner and stretched, cracking practically every joint in regimented order. "Did I miss anything?"

Pygott smothered the wince. "Oh, no. Just the usual, run-of-the-mill train journey. Sitting here, listening to you snore…"

"Is there a buffet car? I don't remember seeing one as we climbed aboard. I should've asked earlier, really."

Pygott only just stifled the harrumph. "So nice to see your stomach's primed and ready for action, if nothing else."

Crone didn't register sarcasm at the best of times, so his few moments after waking were hardly likely to provide fertile landing ground for Pygott's cracks. Crone waited, blinking, unimpressed.

"It's in the *Gold Zone,* apparently. But before you ask, no, I haven't the faintest idea what or where that is."

Crone waited for the information to sink through a few layers of befuddlement and proceeded to vacillate to fill in time. Then, with a resolve Pygott had thought him incapable of, he rose and slung open the carriage door.

"I'd better go find us a few nuggets, then. Would you like anything?"

"Just a cup of the worst tea imaginable, thankyou."

"I believe I can promise you that."

And with a swish, Crone was gone.

Chapter 15:
Northern Wasteband

Something felt decidedly wrong as Pygott's foot settled on the platform.

He turned to immediately recognise the expression that signified Crone felt it too. Doncaster was an oppressive place at the best of times: overburdened with grim horrors and a burgeoning population of monstrosities, but this was far too specific to conform to the general, background atmospheric discomfort.

There was something spongy in the tarmac – actually within the tarmac. Something awkward about the geometry of roof struts and stairs. The station announcer's voice cut through the tannoy system, rough and buzzing like a wasp, to inform confused passengers that the 14.25 TransPennine service to Hull would be 20 minutes late, due to a hippopotamus on the line. In Latin. One of the porters seemed to have collected all the other porters' heads and was wearing them on hurriedly grown, scrawny necks, while heroically ignoring a struggling old lady, who was desperately heaving a suitcase the size of her waiting train up the first step to the next platform.

And of course, the baleful, yellow eye that stared out from the middle of a tan, juddering, gelatinous creature that completely filled the refreshment kiosk was most abnormal. *Walking down the High Street, wearing white stilettoes and half-a-skirt on a Friday night perhaps, but not on a Saturday afternoon, spilling stale biscuits and soda,* Pygott mused.

Crone answered before he'd even rolled his tongue into position to deliver the first word.

"Yes, I know…"

Chapter 16:
Block and Key

Pygott jiggled it, wiggled and prodded, grunted and sweated and sighed.

Please don't tell me I conjured the wrong key, he thought, barely a flash before the locker grudgingly spilled its guts.

Pygott and Crone were both immediately transfixed, slack-jawed and silenced. They were bathed in warm, willowing, pacific light that hopped from one nameless colour to the next.

One day, someone would explain to them why all the most secret places and the trinkets they hoarded, which had to be visited quickly and quietly – in, out, no fuss – were *always* fashioned to be so very *captivating.* How could the average occultist be expected to keep away prying eyes when it took a good five minutes, at least, to retrieve their own AWOL senses from the nearest cloud?

Even Crone's Nu-Eye Anti-Glamour Specs™ had been initially swamped and had to work with every fibre of their own machinations to gather enough control over himself to struggle out a hand and weakly grasp a shimmering ribbon. Even so, he was still afraid that he may not have grabbed the right one. It felt like the right one. It weighed the same as the right one. But there were no second chances if he'd only snagged a similar one. *The one picked is the one chosen is the one used,* remained the rule. And no one had yet found a way to circumvent the convention.

The key slipped first into Crone's hand who palmed it into Pygott's pocket and out of harm's way. Pygott stirred and recovered enough to dreamily swing closed the door, shut his eyes and summon up a memory of breathing, put it into practice and somehow succeeded in resealing the portal. It snapped back into its regular disguise, plopped out a hefty bar of whole nut chocolate - the first time it had worked in such a fashion this month – and promptly broke down.

"No, no. Come on, old man. You have to keep moving. We can eat the chocolate on the train."

"Hmmm," nodded Pygott. "Tired."

"Don't fall asleep! Look – there's the train. Just a few yards now."

Pygott squinted into a yawning, hefty distance a couple of miles beyond the carriage door. "Too far," he muttered, as Crone shoved his drooping figure up the platform, breaking up the chocolate into chunks in Pygott's pocket as they went.

Finally, Crone leaned his friend like a sagging sack of hay against the door frame as they reached the train and fumbled for a lump in Pygott's pocket. "Don't worry; I'm only looking for chocolate," he cooed assuringly. He popped a fistful of sugary revitalisation into Pygott's mouth and shoved him onto the impatient train.

And into Pandemonium.

It seemed that Hell had come to Doncaster to greet them. Which, quite frankly, was a bit of an achievement. Not so much by its arrival, but in that it was so very *noticeable*. Terrific noises belched out of hideous, hulking, stinking creatures, babbling insanely in guttural, indecipherable roars. Intermittently chanting, cursing (Crone presumed), breathing filth and slewing the floors with scum and flotsam, stains and stench.

The portal was packed with them. Jammed in and jostling, mixing malodorousness and rancour to create a seething, cloying fugue that wrapped itself around every filament and choked resistance out of mere mortals.

Smoke stained the air next to every *No Smoking* sign, pitted with traces of sweat and rot and excreta and hate. Crone narrowed his eyes to peer through the throng to try to uncover some clue to wherever any glamour might be hiding. After all, he'd taken this trip once or twice before and though the journey had never been so harrowing, the train had still offered harbour in a quiet corner of magical sanity, away from the day-trippers and unearthly residents.

Crone dragged his attention down a level with none too gentle a dig in the ribs and Pygott strained to see through the writhing clash of bodies to follow the extrapolation of Crone's finger.

Just as a meaty forearm flailed the air, garbed in blood-streak and bruise extensions, Pygott caught a glimpse of safety waning in a far corner, broken ticket bin and his heart sank. They'd never be able to get to it. Not unless both of them suddenly inherited Great Uncle Herbert's talent for teleportation – and quite frankly, he doubted his uncle was all that keen on dying and executing the will just yet. And he was leaving Crone nothing but an old writing desk, so the event wouldn't be any help to Pygott's chubby companion anyway.

No: they were stuck right where they were. Sentenced to reel amid a violent, abusive tumult, under constant threat of belittlement, injury and disgust. And the chanting had risen again. There were missiles fizzing along the ceiling like blunt hornets. And the smells were exploding out in raucous competition. It was only a matter of time before the random element switched as the creatures realised there were beings of another order within their midst and re-centred some of the direction for their hatred.

Crone had grown very pale. And Pygott suspected his own complexion had retreated and sought a layer of shoe leather to hide inside.

For all the spells and protections he'd so fastidiously prepared, he never expected to come up against anything quite so headless, noxious and homogeneously unpredictable.

Still, at least after this, descending into Hell would be like taking a walking holiday in Whitby.

Chapter 17:
Who's the Wamker in the Tweed?

The doors opened and Pygott and Crone stumbled out into muted daylight, into an air of fish and chemical burning. Which turned out to be a positive paradise, after the choking, stifling confines of the portal. It seemed they'd escaped not only with their lives, but also their souls intact. Though somewhat frazzled and chipped around the edges.

They scuttled off as quickly as their cramped legs would race and headed for the relative safety of a dark corner at the end of the platform, accompanied by the odour of cheap coffee and something pretending to be milk, but performing the trick so badly it ought to just give up and join the whitewash union.

"Mr. Crone?"

Sigh. Mop brow. Sigh. "Yes, Mr. Pygott?"

"Should we ever feel the need to make this ridiculous jaunt again, please ensure I buy a newspaper first."

Crone feared the horrors of the ordeal had been too much for his friend and driven him insane.

"A paper? How would buying some fanciful rag help us out of *that?*"

"How? Because I'd be able to look up the football fixtures and check that we weren't going to be jammed into a space occupied by Sheffield United fans on the way to a match against Grimsby Town!"

"Oh, yes, I see." Crone wondered why *he'd* not thought of that. "But I'm sure there's no need to shout at me so angrily."

"What?" His retort was still a little sharp. "Oh, sorry. Yes, you're right; hardly your fault, old boy. I think I need to sit down somewhere quiet for a moment and grab whatever fresh air we can find here."

"You talk as if there is none! The Humber may be chock-full of chemical sludge and the air laced with everything that Stallingborough and Immingham's refineries can throw at us, but I think you'll find a walk along the sea-front quite pleasant at this time of year."

"And bracing, no doubt?"

"No." Crone licked a finger-end and tested the wind. "No. Generally at this time of year, it's absolutely freezing!"

"So I remember. I wonder why Lucifer didn't just camp out *here* for his holiday?"

Crone patted him on the back and they followed the tail-end of a trainful of rowdy football fans off the platform and out towards the town.

"Did you know that Grimsby Town's stadium isn't actually in Grimsby?" piped Crone suddenly. "They officially play all their home games away from home."

Pygott thought to respond, but the gleam of satisfaction that had wrapped itself around Crone's face, in the wake of his burst of surprise trivia, was too glorious to interrupt. So he returned his attention to worrying that it was still not even kick-off time on a Saturday afternoon, when they'd set off from the shop a good forty five minutes later than it was now.

So much so that he didn't notice the sinewy, shadowed form that slinked slyly after them.

Chapter 18:
Fishy Chippery

Contrary to all expectation, a walk along the shore turned out to be not only bracing, but utterly refreshing. Pygott had forgotten how jaded lungs became within the confines of the great city and what a thorough boon it was to be able to suck in great sheaves of briny North Sea air.

For once the bloom across Mr. Crone's cheeks portrayed all the signs of healthy vigour and the old chap was positively galloping along the promenade.

"Do you think we ought to head back towards Grimsby soon? We can't spend all evening enjoying ourselves watching idiots racing souped-up prams along the promenade. We have work to do." Pygott was coming to the conclusion that their endeavour was turning out to be far too much fun and if they hung around, listening to the gentle song of the tide and the screech of seagulls, he'd be tempted to abort their mission here and now. And find an estate agent's window, where he could gaze at retirement properties suitable to sit on the veranda and watch the world end.

"Oh, I don't know, Mr. Pygott. Wouldn't you rather sneak into the gateway after midnight?"

Pygott mused on the question under a rumpled forelock and nodded agreement. "Better the guards half-asleep than deep in the dreamstuff. It's all-but impossible to deal with them then."

Crone halted, his ruddy glow switched to a flush. *"Deal with them?"* He paused a moment, blinking, staggered. Then rapidly caught up with Pygott, who'd ploughed on regardless of Crone's plight. "I thought the usual convention for sneaking into somewhere was *concealment?* Not waltzing about the place, chatting to everyone!"

"Ah, but Mr. Crone, surely the best place for concealment is within full view?"

"But if everyone knows we're there, we'll be prime suspects when Old Nick returns to find His book missing!"

"Which is why we set up an alibi once we're in there. You don't think I only brought hexes and charms and clean underpants in this huge bag, do you?"

"I don't care if you brought Baal's new horn polish! We can't just saunter around Hell without a damned good reason for being there."

"Which is why one of us planned ahead…"

Crone stood exasperated as Pygott turned to his bag and asked it to stop. "What are you…?" he stammered.

"All will become clear," mumbled Pygott, as he ferreted about through the depths of his luggage. "Come on; where are – ah!"

Pygott straightened and waved a hand, first at Crone, then to the bag. "I think that should quell your concern?"

Crone bent as far as his portly frame allowed and peered into the gape. Something moved a little, agitated by the string of novelty lights strung overhead. And finally Crone was granted a clear view of whatever it was.

"Aaah, I see. Very well thought out, Mr. Pygott! No wonder you made the bag carry itself." Crone grinned as though it had all been his own idea. "Just don't let the guards get a sniff of it, or this jaunt will be over almost before it started."

"Don't you worry about that, Mr. Crone. I have all we need to get up their noses. We'll have no trouble tonight, at least."

"In that case, shall we enjoy the evening? Look, there's Cleethorpes Pier. We can buy fish and chips and sit on the promenade annoying the seagulls and breathe in the sea air."

"Greasy food and chemical sludge, is that healthy?"

Crone glanced down at his generous frame and then up at Pygott's sallow complexion. And smiled.

"Are you really going to propose that either of us care a jot for the healthy option? After all, we are on the verge of breaking into Hell and stealing the Devil's possessions."

"Hmm," began Pygott. "In that case, I think I might venture a bag of doughnuts too."

With a smile apiece, they went in search of the nearest chippy, watched over by a boiling cloud of heavenly tentacles and shadowed by a lithe, well, shadow. Just beyond range of Pygott's furthest safety hex.

The shadow demonfully struggled to keep its distance though. *Mmm, fish and chips,* it thought. *I really hope the fat one's not too hungry.*

Chapter 19:
Incense and Insensibility

Pygott wrestled with the almost uncontrollable urge to sharpen his already razor talons and shred his skin into grated cannibal garnish and found that he was wavering a little too close to the line for comfort. Why was it that he still had to use that stuff to ward off the sexual (if what they liked to do to one another, and anyone, or anything else, for that matter, could possibly be described as sex) attentions of Hell Sirens. Although Pygott had to concede that Abulsad was of course mad, from a long, distinguished line of mad Arabs, he really had promised that the new edition of *Daemon Praesidium et alter Carmen* (the title and its errant grammar caused great confusion amongst many a demon, but Abulsad *would not* be convinced to change it: his father had bequeathed it to him on his deathbed, apparently. Pygott didn't believe him for a second) would contain a new spell that dispensed with the need to use *Helvisium balsam.* The old con-man had been as true to his insane word as ever. And so Pygott's fingers kept twitching and his hands crept disobediently towards his waistband every time he did something essential, like pay attention to where he was going. Or, on a more urgent footing, where Mr. Crone was going.

He nearly tripped over a wayward calf again.

"Mr. Crone! Where on Earth are you going?"

Crone stopped, sniffed the air, squinted and quelled his customary panic. "Ha-ha, good one! You had me going for a minute there. I know that stuff plays merry Hell with your skin, but I also know it can't send you insane within the first 36 hours after application. I've read the leaflet."

"I was referring more to your inebriated carriage." He ignored Crone's feebly sarcastic glance around to look for such a contraption. "Can't you walk in a straight line and keep your feet under control?"

"Ah. Sorry. Not after that third éclair, no. Maybe I ought to bring up the rear?"

"If I let you lollygag behind me after three éclairs, it could be Christmas before we get to the Gates of Hades. Still, at least you might be able to fit through by then..."

"Flit-proof bile hens? This is hardly the time," Crone surveyed the territory surrounding him, grunted and nodded to himself. "And certainly not the place to be thinking about fowl again, Mr. Pygott. As I've pointed out many a time, where would we put the coop? There's only room on the roof and chickens don't really fly, you know. The ones that survive the

Wyvern's interest, that is. And the last thing we need is clucking kerfuffle and feathers raining down on the heads of unsuspecting customers. You're best to keep your husbandry dreams in your head, Mr. Pygott; leave them for after we retire to a nice, impregnable pile out in the wastelands somewhere."

So that's it, mused Pygott. *The sugar overload's reached his brain already. There'll be no more sense out of him until morning.* "Very good, Mr. Crone. Right as always." *Sigh.* "You can do the talking when we get to the gates."

"I most certainly shall, Mr. Pygott!"

And while you endlessly gabble the guards into a realm of confused despair, I'll dispense the necessary subterfuge. "And then we're in," Pygott muttered, satisfied.

"Not yet, Mr. Pygott. But we are just approaching the docks. It looks like there'll be lots of lovely fish scales to skate on!"

"Excellent, Mr. Crone. A broken coccyx apiece should set us up nicely for a journey into the Underworld."

Chapter 20:
Hell Hath No Fury like a Demon Scorned

"Bas- erm, grrr, I mean, blaggards!" Mephistophonob growled into its grumbling chest. It was sorely tempted to break its curse prohibition and was getting close to the point where it didn't care what happened should its tongue slip. "After all I've done for those two lately, and all the thanks I get is two fish skins, a tiny blob of dusty cream and one slightly green chip! Greedy bas...reliefs!"

If only they knew what I've had to go through, following their blundering ar-erm, behinds the length and breadth of the country? They, well...probably wouldn't give a toss (that's alright, isn't it? That just means throwing stuff), if I really think about it.

"Bl...asted humans," it grimaced. "Another one of His more cruddy ideas." *Why couldn't He have just admitted He'd made too much clay and left it at that? But, oh no! He can't be seen as making a* mistake, *can He? We all have to pretend like it was part of the plan all along and fawn over how clever He says He is.*

Mephistophonob longed for the old days, after The Fall, when the Earth was seeded with angel's blood, slashed from the ravaged hearts of Lucifer's legions. When the land was young and made of fire and sulphur and there were still noble ideals for which to strive. Battles that were worth waging.

And then along came His 'great experiment' and ruined everything. A set of noisy, clumsy, sweaty, destructive, ungrateful gits. With all the subtlety of Thor's back-up hammer, Bjölnir. And all the compassion of a retarded squid.

Mephistophonob munched disconsolately on a fish skin and shivered at the prick of a North Sea breeze.

"Yes, I know..." it scowled at its master's message.

And now all I have to do is try to keep them safe in Hell, of all places. Who'd be a demon, eh?

Chapter 21:
All Keyed Up

"What a marvellous erection!" Crone announced, neck craned right back to scan as far up the brickwork as possible.

"That's really a phrase you ought not project so loud down on the docks, Mr. Crone." Pygott paled.

Crone squeaked tinily and jumped just as minutely. Then shuffled, abashed, as though he'd flounced like a startled ingénue.

Grimsby Fish Tower loomed majestic in front and high above them. Square and solid and possessed of sturdy girth beyond its reedy appearance at distance. It swelled up out of the shore, reeking of scales and oil and salt and briny decay. It thrust its terraced head to the heavens like a turgid monument to rank fornication.

"Of all the seven Earthly gateways into Hell, this has to be the most apt," Pygott mused.

"Hum?" dribbled Crone, still fondling the brickwork shaft.

"Nothing, old man. Just taking in the foetid air before we make our entrance. Shall we?"

"Hmm, yes. I think we should."

Pygott wriggled a couple of fingers daintily inside his waistcoat breast pocket. Eventually, missing his target, he dropped any pretext to nonchalance and jammed his whole hand in there, scrubbing about in an evermore fevered attempt to catch hold of the squirming talisman.

"Will you *please* forget all this talisman nonsense?" he grunted. "You're a key, remember? There's no point trying to disguise yourself while I'm sticking you into a keyhole, is there?"

The key continued to quiver rebellion in his grasp, unwilling to revert to its true shape.

"Look, I understand you rather like being a grandiose item of ceremonial jewellery – though Hell knows why: even Tom Jones would be hard pressed to show off a medallion so big and gaudy – but I really, *really* need to have you key-shaped for a few moments, at least. Ouch!"

The key had started to protest. Loudly. *Violently.*

Pygott glanced around to locate Crone, all the while wrestling with the suddenly spiky, bristling pendant. Thankful at least that he'd slipped it out from beneath his vest and back into a pocket, before ever assuming that it would be unreasonable about performing its only task during the entire journey. Crone seemed nowhere in sight, almost as he'd expected, presumably having wandered off to inspect an interesting patch of algae, a strip of mouldered deck or lichens on chipped brickwork around the other side of the tower. The phrase, 'each to his own' tended to apply to Crone more than most.

"Please don't make me use the appropriate method of *encouragement.* You know I'll enjoy that as little as yourself." He drizzled a particularly stern owlbrow rebuke down upon the squirming talisman. "But then again, we both also know that the effects will last a damned sight longer on *you,* little key..."

Pygott had no need to even finish his sentence before the talisman, grudgingly, performed a wiggly mutation dance and settled into the form of a large, cold, hard, very heavy, slightly-rust-crumbled, cast-iron key. So black Pygott could hardly discern its outline in the gloom. It emitted a hefty grump so loud that he expected the entire Unholy Host to descend upon them.

It bothered him a little that they didn't. It was strange that they hadn't. But even stranger was the fact that the key had made any noise at all. Because it shouldn't. In fact it couldn't.

"Thankyou," beamed Pygott, shrugging off his puzzlement by virtue of an attack of genuine sincerity. "All this unpleasantness will be over in just a moment." *For you, at least.*

Pygott looked again for Crone, who was beyond perception within the untimely midnight blackness. He wasn't too perturbed, as there was almost no chance that Crone would miss the gate opening: it was hardly the least ostentatious event horizon. And another reason why Pygott had formulated a subterfuge behind knowledge of their appearance in Hell. Sneaking past the vainglorious celebration the gates so enjoyed was, except in the most private and urgent circumstance, far too much hassle to bother with.

He made a final check inside his bag to make sure the necessary props were in place and gently, quietly slipped the key inside the unassuming wooden door in front of his hand.

And turned his wrist.

Crone reappeared beside him with such rapidity that Pygott could almost convince himself his partner had been right there all along. He looked equally shocked and awestruck in spadefuls. And dribbled a suitably appreciative, "Oooh..." that accentuated his wide-stretched kaleidoscopic eyes quite admirably.

They both loitered on the threshold a little too long for secrecy's sake, but not nearly long enough to soak up the opulent splendour of the eyeful scrolling into the distance from beneath their stymied soles.

"New upholstery, I see," nodded Pygott.

"And look at that chandelier!" cooed Crone. "Business down below must be booming."

"It's a far cry from our first visit, when all we received as welcome was a lungful of sulphur dished out by a single, overstressed, damned, ex-hotel receptionist chained behind a charred slab of singed, flaking veneer" Pygott had started forward and his momentum appeared to be coaxing Crone along with him.

They didn't even let him operate the trapdoors," opined Crone, a touch sentimentally. "He was allowed to press the buttons, but that only summoned the guards to throw interlopers into the lava pits, or grudgingly usher visitors onto Charon's boat."

"Indeed! I think I still have the bruise I got upon landing. You'd think he'd at least keep the odd cushion laying around..."

As they proceeded on ever-surer feet into the plush multicoloured, multifaceted reception lounge, the tower door swung steadily closed behind them, issuing its customary snigger of satisfaction at the thought of another soul committed – whether inevitably or interminably – to perdition. Or worse. Pygott and Crone didn't notice, so busy were they surveying Hell's renovations, which had been made almost as palatial – and financed by almost equally crooked means – as FIFA's headquarters in Zürich. They muttered notice of selected features as they passed, like toddlers practicing how to whittle away mummy's will to live with an endless stocktake of the things they could see and hear and still congratulated themselves at knowing the right words.

"Fountain," mumbled Pygott, pointing.

"Pretty chaise," added Crone.

"Gilt nipple-clamp suspension swing," enthused Pygott.

"Nice, but whatever happened to the old ormolu? I rather like ormolu. It doesn't have the tendency to show off like that pure gold monkey penis over there," opined Crone.

And so it continued. Until they forgot all about forward navigation and crumpled against each other like a grunting concertina against the new, gleaming burr-walnut reception desk. Which stretched in a splendid, shallow arc further than Jack Torrance's favourite bar in Kubrick's *The Shining*.

"Mr. and Mr. Oof, was that?" leered the receptionist. Who no longer appeared to be one of the damned. Nor in chains.

Pygott glared across the counter-top in the manner of a man who'd just been rudely abused, possibly, but was too confused to actually register what might have been said or done that so prickled their indignation. *"Oof?"*

"Very good, sir," the receptionist smarmed. "Do you have reservations? I don't seem to be able to find your booking on the roster."

Pygott stirred.

"I'm having more reservations, the longer I stand here. We need to *make* reservations to come and visit a few chums in Hell nowadays? What is the Underworld coming to?"

"We all need to move with the times, Mr. Oof. And what with the surge in admissions over the last century, efficiency is key to keeping track of the damned. I take it your charming euphemism means that you are here to serve your perdition? I'll just bring up the forms..."

"Please don't bring up the forms! I've seen that trick before: it's crude, messy and the smell fair makes Mr. Crone gag."

"Mr. Crone? This is Mr. Crone?" The receptionist dropped his professionally supercilious attitude, along with all pretension to appear human. "I do apologise, sir!" He seemed to have forgotten that Pygott had been present at all. "If only I'd known it was you! I could have all my preparations ready and wouldn't have wasted my time with this oaf, Oof here."

Crone's bewilderment at the dazzling lobby diminished quickly, in direct mirror to the rate his breath had returned. His confusion realigned to centre with perfect precision on the nonsensical twaddle being pushed his way out of the mouths of the moustachioed harpy ill-fitting the receptionist's uniform.

"Surely by virtue of being a preparation, whatever it was must be ready?"

The receptionist frowned across all several of his brows. He was trying desperately to be polite, but really didn't know what was happening anymore. And feared he may be heading towards being vaporised by guests he'd been assured required the utmost courtesy. He really didn't fancy being turned into an evaporated Harpy by an annoyed, powerful wizard.

"I'm so sorry. So very sorry."

"I know that, but what about your preparations?"

"All ready for you, sir. I just don't have them to hand. I was told you'd be accompanied by Mr. Pygott. So when Mr. Oof arrived before you and made his enquiry, it threw me off guard."

"Mr. Oof?" Crone blinked and peered around, unable to locate anyone else within reach who could be misconstrued as accompanying himself and Mr. Pygott. "Who is this Oof? I can't say I remember meeting anyone by that name. Mr. Pygott, do *you* know this Oof person?"

"I can't say that I do, Mr. Crone. I've come across someone who tirelessly considered being called Mr. Irious amusing, but the Oofs have as yet eluded me." He switched his attention to the receptionist, who by now had replaced their sudden switch to deathly pallor with a glittering purple bloat that made him look more like Violet Beauregarde with every passing second.

"Why would this Oof fellow be making reservations for myself and Mr. Pygott," probed Crone.

"Especially as even *we* didn't know we were coming till earlier today? We only had the notion to pop in on our way elsewhere and hardly thought to inform *ourselves*. Let alone make advance reservations!" Pygott peered at the squirming receptionist with baleful, accusing eyes.

The poor, confused – and by now mostly terrified – Harpy had been reduced to emitting a series of cowering "meep" noises, out of which Pygott could make only a few recognisable words. Among them, "expected", "doing what I was told", "warm welcome", "please?"and "not my fault".

"Come, come. As you say, none of this appears to be your fault, no matter how much blame I feel I must necessarily ascribe to you. You're just trying to do your job in a most unusually chirpy manner for a welcome to the eternal abyss. So please don't cry? The counter-top looks as though it's taken many, many hours of patient waxing to achieve such a lovely sheen and your tears are burning awful holes in the wood."

Predictably, having this pointed out only caused him to sob all the more.

No matter how vexed he'd become, Pygott couldn't help but take pity on the poor creature. After all, it was hardly the easiest task with which to be shackled: welcoming an endless stream of travellers who were on the verge of reacting to the news that they were on the cusp of assuming an eternity being toasted on the tines of a rusty pitchfork. Or much, much worse, attempting to maintain a sunny disposition while performing the impossible task of satisfying the impatient desires of incarnately evil, extremely powerful warlocks, demons, despots and demi-gods. All the while wavering on the knife-edge threat of being pulverised by the ire of the least understanding denizens in this portion of the universe.

"Mr. Crone, do you have one of your handkerchiefs handy?"

"I take it you mean the asbestos silk ones, Mr. Pygott? Of course."

Crone fished out a lace-edged square of gossamer finery and handed it across the counter.

The Harpy eyed it with blurry suspicion and set himself to wail anew.

"Don't worry my dear chap. It's just a fancy tissue. Dry your eyes and let's get to the bottom of what has been reserved in our name. And with any luck, find out who was kind enough to grease the wheels to provide some unexpected comfort during our stay?" Pygott smiled his best, expensive book sale smile and hoped it transmitted into a display of empathy, rather than the leer of a hungry exorcist.

After a protracted bout of multiple eyebrow crumpling, followed by a back-and-forth battle of wills between the absorptive properties of the handkerchief and intermittent bursts of eye-gushing, the trio finally arrived at a point where their business could not only be concluded, but actually discovered in the first place.

"So, we have a booking in the Presidential Suite on the inner-ring of the fist circle of Hell. With an uninterrupted view of Judas's frozen stare down on the ninth circle?"

"Yes, sir. With unlimited wi-fi access! I'm instructed that humans get rather tetchy in places that's not available."

"I'm sure we'll be more than satisfied with whatever internet service is provided, thankyou." Pygott slipped Crone a weary look, knowing that he wouldn't have noticed himself being bombarded by low level microwave radiation at all, but hoped Crone might be pried away from all that the Underworld's broadband could provide without resorting to a crowbar, several dangled carrots and a big stick.

"Here's a list of the fire precautions and evacuation route-"

"Fire precautions? I'd hope they exist mainly in the form of six feet of flame retardant cladding? Whereas I would've thought that evacuation into what we all know is a hellish – literally - fiery pit would be more like acting out a certain proverb?"

"Generally, yes. One of the management's favourite little jokes. But the executive suites all have tailored routes to an area in keeping with their particular guest's optimum climate: their comfort is paramount. *Your* comfort is paramount!" The Harpy was back on track and returning to somewhere within reach of corporate comfort. His customers were reacting, finally, in the manner his customer care training prepared him to expect. With no little relief, he handed over a set of key cards inside a snazzy welcome pack and warmed to the prospect of disaster averted and a job well done. Or at least a job that wouldn't result in ritual dismemberment. Not today, at any rate.

"If you'd like to use the elevators on the right?"

"Don't say it!" Pygott hissed in Crone's direction. But too late.

"Would they be Hellavators? Ha-ha!"

Pygott grimaced as much because of Crone's beaming, self-elated expression as the wearisome pun. "Please don't do that again?"

"Quite, sir." The Harpy's eyes were desperately trying not to roll as it forced an insincere chuckle. "Very droll. Whatever you do, please don't use the el – erm, *lifts* on the left."

"May I ask why not?"

"You may. But please, just don't." The Harpy paled even looking in the direction of the granite-clad doors. "One of our partners will be along shortly to collect your luggage."

"Oh, don't worry about our bags! They're happy to take care of themselves, aren't you?" Pygott tipped a smiling wink towards the luggage, which quivered, eager to float off again.

"Please, if you wouldn't mind, allow our partners to convey your accoutrements? They tend to get extremely depressed whenever a customer carries their own luggage. Which means they're Heaven to work with for the rest of the day."

"Well, if you put it that way, we're happy to oblige." Pygott turned to their bags and grinned. "At ease chaps. Take a load off."

The bags settled to the floor. Maybe it was air escaping a seam as they settled, but Pygott could've sworn they'd actually sighed. And their handles drooped in a throng of smiles.

"One last thing, before I collect Mr. Crone and rescue his stomach from that sinful vending machine over there: can I ask who we have to thank for this most generous hospitality? I'm sure we'll find out in due course, but I'd feel more comfortable knowing in whose bed I'm sleeping, as it were."

The Harpy's self-concerned expression had reappeared across his faces long before Pygott had finished the question. It dithered on the edge of fabricating a name, but after a few glances at Pygott's amusedly cocked eyebrow, decided to chance that most uncharacteristic approach: the truth.

"I honestly don't know. My manager gave me strict instructions on how to proceed with your booking, but I only know that he said those instructions 'came from on high'. Which I thought seemed very unusual for a place where the lower you are, the more important your status..."

"Indeed!" Pygott chortled. "Above our pay grade, eh? No matter. But how much is this luxury accommodation going to cost us? I'll freely admit neither I nor Mr. Crone came armed with a great deal of spending power, being but humble booksellers."

"Oh, no sir! Please don't concern yourself over the cost. Everything's already been taken care of and I have strict instructions to provide you with anything you might ask for." The Harpy beamed, presuming this to be the safest pronouncement he'd made all week.

"Ah, well, alright. Erm, thankyou very much."

Pygott turned, juggling the welcome paraphernalia and headed for the lifts, muttering gravely to himself. "Astoundingly, that's the most worrying thing I've heard all week."

Chapter 22:
Hellzavating

The lift doors slid shut, softer than the finest, precision engineered, soft-eject mechanism on an old-fashioned cassette player and a gentle, soothing hum presented the only indication that the contraption had begun to move.

Crone stared nervously at the endless representations of himself reflected in the flawlessly polished, mirrored walls. Each different – unnervingly slightly different – version of himself seemed to be looking back with the tiniest tinge of scorn. He could have sworn that one of them had even tutted as he turned to look at another.

"So, who do you think might be behind intervening in our business and setting up such plush accommodations on this miserably failed sneak into Hell? It can't have been Beelzebub, surely? We didn't tell him anything about where we were going."

"I'm as concerned about this as you, dear friend. Beelzebub might have conjectured we'd pass by, judging by our direction. But even he wouldn't have more than mentioned it to someone in passing at the very most. And he's not the type to organise hospitality, is he?"

"Indeed, no. He certainly wouldn't have attained his position by being so congenial. And I'm sure he wouldn't mind my summation of him as being, not to put too fine a point on it, a tight-fisted old so – erm, scoundrel."

Crone still hadn't looked in Pygott's direction since stepping into the elevator. He stuck out his tongue at one particularly disagreeable reflection and continued to muse. But he was thankfully still paying some attention.

"And what do you think is behind all *this?* When was it decided to convert the upper reaches of Hell into a gaudy, obnoxious pleasure palace? And I seriously suspect there'll be one of those awful, enormous casinos for us to battle our way through on our way to the lower circles." He grimaced. "All that noise and chatter and flashing lights. And the truly hideous carpets, ugh!"

"Which also leads us to the question: *why* have they built this monstrosity at all? What's the point in putting all their time and resource turning Las Vegas into the modern Gomorrah to tempt the masses to sin, if they can have the option of waiting till they're aghast at being slung into Purgatory instead?"

"The Harpy did say they were moving with the times..." Crone piped unconvincingly.

Pygott allowed a wry glance to slither across the space between them.

"And you believe that about as much as I do." His owlbrow cocked so high it almost emigrated into his hairline. "I can't imagine Lucifer signing off on such a carbuncle. He likes the traditional look and the fun of endless puzzles and generally uses brute force to keep people out, not welcome them in! And He certainly prefers the simple styles, not crass commercialism or vainglorious opulence. Granting the denizens of Hell Las Vegas to indulge was a means to deflect such odious nuisance. Installing such a travesty of Hellish tradition at home is definitely something I'd expect Him to put a stop to, most emphatically."

"And it looks funny to me," began Crone, cautiously. "I can't put my finger on it, but everything about it feels so, what's the word...?"

"False?" offered Pygott.

"Exactly!" chimed Crone, with a faltering smile. "It's obviously not a glamour or illusion." He tapped at one of his distasteful visages, releasing a satisfying ring. "But it doesn't feel *real*. It's more like a film set that's been thrown up in a studio. I keep expecting to round a corner and find someone nailing up plywood."

"A distraction, perhaps then?"

"But from what?" Even Crone's disapproving reflections had become interested and were beginning to look more puzzled than offensive. "Has all this been erected for our benefit? Or have we stumbled into some other subterfuge that the Underlords are concerned we might see?"

"Whatever it may transpire to be, we can only hope it won't create even more obstacles to what is already an extremely difficult endeavour."

"Maybe we should just accept all this pretend hospitality and grant ourselves a short holiday instead? After all, the world has to end sometime. Why not be relaxing in one of the safest places while it does?"

"We may not have a choice, dear boy! But who knows?" Pygott clapped his partner on the back with a cheer he surely didn't feel. "For now, here's our floor."

The doors swished open with a self-satisfied sigh that was almost elation. Shortly afterwards joined in harmony by delighted gasps that were pure reflex issuing in Pygott's baritone and Crone's tenor, drifting out of slack-jawed mouths, hung at the bottom of faces bathed in the most beautiful, iridescent light that could never be imagined.

"Oh my. Which button did you press, Mr. Crone? I really don't think *this* is our floor."

Chapter 23:
Raising Hell?

"it doesn't matter how often you stamp those, erm, feet? Nor how much slime the porter has to mop up, I can't let you through."

Aristophonob continued to stomp anyway. Even though its limbs ached, its throat was sore and its eyes blurry under the continual assault of intrusive incandescent lighting drizzling down from what seemed like a million chandeliers. None of its insistence was making the slightest dent in the Harpy's replenished, polished professionalism. He'd been immovable for what may have been the past two hours. And there was no sign that he'd crack anytime close to the demon's onrushing exasperated exhaustion.

"All the flowery phrases and name-dropping in the Underworld couldn't get you into that lift, Mr. Nob. You simply *can't* go where our guests are allowed. It's basically impossible." The Harpy shot a snooty look down all his noses that spoke of finality. And brokered no argument.

Aristophonob took no notice and continued to argue.

"We both know that Pygott and Crone just stepped into that elevator." 'Nob flung a pseudopod in its direction. "So there's no point in pretending that you're preserving the anonymity of what you insist on calling guests! And I have been specifically tasked by Baal himself to follow the pair of them wherever they go. If I have to report back to him that you've obstructed me in that duty-"

"On the contrary, Mr. Nob."

"Please stop calling me *Mister* Nob!"

"As you wish, erm, Nob. You're free to go into that elevator if you wish. I'm not stopping you from going anywhere. I'm simply trying to tell you that lift will not take *you* where it goes."

"You've lost me."

"It's quite simple, Nob. *You cannot go where that elevator goes.* It's impossible."

Aristophonob was finally more confused than irritated.

"But why? Where have they gone?"

The Harpy really didn't like to say the word, but it was his duty to serve his customer to the fullest, however annoying that service may be. So he told it.

Aristophonob paled. Stared in shock at the bank of elevators. Gulped. Wondered how in the name of all things that had ever been evil that it could explain this to its boss. And completely forgot its no-cursing hex.

"Really? *Really?* Oh bolloc – ouch!"

Chapter 24:
Hotel Paradiso

The doors of the elevator grazed apart with the most self-satisfied, pacific sigh. And Pygott and Crone's eyes were momentarily blinded by the beautific eminence of Paradise. Literally.

The pair peered into the centre of all-pervading radiance, gawping uselessly for the moment it took for their senses to truly understand into what they were gazing.

"Is this?" Crone stammered. "Is it really?"

"Oh bolloc-"

"Now, now, Mr. Pygott!" Crone cut him off mid-curse. "That's hardly appropriate language to use in this place."

"Yet entirely appropriate for this situation," grumbled Pygott. "What in Hell's name have we been sent *here* for?"

"Whoever anticipated our entry into Hell has gone to a great deal of effort to deflect our purpose." Crone's brow crinkled even more than it had upon realising where they'd ended up.

"And a deliciously twisted sense of humour to boot," chuckled Pygott, warming to the ruse.

"I don't suppose you prepared any charms or hexes to protect us from anything that might happen to a pair of confirmed sinners?"

Pygott looked aslant at his bag, which was cowering in a corner of the lift. At least their luggage had not been shanghaied en route. "Don't worry, you're not carrying anything that could cause alarm here. You at least are protected from censure." Pygott turned his attention back to the glorious landscape rolling majestic before them. "As for us, Mr. Crone; I have a couple of surprises prepared for an unexpected encounter with the denizens of this realm – but only in case we encountered them *down there*. I fear there'd be little or no effect here. In fact, I don't know if any of the spells I know would work here. Wizardry isn't usually tolerated in such circles..."

"So, we're totally unprotected if we step out of this lift?"

"If we need protection out there, I think the whole concept of the place will be rendered redundant. And anyway, surely whatever they may accuse us of, they're duty bound to forgive us?" Pygott ventured, slyly.

"Of course, Mr. Pygott. If I thought you were a fool, I might just believe you."

"Right now. Mr. Crone, I think I may be a fool. But I still don't believe me."

Chapter 25:
Cold Comfort

Lucifer stared out over the North Pole, tutting briefly at the cluster of adventurers' flags planted at various points, where every expedition had disagreed over the exact location of the true position. Not a single one was quite right.

"Ah, humans," sighed Satan "I did tell You they'd turn out to be nothing but a disappointment, but would You listen? Nah...but what do I know, I'm just an angel?"

Lucifer shook His head wistfully and looked up into an empty, pale blue sky. He was rewarded with a spark of green flame that sputtered and danced and disappeared with a melancholic crackle.

He sat up from His slouch and scanned the horizon, intrigued. Expecting fiery wings and some admonishment from on high. Instead, the green flash returned, stretched, waned and flourished for a few moments. And then exploded into a curtain of wavering hues. Strings of green, yellow, blue and purple accents raced along the sky, reaching up to incite their brothers and sisters to emerge into view and join the chorus. Herne's hunting horn blasted a refrain and the thundering hooves of his retinue roared across the aether in frantic pursuit of an unseen, celestial hart.

The aurora tracked its progress, like God's own graphic equaliser and treated the Lord of the Underworld to a breathtaking five minute vaudeville performance, graced by singers, acrobats, jugglers, magic lanterns and thrilling derring-do, all amalgamated into a single, awe-wrenching atmospheric display.

By the time the last flicker died softly away, with what could almost be the sound of the stage curtain swishing closed again, He found He'd raised Himself off His deckchair in silent standing ovation.

"Damn You," He grinned up to the Heavens. "For all Your faults, You're still a faultless artist. Thanks for that, Old Chap."

And with that, He settled back into His chair, gratified and satisfied that He'd picked exactly the right spot to sit down, gaze through the ozone halo up into the deepest black of the upper atmosphere and relax Himself into a well deserved nap.

He closed His eyes after a while, snoring out steaming clouds of breath that boiled off into the sky like Hell's favourite steam train, *Dante's Allegory*.

And was, for the first time in millennia, truly at ease.

Chapter 26:
Reservations About Reservations

"Mr. Crone, Mr. Pygott, welcome to Heaven."

The angel beckoned to them, its face beaming with benevolence and wings fluttering gently, issuing a dazzling, golden rainbow. The breeze that whispered from the feathers at the tips settled in the small of their backs and nudged them irresistibly out of the elevator.

"There, doesn't that feel better? There's no need to hide away, is there? We're all friends here."

Pygott and Crone both returned looks which they hoped appeared convivial, but were mutually certain displayed more as scathing glares. Pygott glanced back behind him, ruing both the fact that the lift doors were sliding shut and that he'd only just had the presence of mind to consider pushing one of the disappearing buttons, which might have taken them back down, or at the very least retained the option of access.

"Thankyou for the welcome," ventured Pygott. "But aren't uninvited visits to Paradise strictly forbidden? We're not about to be incarcerated for trespass, I hope?"

Crone visibly paled. Which for one of his pallor was quite an achievement.

"Oh, my word! Of course not! You are entirely welcome. And expected."

"Not just expected, it seems..." Pygott's brow formed a deep trough atop his nose.

"Indeed! Careful preparations have been made for your visit. And your every comfort will be catered for. Within reason, of course." The angel beamed, angelically, practically simpering.

"This is all too surreal," muttered Crone, lost in gawping at the secret entrance to Heaven.

"While we appreciate all the hard work you've no doubt put into readying yourselves, we'd very much like to know why we appear to be the only ones who weren't aware we'd be here at all?"

Neither Pygott or Crone had ever seen a confused angel before. They were entities simply not equipped with the necessary tools to cope with concepts such as uncertainty.

"Your reservations were made in all good faith..." offered the angel, already shifting nervously, as though weighing up whether or not to turn tail feather in the face of an angry gryphon.

"That's as may be," growled Pygott. "But whose good faith actually made those reservations? Because it most certainly was neither myself or Mr. Crone, was it, Mr. Crone?"

"The deja-vu is killing me," wailed Crone.

"Indeed," agreed Pygott. "And since when did Hell have an express elevator to the Promised Land? Are you hiring out sections of Heaven to Satan to use as entertainment suites?" Pygott snorted.

"Actually, yes," stammered the angel. "In these austere times, we've all needed to tighten our belts a little and seek more compliance between ourselves and our Underworld partners. We're all on the same team, after all."

This time it was Pygott's turn to look confused. *"The same team? Saints preserve us..."*

On the one hand, he was utterly exasperated, while the other was desperately trying to recall whether members of the Heavenly Host were capable of leg-pulling.

"I need to lay down," whispered Crone, mopping his brow.

Pygott agreed. But found he was incapable of more than the tiniest nod in reply.

"Splendid!" The angel had already forgotten there'd been any objection or difficulty and launched seamlessly back into overbearing genial host mode. "Let's get you to your rooms, shall we?" The angel set off, fully expecting the guests to follow, without the slightest recognition they were still standing shock-still. "I take it your luggage can take care of itself?"

Pygott finally roused, a little more irk reinjecting into his system. And looked around to address the hunkered, equally stymied bags.

"Yes. The service was much better in Hell."

Chapter 27:
Buckets of Baal

Baal remained utterly silent.

Not even the sound of his horns rattling or the clang of dangleberries swinging on his hairy haunches came Mephistophonob's way. The little demon had never, ever heard – or *not heard* - the like in aeons.

And it was currently much too scared to recognise the depth of its terror.

The anticipation was driving it bonkers, prompting it to dare prompt Baal himself to speak. An urge it beat down furiously. Baal's silent rage was already terrible enough and Mephistophonob *did not* want to be the minor demon to crack the seal and free its full-formed, pressurised fury. No matter how jittery the seemingly endless waiting made it suffer.

Oh, to be back to the normal course of howling and ranting insults and blind ignorance of anything 'Nob said! Anything had to be better than this awful, empty, aggressive void.

"WELL..." came an almost impossibly quiet rumbling from below. More tremor than a sound, vibrating up through miles of strata.

Mephistophonob tried its best to keep from squitting as the grumble broke the tension. There were no splats, but it was left with a most uncomfortable, warm, damp squelch between at least a couple of buttocks. With an immense effort of will, 'Nob succeeded in holding back the squeal of fright that leaped into its throat. Better to remain silent until it was asked a direct question. It may be tethered to the lowest demon rung, but that by no means made it stupid.

"SOMEONE SOMEWHERE IS PLAYING THE FOOL AFTER GETTING WIND OF OUR LITTLE SURVEILLANCE OPERATION. WHO WOULD WANT TO KEEP PYGOTT AND CRONE AWAY FROM US? AND WORSE, US AWAY FROM THEM? HMM?" Baal was in uncharacteristically focused mood.

"I don't know, Your Pulchritudinousness. Maybe one of the other council members scoring points? They *were* talking to Beelzebub on the train..."

"AH, YES! THAT OLD BOUNDER, INDEED!" Baal's cacophony had returned to its more usual deafening pitch. Mephistophonob found it almost comforting. "WOULDN'T I KNOW IF BEELZEBUB WAS PLANNING ANYTHING THOUGH? WE ARE ESSENTIALLY THE SAME DEMON, AREN'T WE? IT'S BEEN SO LONG SINCE THE OLD DAYS, I CAN'T REALLY REMEMBER. IN THE BEGINNING, IT WAS JUST ME. AND THEN ALL THESE NEW RELIGIONS

CAME ALONG AND SPLIT ME UP. I HARDLY KNOW WHAT'S ME AND WHAT'S SOME OTHER MALEVOLENCE ANY MORE!"

Baal returned to silent pondering.

Mephistophonob waited. This time, not afflicted by trembles.

"NO, NO. I CAN'T SEE 'BUB BEING INTERESTED IN SUCH INTRIGUE. TOO BUSY RAISING MISCHIEF WITH THOSE FLIES OF HIS. THIS STINKS OF SOMETHING, OR SOMEONE MORE DEVIOUS. MAYBE PYGOTT AND CRONE RUMBLED YOU?"

Normally the little demon would have been petrified at such a notion. But its joy at being asked, rather than the subject of hurled accusation actually buoyed its spirits.

"Not a chance, Your Despoilment, if you'll pardon my candour? Pygott hasn't cast more than a few discovery charms. I've been able to keep well out of range and if I *had* mistakenly triggered any of those charms, I don't think I'd be capable of speaking by now."

"HMM, YES, INDEED. CLEVER CHAP, THAT PYGOTT. NOT CLEVER ENOUGH TO AVOID BEING PARCELLED OFF TO HEAVEN THOUGH, EH?" Baal laughed. Long and hard. And to Mephistophonob's surprise, with genuine amusement. He was actually *sharing* the joke! It was almost – very cautiously – starting to enjoy itself. The job had suddenly become rather more interesting.

"What if it's *them? Up there?*" 'Nob suggested.

"WHAT DO YOU MEAN, *THEM?*"

"What if some sneaky do-gooder discovered what Pygott and Crone are up to and tipped off the Heavenly Host? It must be something *really* important to lead them astray so drastically."

For the first time in Mephistophonob's long and miserable existence, it felt an entirely alien sensation. It was so unprecedented, it had to force itself to recognise what was happening. And even so, didn't actually believe it.

Baal was listening. Asking questions. Taking notice. And somewhat impressed.

"I REALLY HADN'T CONSIDERED SUCH A THING. YOU'RE NOT SUCH A DIM LITTLE DEMON AFTER ALL, ARE YOU?" Baal almost sounded like he was smiling. Mephistophonob's head spun.

"Erm, no, Your Enormous Contemptuousness. My reputation hasn't ever done me justice."

"WELL, MY DEVIOUS LITTLE SERPENT, I THINK IT MAY BE YOUR TIME TO STEP OUT OF THE CAREER SLURRY PIT. IF I PRETEND TO BE JUST AS CLEVER, I MIGHT JUST BE ABLE TO SIDESWIPE THESE POISONOUS NOBS." He chuckled. A horrific, powerful, guttural, amused growl. "DO YOU FANCY BEING THE FIRST OF YOUR KIND TO SERVE HELL IN A VERY SPECIAL WAY?"

"That sounds exciting, Your Indifatigableness." *That sounds a tad dangerous, you old bullock!* Mephistophonob was well aware what Baal normally liked to do with a poisoned nob. "Is it some other secret mission I can assist with wile we wait for Pygott and Crone to descend from Heaven?"

"NOT EXACTLY. I HAVE A FEELING THOSE WINGED SNOBS HAVE NO INTENTION OF ALLOWING THEM OUT OF THE SILVER CITY FOR A WHILE AT LEAST."

Suddenly Mephoistophonob had the feeling it was better remaining an eternal family embarrassment and Hell's favourite kicking stool.

"What do you have in mind, Your Indescribableness?"

"I WANT YOU TO DO SOMETHING NO DEMON HAS EVER DONE BEFORE."

The note of triumph was far too serious for 'Nob's liking. "I like the sound of that a lot," it lied. Hoping none of the utter trepidation it felt had filtered into its voice. "What exactly do you want me to do?"

"MY BOY, GIRL, THING, WHATEVER – GET READY TO BECOME A LEGEND IN HELL FOR ALL ETERNITY."

Argh! Will you please put me out of – or into – my misery?

"YOU'RE ABOUT TO BECOME OUR FIRST SECRET AGENT IN UNCHARTED ENEMY TERRITORY."

"I'm not sure I understand..." 'Nob really couldn't bear the tension any longer. It was in danger of crumpling under the weight of intrigue.

"GET READY FOR A TRIP. I'M SENDING YOU TO HEAVEN."

Mephistophonob's mouths hung slack. Too shocked even to pretend to voice the thanks it was supposed to convey at being granted such an honour.

Such a suicidal, agonising, insane honour.

Oh someone's good God. Why do I never learn to keep my big mouths shut?

Chapter 28:
Pent-up Suite

"Is 'wi-fi' all anyone cares about these days? If I hear anyone tell me the free connection is excellent once more..." Crone wasn't feeling at all Heavenly.

And neither, for that matter, was Pygott. While he'd been briefly happy to enjoy whatever soporifics Hell had conjured to stall them – just long enough to formulate a fresh stratagem – he wasn't in the least comfortable with being forced to navigate a path from entirely the opposite direction.

"I fear I may drown if there really are as many hot-tubs as our over-eager attendants suggest. I can't imagine there'll be any solid ground left inbetween them all." Pygott's expression was more doleful than a bereaved bloodhound. "Who could have predicted Paradise could be so – what's the nicest word - *tacky?*"

"They were always a little excessive with wanting to gild *everything*," offered Crone. "but apart from the odd, gaudy corner, it was bearable. Whereas this..." He peered around and shuddered. "It's like being locked inside the world's sickliest *Build-a-Bear Workshop.*"

Pygott glanced up from the pamphlet he was perusing with some distaste.

"Apparently there's a *Build-an-Angel Workshop* around the corner, in *Hallowed Mall.*"

"Sounds positively hideous! The sooner we're out of here, the better, Mr. Pygott."

"We are entirely in agreement, Mr. Crone. Though Lord knows how we go about achieving that."

"Then maybe we should ask Him?" quipped Crone, without the slightest hint of humour.

Please don't, Pygott kept to himself. *It may yet come to that.*

Chapter 29:
Mall Adjusted

"I know, Mr. Crone. I'm starting to shrivel up like an upturned tortoise in the desert."

Pygott had tried his damnedest to distract himself from Crone's persistent bellyaching about the oppressive lighting, sub-tropical heat, nose-twitching artficial odours pumped out through skin-crackling air-conditioning and the bland, irritating background music that was just – *just* – loud enough to be unavoidably intrusive, that couldn't make up its mind if it was optimistically jingly or unchallenging and soporific. And most of all, the endless troupes of people, souls, cherubs and seraphs all blundering around the aisles in aimless non-direction. Devoid of purpose, utterly alien to the concept of spatial awareness and ignorant – *rude* – in a way that was so absently passive, it was impossible to rouse them to a level of consciousness where Pygott and Crone's impotent rage might gain some manner of useful release.

If just one more numpty stopped dead in front of them though, gawking blankly at another shop window display on one side of the aisle (all of which they appeared able to block with their puny forms), then just as suddenly dart in the opposite direction towards another equally sappy store, just as the pair attempted to walk past, one or both of the booksellers was going to lose control and become the harbingers of some most unHeavenly rebuke.

"Doesn't this labyrinth ever end?" Crone huffed through exhausted breaths. "At least in the old days they made puzzles and mazes that could be solved, so there was at least a chance of escaping! But this is just interminable."

"I've been keeping my eyes open to look for a chink in the structure. Something that will let us through to the - how can I put it - back office, if you will? Ouch! Madam, will you watch where you're going?! And to you too!" Pygott shook a fist. "Where was I? Ah, yes. The back orifi, erm office. From there, we should be able to fashion a viable route back to somewhere less mind-numbing."

"And have you found a way out?" There was already a worrying note of desperation in Crone's tone. Mainly because Pygott was starting to feel the same twitch.

"Though it pains me to admit, my dear boy, the answer is a decided no." Pygott tried manfully not to look directly at the effect of his honesty, as he couldn't raise a reassuring expression in response. "Please don't cry, Mr. Crone?"

"I'm not crying," sobbed Crone in protest. "It's this damnable strip-lighting setting off my aversion. I swear I'll be blinded before we get to the next hideous fountain."

"Fountain?" Pygott brought his attention back to the broad, spangle-paved avenue they traversed. "Ah, that gruesome thing? Didn't Lucifer force the 80's to end specifically to be rid of that sort of – oh?"

Pygott stopped dead, causing several slack-jawed amblers to crumple into his back like a flesh concertina. They eventually, after standing confused, blinking blankly into his shoulder blades, slid past and waddled on their way like amoebae feeling out a morsel. Crone was a dozen steps forward of his partner before realising his next statement was about to be delivered to nothing but recirculated air.

He pirouetted like Mavis Cruet dancing atop a tree stump and peered back at Pygott, who appeared to be doing his best impersonation of a fiendish genius. Before he could make any utterance, Crone was fixed with a flashing, triumphant wink.

"Fountains, Mr. Crone!"

"You've lost me again, Mr. Pygott."

"I have a ruse bubbling, Mr. Crone. Which may just give us what we need to find a way out."

Chapter 30:
All Hell Breaking Loose?

Hell was in uproar.

And the Reception Hotel & Transport Interchange Complex (or 'HeReTIC' as the corporate punsters smugly referred to it, no matter how strained the acronym) had barred the doors to keep out the tsunami of damned and demons clamouring to find out not only if the rumours were true, but also to seek the golden pig that confirmation might deliver.

Of course, this was causing merry chaos.

Much as the souls of the damned being forced to stand around in a seemingly never-ending queue was a handy addendum to their prescribed course of suffering, it really wasn't doing any favours for the Grand Arch Torturer's dyspepsia. Especially as she'd climbed the ladder so high that it had been a very long time since she'd been forced to get her talons dirty or flex a muscle to lash a screaming soul to ribbons. Sitting in a plush office, overseeing a pool of beavering administration demons and suffering office sinners had always been sold to her as a faultless career move, stuffed with perks: a position of influence and power. A relaxing, executive post with a key to the VIP bathroom and holidays in the company villa in Nuevo Gomorrah.

Instead, it had turned out to be the very worst decision she'd made in her entire unlife.

She hated it.

The air conditioning sucked the life out of the fiery pits to such an extent that on most days that there was hardly even a comforting whiff of sulphur. The atmosphere control not only stopped the endless reams of paper pushed back and forth across her desk from bursting into flames, but also, no matter how many layers and unctions she wore, nor heating dials she spun, she was constantly bathed in cool sweats as her body protested at not being slaked with regular, skin-scorching magma splashes. It was bloody freezing all the time!

The inane chatter drifting from the boring rut of aspirational half-wits across the office made her want to rip out her own ears and nail them inside a distant volcano. And the pressure to meet pointless targets shifting souls and filing completed paperwork was incessant: demands flung down from the kind of bosses who, quite frankly, no one should ever disappoint. It was almost impossible to fabricate acceptable excuses for delays and worse still, Devil forbid she could ever risk failure.

The present backlog of entry visas and incomplete admissions was planting ulcers on top of ulcers on top of burst ulcers. And though she knew there was absolutely nothing she could do to change the situation beyond being granted a fanciful tenfold increase in staff budget, that didn't stop the endless avalanche of passive-aggressive messages and surly visits from irate heads of each level of Hell, roaring out demands for their fresh influx of trident fodder. *'We have targets, don't you know?!'*

"Urgh." *There goes another popped ulcer.* "I suppose I ought to go out and deliver some sort of pep-talk and organise another meeting." Oh Hell, how she detested having to chair meetings!

Chapter 31:
Trouble at t'Mill

Someone or something, so the whispers went, had found a direct route between Hell and Heaven. But not only that, they'd used it!

And according to the rumour mill – which had completely stopped the grinding mill that spun at the centre of Level 3 to make soul-mince for Level 4's long-pork pies – whoever had succeeded in piercing the veil was currently swanning about in Paradise, having the time of their lives, or deaths! Indulging in all the pleasures that eternal Eden could provide. Bathed in the milk of angels, swathed in the finest silks and gold, eating manna like it fell from the skies (which, infuriatingly, it no longer ever did!).

But the most annoying – and hottest – rumour claimed that they had made absolutely no secret of their presence amidst the righteous. The latest tattle hinted that if someone found the right portal, *anyone* could make the same trip, without security controls or border posts to negotiate. Supposedly, everyone could now be free to go where they wanted – up, down or sideways – with all the freedom they wished. The only thing that had stood in the way all these years was bureaucracy. And the belief amongst the wider populace such that they were stuck where they'd been dumped solely because they'd been *told* that's where they were meant to be.

Predictably, everyone was livid.

The damned were incensed that they should have been able to take a break from torment if they pleased, if only they knew how. And so were rebelling against their convictions and refusing to turn up for daily punishment in droves. The pain-dealing crews were furious that their domination had met with pointed interference by their clients and in turn were becoming increasingly tempestuous, the longer their sadistic impulses failed to be tempered by the everyday, measured release. Some had even started thrashing each other, which further antagonised those involved.

Arrivals and administration were all tearing their horns out as fresh meat continued to arrive, then hit a log-jam of already delayed souls on one side resisting being forced in, versus most of the rings of Hell clamouring to get out. And once the newbies had been tapping their feet and tutting, concerningly for much shorter periods than was politic, the wildfire gossip was burning their ears and prompting them to turn around and spark sporadic skirmishes as they were prevented from going back the way they came, at the very least.

The bigwigs were fuming at operations stalling and running far from smoothly, if at all, and grumbling loud about the reign of chaos. The irony of the Lords of Hell complaining about submitting Hell to the machinations of chaos seemed utterly lost upon their annoyance. Every mention of the situation stoked up further plumes of wrath, all of which was in turn heaped on the heads of their over-stretched subordinates.

Poor Xenophon had already been reduced to steaming tears and was becoming more and more desperate as he watched his beloved Hell-fires dwindling hour by hour, starved of the blood and flesh suffering that fuelled the furnaces

Baal himself was even more exasperated than usual, as he couldn't find anyone to blame for starting the rumour. Especially important being that it was, in part at least, true. No one was directly aware of Pygott and Crone's diversion, as even Baal himself had been unable to find how or by whose hand it had occurred. And he'd been very, *very* careful, devious in slipping Aristophonob into one of the regular ascendences from Purgatory. Plus, as he'd monitored the operation intimately (much to the little demon's express discomfort), just in case any difficulty should interrupt proceedings, he already knew that little 'Nob hadn't given itself away. And no one appeared to twig the deception at least as far as the point Baal lost contact with 'Nob slinking through the Pearly Gates.

He was systematically venting his frustrations on various lesser demons, through no fault of their own. But even this was already becoming tiresome. He wanted to get his horns on the scumbag who'd practically placed him in the line of Satan's ire and left him to dangle on the edge of a precipice from which he'd spent aeons chucking the unrighteous to their ultimate doom. He really did not like the sensation one tiny bit. And the sooner he could get back to the secure role of chucker, rather than potential chuckee, the less fraught he'd feel. He'd never experienced dyspepsia before and fully understood the bellyaching – literally – that stomach ulcer sufferers like that nincompoop in the visa and immigration office constantly harped on about.

"IT'S WORSE THAN I THOUGHT," Baal ruminated "NOW LOOK AT ME: ONE OF THE MOST IMPORTANT DEMONS IN ALL THE UNDERWORLD AND I'VE DEVELOPED A SUDDEN STREAK OF EMPATHY!" *Shudder.*

Chapter 32:
The Fount of all Knowledge

"Mr. Pygott, I'm confused." Crone was doing his best to keep up as his partner nipped from pillar to post to desk to pointless electronic display.

"Don't fret, Mr. Crone. I've got used to that over the years."

"Thankyou, Erm, I mean, no. You're confusing me! Stop it."

"What is there to be confused about, Mr. Crone? We set off for Hell to retrieve a book that nobody believes really exists, only to find that Hell has turned into a faux Las Vegas resort hotel that unceremoniously bundled us up to Heaven, which appears to have been rebranded as a New Jersey shopping mall, which to all intents and purposes is keeping us imprisoned for no discernible reason. Surely that all seems a simple set of circumstances?"

Crone folded his brow, which made his nose wrinkle into a florid walnut and shook his head.

"No, no, no! Fountains!"

"Not here, no."

"Why ever not? You said you had a plan that has something to do with fountains! Yet we've walked past several this morning without even pausing to notice."

"That's because we aren't looking for fountains at the moment."

"Then what *are* we looking for?" Crone's flush was rising to the point where restaurant diners were pointing him out as the lobster they'd like to be served for dinner.

"We're looking for a hardware shop."

"Are you intending to build a fountain yourself? Is your plan to show-up the designers of all these other fountains with a ravishing display of artistry? Because I'm off to ruin my digestion amidst the plastic foam of a mocha latte until you finish the project. I for one, forgot to prime my builder's-arse crack this morning!"

"On the contrary, my dear Crone. Building is the last thing on my mind. What I really want is a nice, hefty sledge hammer. But in this pathetic place, where no one is required to lift a finger, 'God helps those who help themselves' seems to have become anathema. But as a simile for shopping malls on Earth, there should be a token version of *everything* that one would expect to find, yet all I've seen as yet is some dainty nonsense that would hardly dent a tray of bonfire toffee. How in God's name can they call this charade Paradise?"

"And I always described these places as Hell on Earth," opined Crone. "But in past experience, Hell is so much more cosy."

Pygott had already stopped to fidget over yet another exploded diagram surrounded by a thicket of lush palm fronds, that seemed to detail only endless opportunities for the idle to consume. The increasing angle of the hunch in his spine and proliferation of grunts and sighs indicated that he wasn't being offered the single product he actually wished to consume, as it were.

"Right, we're going to chase one more wild goose before I resort to desperate measures. Normally that might involve ripping out one of those seats and using it as a substitute, but they look so flimsy, I'd have a better chance using my dickie-bow."

"It wouldn't be the first time, Mr. Pygott."

Chapter 33:
Hallowed Be They Nob

Mephistophnob couldn't quite work out if it was having the time of its non-life. Or affliction by some hideous malady that might pervert its nature forevermore.

It was shopping – in full, undisguised view of everyone – around exactly the kind of environs it would normally avoid like a herd of Jehovah's Witnesses on a door-knocking crusade. There was intolerable, air-conditioned, humidity controlled heat. And cold, depending which retail habitat zone it was skipping about. There was light. *So* much light. Artificial strip lighting that hurt and dulled the eyes of even the human souls it saw milling around aimless in its way. It hadn't found a solitary dim nook anywhere since it breezed through the swishing, automated entrance doors.

What it had found was sweet, bordering on cloying, floral, entirely manufactured aromas wafting from vents that bordered every aisle, along with intermittent tsunamis of coffee and caramel and curry and more comfortingly, now and then a hint of too-long exposed fish from scattered sushi bars. And in the background, harmonising blandly with the hubbub from shuffling feet and mumbled, grumbled non-conversation below, there was a ceiling of insipid, tinkling Muzak, that neither soothed or entertained. It was simply, unavoidably *there.*

Normally, by this point, Mephistophob would have been scratching off its scales and gargling its own bile as its corporeal body vomited resistance to the overloading hideous stimuli.

But instead, to its utter surprise, it found itself flouncing atop the composite paving, gazing through shop windows filled with trinkets and baubles, sauntering idly up and down packed display racks to try on clothes that couldn't possibly fit its highly unusual body shape and hats that weren't big or shapely enough to cover all its heads. It was wolfing down takeaway foods that should be churning its stomachs to clotted bilge and generally gambolling about wearing beaming smiles across all its mouths like a debutante heiress who'd managed a sly manoeuvre to give her gaggle of nannies the slip.

It was elated. Enthralled.

And filled with the most unnaturally beautific enthusiasm for, well, *everything.*

It didn't care where it was going or what it was seeing and certainly had forgotten all about what it was supposed to be doing there in the first place.

Heaven was flipping brilliant!

And if it had been aware of the rewards for piety or slavish obedience or whatever classified that religion stuff these days were anything like this rush of feeling, it might well have repented and done its utmost to defect to the other side centuries ago.

If it *had* done so, Mephistophonob would have been very disappointed.

Heaven in those days was a spartan, grim-faced, pious enclave. More like Lady Whiteadder's boudoir than the new Eden. And Mephistophonob itself would have been thrashed daily with nettles and birch sticks for several hours to ensure that its demonic nature was being thoroughly vanquished. And as punishment for having been demonic at all.

And of course, because the citizens of Heaven back then were all antisocial sadists.

Either God had become doddery, soft in His dotage or Nietzsche had been right after all and He was lying in state on some distant, ceremonial cloud. Or, possibly, He really had got fed up with looking down on the sorry mess the human race had made of His glorious creation and decided to sublet the real estate through a profiteering realtor and had buggered off to sunny, uncaring retirement in Lanzarote.

Whichever, Mephistophonob didn't care.

As long as it could get away with staying in this particular assignment, the logistics mattered not a jot.

Which is when, annoyingly, common sense gingerly, grudgingly raised its hand.

If 'Nob was to grant its own wish and remain skipping gaily about the aisles of *Hallowed Mall* – naff name, but catchy – it was essential to maintain at least two circumstances. First, it had to keep Baal onside. Which meant at least presenting the appearance of doing the bull's bidding and carry on reporting tabs on Pygott and Crone's where and whenceabouts. Even if the information it passed on wasn't entirely accurate or up-to-the-minute. And secondly, *vitally,* do whatever it took to keep the booksellers trapped here with it. With any luck, for eternity.

I'd better get my noses back in working order and find them. They can't be up to any mischief here though, I imagine?

Chapter 34:
You Take the Low Road...

Pygott leaned nonchalant on the smooth ash handle of his shiny new sledgehammer. Calm, satisfied by a job well done. Manfully hiding his discomfort at realising though he'd taken careful steps to protect his favourite suede shoes from everything Hell might throw at them – molten lava, demon sweat and spit, boiling blood, brimstone and Turkish Delight – save for an initial brush with Scotchguard, he'd not reckoned on a fountainsworth of lavender coloured water lapping over his instep.

It had already begun to seep into his socks. And what's more, it was uncommonly cold.

Crone was inching ever backward, away from the steadily spreading puddle, mouth agape as his eyes darted back and forth between the head of the flood, the immense hole in the base of the fountain and Pygott's unblinking, expectant expression.

The whole mall seemed to have stopped.

Time itself, as much as it existed here, had ceased and the silence was palpable. Even the perpetually piped snooze-music had called a halt to itself and held its electronic breath in anticipation of what might happen next. Along with everyone and everything else on that shopping mile.

Until suddenly, all Heaven broke loose.

Angels appeared from everywhere.

As though the entire host had all being playing a particularly skilful game of hide-and-seek amongst the pillars and potted ferns, but had just realised en-mass that the seeker was cheating and had found them all at once by nefarious means. They used to play the game with God Himself in the early days, but His omnipresence made hiding a fruitless endeavour and the game proved continually dissatisfying for all involved. Even though they persisted in trying to keep the game alive so long that God was forced to invent the concept of common sense to put a stop to the escalating nonsense.

The angels flapped and fussed and ushered bystanders out of the way and threw a forest of *Caution: Slip Hazard* signs across all four cornerless spaces, blocking off seats and walkways and shop entrances in a flurry of organised panic. Lest anyone should suddenly reverse their instinctive decisions to get as far away from the contretemps as possible, in an attempt to finagle dubious afterlife litigation. Because, contrary to all expectation, St. Peter still allowed Pearly Gate access to an inordinate amount of ambulance-chasing shysters. Who all carried on in death as in life.

Eventually, satisfied that they'd fulfilled every health and safety procedure on the tick-sheet, a gaggle of angels danced around a pinhead of whipping mops and surrounded an unmoved Pygott. Most of them were totally unused to scowling and the expression really didn't sit well on their angelic faces.

The presumed Archangel (though more likely, simply the designated team leader of the mass of minions) stepped forward, planted feet firmly in hero pose, thrust forth gossamer-clad hips and sucked in a brawny breath, ready to bellow with all the righteous fury that Heaven could muster.

And was rudely interrupted by a decidedly unrepentant perpetrator.

"There seems to be an awful mess here. Caused by terribly shoddy workmanship too. I barely brushed against this carbuncle and it burst like an author's dreams of stardom. You're lucky I'm not the type to sue."

The angel's expression fell like Lucifer Himself plunging out of the clouds, long before anyone had the presence of mind to write about it.

Stupefaction, it transpired, was another expression that didn't cling too well to an angelic visage.

Pygott had introduced a whole new experience to the trainee angels charged with perpetuating a harmonious environment within the galleries of Heaven's gleaming, eternal distraction.

No one had told them there were such things in the hereafter as consternation.

Souls allocated to swanning around the malls and lidos and plush apartments above cloud level weren't wilful, didn't cause trouble or damage the facilities with intent. And certainly didn't impertinently provoke innocent angels who were blithely flitting around being generally pious and only trying to do God's bidding.

"My feet are getting very wet," pouted Pygott. "Don't any of you sorry creatures know where the stop-cock is?"

"We're doing the best we can, sir," offered the exasperated angel. Edged with just a hint of sharp irritation.

"Those mops are just swilling it around and making me even wetter. Who's in charge of this sorry display of incompetence? These are new shoes! And you're ruining them."

Pygott extended a bony finger and jabbed it into the centre of the angel's puffed chest. And made it flinch with each stabbing contact.

"This is Heaven, sir. We are a socially aware, self-regulating construct and rely on our-"

"So *you're* not in charge then? I'll talk to someone else." Pygott buried his palm square in the angel's chest and shoved it aside. Aloof and unconcerned, Pygott tossed his eyes around the galleries and boomed haughtily. "Who *is* in charge of this *deplorable* mess?"

A valve popped. Blew somewhere down deep in the angel's psyche. It's face burned redder than Lucifer's left butt cheek and where its sandals were planted in the still ebbing puddle of escaped water feature, there were wisps of vapour forming tendrils up between its toes.

It was angry.

And had no idea either what such emotion meant or how it had arisen at all. It had much less knowledge still about how to control or release it in an appropriate fashion. Accordingly, it reacted in a fashion that was entirely inappropriate.

It practically exploded.

And Pygott — more impressed than he imagined he could be at snapping the creature's resolve — really thought that the angel might spontaneously combust, detonating itself, and send scorched chunks of angelic shrapnel flying into the aisles and shops and faces of aghast shoppers.

Perhaps Pygott's swift triumph had been a little too successful?

Everyone in Heaven heard it go off.

In fact, Pygott suspected more than a few sensitive people on Earth and possibly even the upper levels of Hell possibly felt the shock-wave and winced at the titanic, shrieking roar that had erupted from the angel's astounded, terrified, fulminating mouth.

He definitely hadn't expected he'd have to put only minimal effort into cracking the angel's shell to prompt him to commit a mortal sin. But if this was all it took to tempt the poor creature into becoming consumed by wrath, he'd raise not the slightest grumble. The poor thing evidently already had unresolved issues.

Pypott risked a glance around to locate Crone, hoping he'd not melted too successfully into the scattered palm frond jungle jutting out from the base of each pillar. He needed to be close, as this opportunity might evaporate at any second and accidentally leaving Crone behind would be of no help to Pygott's plans at all.

The main problem was that being within the blast radius of a detonating angel required no mean level of courage. And for all his virtues, his partner Mr. Crone's most successful survival ploy was to defer to cowardice. Though Crone's methods had worked beautifully at least until now, that might prove an unfortunate complication in this scenario.

Predictably, Crone had eased his way into a large frond a short distance behind Pygott and camouflaged himself astoundingly well as a stumpy palm trunk.

Pygott, satisfied Crone was within reach returned his full attention to the fuming angel, who was already in full, fury-bitten flow, turning the air a deep, undignified shade of blue. Pygott almost felt sorry for it, but it was too useful to him to indulge in fripperies such as compassion. And he really needed to shepherd it nearer the hiding Crone with some haste.

Pygott turned his back on the angel and sidled off in Crone's direction, splashing water as hard and high as he could, causing a wave that flooded an area one of the minions had just managed to mop dry.

"Tut-tut, look at the state of this place. My feet are getting soaked all the way over here too."

The angel stopped its tirade for a second and gaped, glaring after Pygott with undisguised loathing.

"Where the bloody Heaven do you think you're going, you odious, insignificant spurt of monkey spawn? I was talking to you!" Spittle was flying from flecks of foam gathered at the corners of its mouth.

Screaming, more like, noted Pygott. *And I believe you've just added a dash of pride to your rap sheet. It's just getting better! Or worse, in your case.*

"I believe I said I was going over here to look for someone competent enough to be in charge," Pygott prodded in the most obsequious voice he could muster. Which turned out so potent he found even himself irritated by the tone.

"*I was talking to you!* Have the decency to pay attention while I'm finished!"

Pygott had finally managed to pique Crone's heed. And inbetween paying enough lip-service to the angel to crank up its ire, had succeeded in transferring enough subtle hints that Crone had realised this was a plan in action, rather than just bewildering melodrama. And if nothing else, Crone had recognised that he needed to be back beside his partner to be involved in whatever manufactured chaos Pygott had set in motion.

"Well, I decided you had nothing to say that was worth hearing, so I-"

"I am *the* most important one in this entire place!!!" The angel bellowed, rattling the roof stanchions in order like a domino xylophone.

Bingo! Pygott rejoiced. "Mr. Crone, ready yourself."

The angel opened its spume-drooling mouth to unleash another torrent of rebuke in Pygotts' direction. Just at the same instant it realised that it had become utterly paralysed. Larynx and all.

And there was a pair of humans – flesh and bone, living humans, for Heaven's sake! - gripping tight to its immovable elbows.

Even worse, not only were they flagrantly not discarnate souls, like every other non-angel that strolled the artificial avenues, they were smirking! In a very self-satisfied, patronising and *infuriating* manner.

A fury that the angel was frustratingly unable to release.

Pygott had fully expected the event would be marked by, at the very least, a cavalcade of lightning bolts, thunder claps, flashing lights and wailing souls. Possibly even the deafening boom of Metatron - if not such embodiment in person – proclaiming the poor angel's damnation. It was in the process of being punished for one of the ultimate transgressions and banished from Heaven, to be cast into eternal exile within the molten pits of Hell – the absolute nadir on any angel's career. And it had already missed the boat for inclusion in any book that would make it famous.

So it really was most impolite that its boss – God – couldn't be bothered to announce what was being done to it by some sort of proxy, let alone snubbing it in person.

All that happened was a grave chill enveloping the trio, bringing with it an inferred cone of darkness that descended, paradoxically, from above. And then continued to descend after swallowing its target.

The angel's outrage mutated into sheer exasperation. All of which it could only convey via wide-staring, tearful eyes. It seemed its cat-like irises were the only part of its being that had escaped incapacitation and they compensated by retreating as far towards the corner of its eyes as its face would allow.

Pygott actually felt a glimmer of guilt and no small measure of sympathy.

Still, needs must!

As the cone descended, illuminated numbers appeared and rolled upward past them, presumably thought Pygott, to tick off the myriad levels of reality they were falling through. The angel's unblinkiing eyes followed each digit until it disappeared and refocussed on the next in the sequence rising from the non-existent floor. It took what Pygott considered far too many numbers for those panicked eyes to flush with comprehension. And even then only once the quite irksome, repetitive mechanical voice repeating "Fall" over and again sank into its stupified ears did its hardened crust of ignorance finally shatter.

The angel's jaw dropped.

Its eyes responded in a way that suggested it wasn't at all sure it was free from paralysis and had managed to perform the task itself, or that perhaps the *Fall Portal* (as it appeared to be labelled, judging by the shiny plaque projected beneath each successive number) had taken some pity on its passengers and granted the gift of a gasp to help with shock management.

Pygott turned his attention to Crone, who was still gripping onto the angel's arm with pearl-white knuckles, using what looked like sufficient force to crush ordinary mortal bones. The colour of his face was underlain by a similar whiteness, but even that was underlayered by a grey, slightly green pallor that reminded Pygott of a monkfish that was one gasp short of suffocating.

"Please don't vomit until we land, Mr. Crone? I shudder to think what the contents of your stomach might do to the interior of this portal. I can't see any vents..."

Crone nodded, teeth clamped and lips sealed with the same force his fingers exerted on the unfortunate angel. He was already well ahead of Pygott in estimating the consequences of conceding to his body's diaphragm-jerk reaction and had about him the air of a man worried the portal wouldn't stop before his resistance broke.

He managed to summon a modicum of humour though. Much to Pygott's chagrin.

"I almost preferred the other Hellevator."

Pygot did his best to ignore the pun anew, distracting himself by noting that the level numbers had already turned to a fire-licking red colour.

"Stay strong, Mr. Crone! We're already plummeting through the seven rings of Hell, it appears. We'll soon arrive!" He threw a smile across the angel's twelve-pack. And realised that he really shouldn't have used the word, 'plummet'.

The very lowest number rolled up and wavered for a second at everyone's eye level, simultaneously. Then blurred into incomprehension as the portal crashed to a shuddering, bone-jangling jolt.

Crone, to his eternal credit, held onto the spasm that rocketed through his abdomen and at least for now kept the inevitable tsunami of biliousness inside his jiggling belly.

The portal's tone changed from bland, corporate information drone to gleeful, demonic mania. It practically showered them in oily information of their destination, now repeating, "Fallen". It almost sounded like a chuckle.

The portal withdrew, to reveal a sea of ice that roiled and writhed like an angry ocean of wind-thrashed water nonetheless. And was surrounded on all sides by a whirlwind of liquid fire.

Pygott had heard tales of the Ninth Circle of Hell, but had never been there himself. Nor ever seen an accurate depiction, it seemed.

It was beautiful. And utterly breath-taking in a way that the blandishments of Heaven could only envy, had that been allowed up there. Pygott found the entire vista very calming and sedate. It looked as though everything here moved in a vacuum of slow-motion and silence. There were no crackles bursting out of the flames, no creaks or grating from the ice waves crunching around and over one another. Not a single scream from a tortured, frozen soul. There was perfect, dignified silence.

As the veil lifted completely, their drying eyes could see one of Hell's guardian angels step forward to greet them. It was clad in a scarlet monk's habit and endlessly ran a set of pentagram-embossed rosary beads through its scaly fingers. It smiled paternally at the confused angel. Whilst failing to make it plain that it really hadn't expected there to be a pair of breathless booksellers bookending its bemusement.

Keeping itself as unfazed as possible, it launched into a speech it hadn't been able to dust off in millennia.

"Good day. Thankyou for choosing Hell for your eternal serv-"

SPLAT!

Crone finally lost control of his volcanic anti-peristalsis as the portal sank to rest with a final jerk. And painted the plush velvet garment with acid carrots and sweetcorn.

"Ugh! So very, very sorry, dear boy!" Crone looked as green as the habit had been red. "I can't even remember eating any sweetcorn..."

Chapter 35:
No Relaxation for the Wicked

Aristophonob stopped giggling. And looked around the shop to see what had caused the sudden change in atmosphere.

The tickle that had been, well, tickling it as the tank of little fish nibbled furiously at a millenniaworth of corns and scales on several tentacles had stopped being the only tickling sensation and it was distracting it from the severe pleasure of indulging in a piscine pamper.

Something was niggling at the nape of its necks. And spoiling the enjoyment generated by the relaxing, entirely gratis spa session. Which was doubly irritating, as Aristophonob was only just getting used to the concept of Heavenly pleasure.

It was a little disturbing, as the intriguing sensation felt alarmingly normal. Exactly the kind of notion it was used to feeling as part of its pre-Paradise existence.

Aristophonob raised its limbs out of the tank, taking the opportunity to snaffle a few attached, still ravenous fish before realising that halving the aquarium's population might be noticed and cause some consternation. There didn't appear to be any 'Please don't eat the fish' signs, but 'Nob reasoned that eating the cleaning staff might possibly be frowned upon.

It brushed away as many of the rest of the rasp-toothed marvels as possible from out of its nooks and the odd cranny and slithered off in search of clues. Already far too distracted to notice the torrent of wails left in its wake as the shop staff discovered the river of slimy ooze despoiling a fish tank and trailing out of the door.

Aristophonob sniffed the perfumed, filtered air, peered around the banks of soft-tone, unrealistic lighting arrays and scanned the ranks of generic shop-fronts. And peered into the blankly enthused faces of shopping zealots filing endlessly past. Such an easy, nonchalant existence! Why would any demon not opt to spend eternity free from toil, responsibility, ambition or desire? Free to wander aimlessly forever amongst a constant barrage of wish-fulfilment and a belly that was never empty? And the temperature that wouldn't vary from the temperate median?

Whatever soporifics they pumped into the constantly churning air-con had certainly worked their pacific magic on the little demon. Barely days ago, having to spend five minutes in such an insipid, cutesy environment would have had it breaking out in blotches and a rash of hives, squinting in ocular pain and scratching itself to frantic ribbons in its efforts to remove itself from the unctuous stimuli.

But against all the odds it felt inordinately comfortable here.

And it sensed that comfort was in danger...

"I haven't contacted Baal in while. Maybe it's just a niggle there'll be trouble if I don't send an update on...oh?!"

The truth about the prickles and prods at Aristophonob's twitching nostril cilia flumped down with brutal weight.

Pygott and Crone are gone.

It couldn't detect any sense of them anywhere.

The last time it could remember sensing them, they were strolling around the mall without a care in the unworld. Dipping in and out of shops, Pygott striding like a Greek God on holiday at Universal Studios, tutting at the Disney caricatures of himself, while Crone bumbled along behind like Bubo the mechanical owl, displaying an ever-shifting mix of excitement at each emerging marvel he wanted to trial and grumps of dejection each time Pygott pooh-poohed the suggestion, and marched onward with little more than a cursory nod to his partner's protestations. He did though concede to Crone's earnest pleas for ice cream, even though he hadn't partaken himself. And appeared utterly at ease throughout each devouring as Crone gobbled Flakes, wafers, nutty sprinkles and fruity syrup like a hyena rushing through a boar's ribcage.

They had presented the picture of normality and gave Aristophonob all evidence needed to satisfy itself that it could relax and have the afternoon off, at the very least.

Hellfire!

Just when it thought its luck may have finally turned, the brimstone had noticed and gathered together a posse of fiery, stinky rocks to hurl themselves at the little demon and ruin its fun.

Humans! Can't trust them with anything, bah!

In a titanic grump, Aristophonob gathered its resolve into a trudge back to unappreciated servitude. It wondered if the ban on cursing that had hovered with menaces above its heads was still active in Heaven? Because it really, really wanted to kick inanimate objects and have a seriously good, bad, hard swear. But still daren't test that hypothesis right now.

It had enough woes to contend with.

Chapter 36:
Loss Adjustment

"I really can't apologise enough. If only we had our luggage, I'd offer you a towel..."

The sodden angel - who had finally managed to sluice enough sputum from its chin to dare open its mouth and announce its name, Vassago – issued a rasping snort that belied its extreme, suppressed annoyance. But turned its gritted fangs to Crone and forced a smile.

"Don't worry about it, young man. These things happen." There was a weariness behind the statement that served as mild comfort to Crone, if only because it indicated he didn't bear any personal grudge. "In fact, these things happen practically *every time* someone arrives in that Satan-forsaken contraption..."

Vassago picked another gobbet of misidentifiable luncheon from the semi-liquid beard it seemed to have grown and flicked it aside. Inadvertently knocking down a small, stone hut and crushing a miniature bellows pump attendant in the process. It crawled out from under the wreckage and rattled an enraged fistula at the receding group. And squeaked a torrent of oaths that turned the flames in the air bright blue.

Pygott, still under the influence of a translation glamour, reacted by turning a phenomenal shade of pink.

The group pressed on regardless; Vassago on point and setting a tremendous pace, Pygott and Crone skipping confused at its ankles, entirely oblivious to where they were being led. And a most bemused fallen angel, who until barely moments ago had been wandering around Paradise, herding sickeningly contented souls around an endless, sedate retail experience, brought up the rear in open-mouthed disbelief, dragging the tips of its forlorn wings along the springy, tacky basalt. It's only cogent thought was to consider changing its name to 'Despondent'.

"Now, now, Dys! Don't be despondent, my lad! There's a wealth of opportunity awaiting you in Hell." Vassago aimed an agricultural wink at the ever-dropping jaw of its counterpart. "Your punishment was doled out by that po-faced lot up there, whereas with the right attitude, an eternity here can actually be *fun.*"

Dys – reeling at the notion that its name had officially been changed within moments of its descent to Hell – boggled and paused. At least that's what it thought, though its feet thought otherwise and kept it moving. Bringing it further shock when it swam back to lucidity and startled itself by realising it appeared to have teleported twenty yards forward. It shook its head, stuck out its bottom lip and decided to ignore Vassago's infuriating optimism and instead turned its attentions to surveying the iciily fiery view scrolling past instead.

Pygott, on the other hand found a sudden spring to his step. And raised a cloud trail of fiery stripes in his wake that came close to breaching Stephen Spielberg's copyright.

"Excuse me!"

Crone wandered on behind. Wondering why they were following this vomit-encrusted angel at all, instead of slipping away to continue with their more urgent assignment. After all, it was so self-assured and setting such a bruising, never-look-back pace that it wouldn't likely notice their absence before they'd bumped into Judas's commemorative, David Blaine inspired ice-coffin at the very least. He also wondered why Pygott had suddenly become so irksomely chirpy and wondered – yet more! - just what the Dickens he was up to.

"Hello, Mr. Crone! Lovely day for a stroll!"

Crone rounded, recognising the voice. Though nonplussed to hear it in this setting.

"Ah, good day, Charles. What the Dickens are you doing here?" The same pun out loud. Crone cringed.

"Ha! Good one, Mr. Crone, very droll. Can't stop; I have urgent business. We'll catch up in the shop soon, I hope?"

"Yes indeed. The kettle's always on..."

And he was gone.

Crone frowned. This trip was becoming less predictable by the minute.

Pygott, on yet another hand, was grinning ear to earring.

"Vassago, isn't it?"

"It is indeed." The angel boomed, puffing out its chest. Puny humans didn't usually recognise or remember it. It swelled with a sense of pride at the suggestion its name was once again being placed on the tongues of the upper-worlders. "Mr. Pygott, isn't it...?"

"So it is. You really *are* Vassago. How did you come by this job? I've heard it's extremely difficult to secure a position at this level, even for a trusted old footsoldier such as yourself?"

"Ah, well, I'm perfectly positioned for this post, what with my special skills." It winked broadly from beneath surprisingly beautiful, lush lashes.

"I imagine so!" trilled Pygott.

"And it's not like I'm stuck down here waiting for that lift for all eternity! Good job too, really. You're the first ones to arrive that way for a two hundred years, I reckon."

"That long? Well, it was a very smooth ride. You must have a most talented maintenance team?"

"Impressive, isn't it? And all down to the original engineer. It hasn't been touched since Leonardo got into that argument with Dantanian. That was before the sneaky angel absconded and joined the Musketeers, of course!" He laughed too hard at his own quip.

"Really? How fascinating." *You really are quite mad, aren't you?* Pygott succeeded in keeping the question silent, but had no control over one sharply raised, querulous owlbrow. "I hope being on call for such a vital task doesn't interfere with your other, equally important role?"

"Oh no, not at all!" Vassago was relishing the attention. No one had taken such an interest since, well, since Leonardo first arrived. "In fact, it's all part of the package. Everyone that arrives via that portal is essentially lost. And it's my job to find them and reunite them with the place they should be. So I turn up quick-smart to set the wheels in motion."

"Indeed! And it works a treat, judging by our smooth passage." Pygott gave Vassago a hearty clap on the back."You should receive far better recognition for your efficiency. I'll see if I can put in a good word with the Big Man the next time He's in the shop."

"That's *very* kind of you, old boy. I bet no one offered you the same kind of support up there, eh?" He pointed a thick, taloned finger that almost cleaved Pygott's forehead in twain as it reared upward.

"Indeed not. A more aloof, unhelpful bunch I've never come across, I'm sure. In fact, this poor being behind us seemed the only one who cared at all. Such a shame it was too sudden to do anything about our left luggage though."

"What? You've ventured out without your essentials? Oh dear, oh dear. I would have thought better of you, Mr, Pygott?"

"A terrible oversight on my part, I'm afraid. I was so busy taking this bull by its horns that I completely forgot to bring along the shields to blunt those dangerous prongs." He shook his head, sighed. "Alas, our poor cases are utterly lost now..."

The angel grinned. "Lost, eh?"

"Completely."

They strode on. Vassago offered a quick glance back, finally, to check that its charges were still keeping up (or within distance, anyway). Pygott stole a swifter glance to wink in Crone's direction. Which Crone had no understanding of whatsoever and remained utterly oblivious to the whole affair.

Vassago looked back, sidelong at Pygott and smiled again.

"You're a wily one, Mr. Pygott. I'm surprised you're not running this place."

Chapter 37:
Excessive Baggage

Mephistophonob peeked around the door of the room it found had been allocated to Pygott and Crone during their unwilling stay. The coast appeared clear, so it slithered inside, pocketing the keycard behind a handy scale and gently clicked the latch.

It still couldn't believe how gullible the 'good side' could be! Not only had 'Nob managed to blag its way into securing entry to someone else's room, it'd even been practically forced into convincing the hapless angel on reception that it was both Pygott *and* Crone and could expect full gourmet room service to arrive shortly after it sneaked into their suite.

Apparently, there was also VIP access to all 'Heavenly TV' channels, which, much to 'Nob's disbelief and, quite frankly displeasure, included a slew of 24hr non-stop porn extravaganzas.

What's the universe coming to (pardon the pun)? All the collective saints turning in their graves must be what keeps the world spinning...

Mephostophonob checked the bathroom, which happened to be first right. The stark shock of strip-lighting blinking on was blinding for a few seconds. But once the purple blob creatures had died away, all that was left to see was a pristine set of fresh towels in a neat pile atop the toilet, gleaming bathroom furniture, a freshly pointy-folded roll of tissue in the dispenser and a pair of abandoned toothbrushes standing in a glass tumbler that resembled a beleaguered nylon bouquet on the sink-top.

'Nob flicked off the light and switched across to the room to its first-wrong. This was a small kitchenette, equipped with a waist-height fridge, sink, a combination grill/oven/microwave/toaster/forehead-massager and what with Pygott and Crone being extremely British, that essential home comfort: an electric kettle.

No clues there.

Turning around, there was a plush lounge bedecked with couches, a needlessly large TV, squishy armchairs and a coffee table that appeared to be daily supplied with unnaturally old-fashioned newspapers and periodicals. There wasn't a soul around. Which was a strange experience amidst the suffocating overdose of spent Earthly essence beyond the walls. Instead, 'Nob found only a school of dust motes, dancing to a silent tune around the streams of light flowing gleeful past the drapery.

Dust swirling around a space entirely free from dirt.

"This place is far too confusing."

And for the first time since arriving, Mephostophonob felt a painful stab of homesickness for the dank, dark cold of its underworld realm. A pull strong enough to countermand the wrath it knew it would suffer at the hands of an irate Baal. No matter that none of the blame could reasonably be pointed in its own direction.

For all the desertion that hung about the apartment, Mephistophonob couldn't shake the feeling that it was being watched as it shuffled around each of the bedrooms. Casting a check for people, souls, vermin or hidden cameras yielded nothing. Had there been a sneaky camera secreted about these rooms, 'Nob would've truly worried about the content of the purported porn channels. They wouldn't, would they?

But there was definitely *something* scrutinising the demon's every move.

It exited back into the lounge, where the feeling subsided. As soon as it jumped around the door of the next bedroom, though it could see no one, the sensation hit back with a vengeance.

But there's nobody here!

Not a single sign of life. In fact, Pygott and Crone had left no personal clues laying around to suggest that one of them had ever been in the room at all. There were no books or magazines. No glasses or combs on the bedside tables. No litter in the bins. They appeared not to have picked up and scrutinised the free pen and notepaper laid out on the standard work desk. Though what corporate communication or administration anyone might desperately need to send out from a Heavenly hotel room fairly made Mephistophonob's brains boggle.

They seemed not to have even taken a squint at the little card bearing the Holy wi-fi password.

There weren't even any suits in the wardrobe, trousers in the essential trouser-press or socks in the drawers to smother the Gideon Bible (why they felt the need to spread their gospel amid absolute proof of the existence of God, Heaven only knew!). In fact, there was no evidence to suggest that either of the booksellers had bothered to unpack their bags at all. As though they had no intention to stay from the off.

Which is when recognition tugged at Mephistophonob's ankles. It settled attention on one of the bags and stared intently into its brass catches. Then, nodding in half-confirmation, slipped – as best a scaly, slimy demon can – around to the next room and sought out Pygott's valise.

It was found hunkered down at the base of a pedestal table that held aloft a brass lamp and chunky, Bakelite telephone. The valise was neat, tidy, smoothed by age and use. And quite obviously much larger than its outer appearance betrayed.

It glared at the demon through burred brass buckles. With nothing short of malice.

Mephistophonob sensed there were teeth hidden under those catches. The idea forming at the back of its brains was going to require some measure of diplomacy.

And a very careful approach.

Chapter 38:
Onward Circuitous Direction

Leaving behind their warmest wishes – a not too difficult task within the fiery, infernal furnace – and a bemused, if increasingly re-angered angel, still coming to terms with an entirely new name, situation, future career prospect and a decidedly reconfigured personality, Pygott and Crone ventured on their merry way.

"You seem surprisingly merry, Mr. Pygott!" Crone ventured.

"Well, all things considered, our progress has been surprisingly uneventful as yet. Perhaps this wasn't such a perilous endeavour after all?"

"I do hope you're not tempting fate with such a proclamation Mr. Pygott?"

Crone looked around them, like a club-circuit comedian awaiting an aside from their stooge. Fully expecting disaster to leap upon them from all sides at once.

Pygott breathed a hearty lungful of sulphur and seemed genuinely relaxed. For the first time since leaving the shop.

"If there was ever a more appropriate place in which to tempt fate, I for one can't bring it to mind." He cocked a satisfied wink in Crone's direction. "And from here-on, the adventure can only become more exciting. We have only a few basic hexes and our own wits to rely on to see us through."

Crone blanched.

"I fear my wits expired somewhere between Doncaster and the Humber, Mr. Pygott."

"Understandable, Mr. Crone." Pygott whirled an understanding smile in the direction of his partner. "But I'm sure your esteemed intellect will rise to the fore and relish the next challenge we face. After all, we still have a way to go before enacting our plan to intrude upon the Big Guy's inner sanctum."

"We really are still going ahead with this, aren't we?" Crone grizzled.

"Indeed we are, Mr. Crone. You insisted on it, if you remember?" The smile remained playful, but edged with a wicked gleam. "Although I wonder if we're perhaps too late? It's normally a hive of deplorable activity down here. Yet we haven't encountered a single soul since departing Vassago's company."

"You don't think Nick's opened the main gates and let everyone out to ravage the Earth already?" Crone's pallor practically washed all the colour out of not only his face, but their immediate surroundings.

"It really is a little quiet. What under Earth do you think is going on around here?"

"Perhaps this is what always happens on the rare occasion Nick takes a holiday?" Crone looked utterly unconvinced by his own suggestion as it collected a most discouraging brow twitch from Pygott. "I know, but what else could it be? When the Serpent's away, maybe the rats have a non-stop party?"

"A party in Hell? Surely there's not a chance in, well, Hell of that being sanctioned? Baal certainly wouldn't put up with any sort of racket. Unless, of course, he was the instigator."

"Last I heard, he'd gone into hibernation for tax reasons."

Pygott briefly opened his mouth...then thought better than to ask the question. He feared Mr. Crone might try to formulate an earnest answer. It might just be true.

"Even the fires don't seem as hot, for some reason. And Xaphan is nothing if not dedicated. He'd never let the furnace suffer."

"Perhaps we could ask that gent over there, Mr. Pygott?" Crone pointed into the distance, where what looked like an angel could be heard tutting in a loud, most displeasured manner. And throwing its arms up and out in apparent despair at explosive intervals. Then scrabbling with some great difficulty to collect and reattach them.

Against all his better judgement, Pygott agreed and approached. Having returned to Hell, the fire insulation hex had retuned itself. Which was proving to be most uncomfortable in the suspiciously temperate Hell-base. And Pygott was most keen to wrap up proceedings and return to the welcome, mildewed aisles of the shop as soon as unearthly possible.

"Good, erm, day?" Pygott called. And waved.

The fallen angel turned to wave back, before realising that particular arm was still squirming on the floor a few yards away. The angel did not appear to appreciate being made aware of its faux-pas. It wagged the other fist in Pygott and Crone's direction, wearing an expression of rage scripted for a US sitcom scene in 1956.

Then realised that the attached arm had been sealed back into the wrong socket and was actually admonishing swathes of empty space at its rear.

Which didn't at all improve its demeanour.

"Filth!" It screamed at them. In the midst of shaking off the offending arm and stooping to collect the other. Hoping that would do a much better job of gesticulating.

Pygott and Crone looked around to see what manner of degradation so offended the angel. Instead, they saw only what they'd expect at Hell's deepest quarter: earth scorched clean by the continual blasts of inferno heat and freezer burn and everything kept strictly in place. There was no scope for stepping out of line within such close proximity to the many important denizens of the Underworld. If anyone ever thought, *I'm in Hell, can it get any worse?* they'd obviously never put a foot, cloven hoof or tentacle out of line amongst the well-oiled, clockwork machine that kept damnation ticking along at peak efficiency.

Although, as they'd already noted, the cogs all appeared to have sprung out of the clock case.

"Look at those disgusting footprints you're leaving! Did no one ever teach you to wipe your feet?" Improbable though it seemed, the angel's rage seemed more incandescent than the fiery pit that should surround them.

"I assure you, if there was a *Welcome* mat available upon our arrival, we would have used it." Crone looked behind them. "Though I can't see that we've tracked any dirt from Heaven. It's even cleaner up there than here. Spotless to the point of unpleasantness, in fact."

The angel's fire paled to waxen pallor.

"Heaven?" It's jaw lolled a moment while its brain desperately tried to catch up with its colossal depth of shock. "*Heaven?* Oh my Hell! That level of stain might never be cleaned away!" It began to thrash at itself as though poisoned, carnivorous ivy was wrapping a stranglehold around its shoulders.

As it centred its glare upon them, recognition blossomed within Pygott. And for the first time since returning to Hell, genuine concern bubbled up alongside.

"Mr. Crone," he whispered. "Try not to worry, but I think we may be in for a spot of bother."

"With this fellow? He doesn't seem all that dangerous to me. Quite armless, in fact, ha-ha."

"Coming here, bringing your filthy, pious infections with you! Sullying our perfectly corrupt environment. You must be cleansed!"

As the angel reattached the second arm the right way around and spun to advance on them, Crone's memory also soldered the link. And he squeaked.

"Oh my! That is, isn't it?" he stammered. "It's the damned fallen angel of OCD! Banished from Heaven for constantly bleaching out Archangel Gabriel's china teapot collection. What are we to do?"

"We brought protection for just such an emergency, Mr. Crone! I took the precaution of packing the holy relic of St. Bilius. The only known protection against our friend, Trebus here."

"*You* own the relic, Mr. Pygott? The sacred poop squeezed out on the top step of the Vatican by St. Bilius to protest at the rescinding of the rights of priests to use novice nuns as bed-warmers?"

"The very same, Mr. Crone. Or should I say, *we* own it. After all, it's one of the Third Left Tentacle's prized secret assets. Full marks for your history assignment, by the way Mr. Crone. But I'll have to advise you to do more revision on your stocktaking methods."

"And I shall have to watch the acquisitions ledger more closely for expensive, likely unethical purchases you slip through without consulting me!"

"Touché, Mr. Crone."

"Have you two finished prattling?"

The pair paused, turned indignant expressions towards the snarling creature and glared.

"No, we have not completed our discussion, thankyou."

"How rude of you to interrupt!"

"Standards are slipping here, Mr. Crone."

"Indeed, Mr. Pygott. Hell used to be such a welcoming, efficient, polite place."

"Like Switzerland."

"But warmer"

And they turned back to their conversation. Leaving Trebus momentarily stultified.

"Well then, Mr. Pygott, I believe this is your cue?"

"My cue, Mr. Crone?"

Crone tipped a non-too covert series of nods in the direction of the steaming Trebus. "Yes, Mr. Pygott, it's high time you produced our unfeasibly appropriate trinket."

"Ah yes, that cue." Pygott turned, squinting. And hissed at Trebus. "Will you please blow your steam elsewhere? It's causing havoc with my anti-frizz hair balm!" Huffing and straightening his cravat, he returned his attention to his partner. "Much as I'd very much like to respond directly to your suggestion, I fear I'm unable."

"Are you playing some sort of mindgame with me, Mr. Pygott? Because if so, I'd like you to explain the rules."

"What I'm saying, Mr. Crone, is that I don't appear to have the holy relic of St. Bilius directly to hand."

"Are you worried you can't reach it without arousing suspicion?"

"I'm already suspicious!" The increasingly frustrated angel roared.

Through pursed lips, attempting to ignore the lances of soaring spittle flying past, launched by Trebus's flapping tongue, Pygott attempted to tweak his partner's comprehension.

"I packed the relic safely in a specially concealed pocket in our luggage."

"And you're worried you'll be intercepted before reaching the particular bag?"

"Very much so. As our luggage went with us on our unexpected detour *upstairs.*"

"I know *that.* But we didn't have time to bring our bags with – oh." Finally, Crone's understanding caught up with his bluster. "So that means...?"

Pygott nodded and they turned as one, grimly, to face the looming angel.

Crone gulped. "Oh Hell."

Chapter 39:
Midnight at the Lost and Found

It wasn't a pleasant feeling. Not in the slightest.

Like having one's oesophagus served for dinner inside a well-baked pie, slathered with onion gravy, by some surreal process where it remained inside the chest cavity, but had somehow been jammed solid inside the ear canal.

Aristophonob particularly didn't care for it.

If this turned out to be Baal's way of repatriating minions, Aristophonob would...well, suck it up and hope it wasn't yet in serious trouble. And anyway, how could Baal have found out about Pygott and Crone's disappearance without 'Nob filing any report? He had to be – dangerously – woken every time there'd been a necessary update. So he could hardly be suddenly on the ball now, surely?

Twisted forms morphed in and out of existence in front of its bulging, squashed, stained, disbelieving eyes as it tried demonfully to keep down the remains of the very tasty bars of posh soap it'd eaten in the booksellers' bathroom whilst musing over how to convince the luggage to conspire in their escape. Before finally, the sensation of being transformed into Stretch Armstrong moulded in bile began to subside and Aristophonob recognised substance cushioning its many-buttocked frame once again.

"Excuse me?" came a discarnate question from somewhere the other side of the Mouldy Milky Way.

Aristophonob attempted to focus and found that all that swam immediately into view was the street sign itself. And the adjacent gutter of Mouldy Milky Way. And its mind seemed to be still at least two ethereal planes behind its sagging, creased body, it squinted again in pure reflex.

"I said, now I know how kebab meat feels when it's projecting the morning-after hangover."

"And you brought the smell too!" chimed the voice. With far too much cheerfulness. "Now, if *you* could please stop harassing my friend, Mr. Pygott here for a moment..." The voice boomed with unexpected authority.

Pygott? He thinks he's talking to Pygott!

"Will you please keep quiet? We're trying to hold a conversation here! Where did you come from anyway, crinkly creature?"

Oops! Did I speak out loud then?

"Yes you did!" the voice chortled. "Now can you please learn to think in silence?" Muttering exasperated oaths, the voice's owner turned away, out of Aritsophonob's antenna-shot.

Their was a nudge on 'Nob's midriff and it got the impression there was also a "Shush!" But it couldn't swear to have heard anything. And whatever jabbed it had sharp corners. *Corners?*

Aristophonob decided that, as it didn't appear to be in direct danger – no matter how painfully angular its neighbour seemed to be – its best recourse was to sit still, shut up and wait until it recovered enough sensibility to discover what was going on. It resolved itself to toying with the basaltic scree that layered the ground around its tentacles. If it concentrated steadily returning vision solely on the floor, it could almost convince itself it looked like home.

Come to think, it almost *felt* like home.

Aristophonob dared to look up and its focus was greeted by the surly indignance of a travelling case, briefcase and satchel. It all looked startlingly familiar. And appeared to be annoyed at the demon's unexpected presence.

Through a sliding curtain of bleariness, it steadily dawned that across the road stood a pair of angels – one hurling insults while the other batted away the barbs with cheery indifference. And the snatches of landscape beyond looked very much like the background scenery to the Water Margin, as Ling Chung was dragged in chains across the black, volcanic sands to prison, after committing the sin of drawing his sword inside the Governor's palace. They also looked alot like Hell.

And then, "Oh my!" Pygott and Crone wavered into view,

Chapter 40:
The Papal Protest of Saint Bilius

"Now, if you two wouldn't mind?" Vassago pointed what for the angel constituted a glare at both Trebus and Mephistophonob. "I'm trying to speak to my friends here." Vassago smiled as it turned to Pygott and Crone, satisfied that there'd be no further interruption.

Leaving in its wake a spume of sparkling steam that enveloped an all ready to explode angel, which would have infuriated Trebus even further, as projecting all its body parts and innards would create such a scummy, sticky mess. Mephostophonob, for its part had recovered sufficient nous to realise what was actually happening. But really wanted to find out what was *really* happening. Because that wasn't yet becoming any clearer.

"Mr. Pygott, Mr. Crone, it's very good to see you again so soon. I hope your impromptu return to Hell is proving advantageous?"

"Thankyou Vassago. Our furlough remains as unpredictable as ever. All present company should serve as illustration." Pygott gestured at the throng.

"Myself included, I shouldn't wonder!" Vassago beamed with pride. One of the niceties of being cast out of Heaven, felt the angel, was finally being allowed to take pride in its work. "But as is my bond, I located your lost luggage and returned it forthwith. I hope you'll forgive my tardiness? But I had The Devil of the time getting them to move between realms, for some reason."

"Possibly our strange little friend there?" Crone queried, indicating a still bemused Mephistophonob. Who now also had to deal with the incalculable notion of being referred to as someone's friend for the first time ever.

"You may be correct, Mr. Crone." Vassago pursed its lips and regarded the blinking creature. "I tried angelfully to send it where it ought to be. It was obviously lost, otherwise it wouldn't have become attached to me in the first place. But no matter what I did, it ended up coming here. I take it you're sure it's definitely not yours?"

Crone appeared to be eyeing the creature with some measure of both suspicion and kindling recognition, sparking a tremor of panic inside one of the little demon's stomachs.

"We certainly didn't take him up there with us, to our knowledge," offered Pygott, with a shrug.

Him? Mephistophonob was now being considered in the same vein as a *person?* Which it was rather chuffed about. Though that emotion was tinged with a little chagrin at the instant presumption of being male. Would it prefer to be a bloke? It had never given thought to such notions before. Apparently humans saw it as a great advantage to be able to urinate standing up, especially the joy of being able to splash jets of liquid onto trees? That hardly mattered in the case of 'Nob's adaptable demon vents.

Though its several supernumerary testicles might have something to say about any choice it made.

"Certainly not intentionally..." Pygott peered more closely, seemingly right through Mephistophonob's scales and into its nervous jelly. "But I believe you'll have to wait, little chap." Pygott cocked one last inspection over 'Nob and turned back to an intrigued, beaming Vassago. "We have far more pressing matters that require attention!"

How did that get there? Thought Mephistophonob, as it watched Pygott reach down into one of his bags, rummage briefly, then pull out a quadrate, wooden box, lavished with ornate gilt-work.

Vassago's eyes glinted as it goggled at the casket.

"My word! Is that *really* what I think it is?"

"Indeed it is." Pygott purred.

"I thought it was lost decades ago. And you've been hiding it away all this time?"

"I prefer to think of it as preservation," he grinned. "Which, under our present circumstances is most appropriate."

"Ha-ha! Very good!" Unleashing a mighty wink - that happened to replace a paper bagful of gobstoppers in Crone's pocket he'd lost as a younger, sprightlier man, whilst running from a particularly mean basilisk – Vassago stepped aside and turned the diamond smile toward its compatriot of sorts. "Trebus! Stop snorting down my neck and prepare for battle!"

Trebus roared in frustration-relieving triumph and launched itself forward, rubber gloves squeaking a contorted symphony as the angel's talons flexed inside them. Accompanied by a cloud of sparkling basaltic dust that kicked up around its feet as it scraped to a sudden, quizzical halt.

"Battle?"

"More indiscriminate slaughter, old chap." Pygott thrust forth the casket in one hand and readied to flick the clasp. "This is your cue to retreat and leave us to get on with our day, by the way."

Trebus weighed up its options and chanced brief glances towards the amused faces dotted before it. None of which seemed to be retreating themselves, in response to its unleashing righteous wrath. Even the little, nondescript demon, who appeared to be the most timid bugaboo ever spawned by, erm, Hellspawn seemed to display only mild confusion as it backed away. In fact, if Trebus were to be entirely honest, it would swear he demon was sneaking off while the others were distracted. Even the ever-vigilant luggage hadn't noticed it fashioning escape.

But the pumice dust settling on Trebus' arms vetoed any possibility that common sense might intrude upon the path of angelic righteousness! These messy interlopers were cluttering the place, leaving unattended bags *and* filthy demons laying around. And no doubt all this dust was their doing too.

The Marigold mist descended and Trebus launched anew at its presumed tormentors. All teeth and talons and rage and whirling scrubbing brush.

"Behind me, Mr. Crone," assured Pygott. And calm as several cucumbers lofted the casket to beard-lip height in front of himself.

Trebus didn't pause to consider there may be serious resistance to its will. And flayed wild at the steaming air, ready to claw away the box, crush it into its bulging refuse cart and dispense with the filthy beasts littering the path and retarding its clean-up crusade.

Pygott held his nerve and his hands steady as one of the angel's thrashing claws slashed the air apart a fraction from the clasp of the tiny chest. And thrust forward in a graceful, piercing assault into Trebus' personal space. He flipped the lid open a steel nostril hair's breadth from the angel's curled upper lip.

And it froze like the Gorgon's date on Prom Night.

Slowly, stutteringly, Trebus allowed its eyes to inch downward to look at what was throwing out the soft, stultifying mustard glow from atop its velvet throne inside the reliquary. It stopped its approximation of breathing and if it had a heart, the poor thing would've ceased beating in an instant.

Never had it known such sensation as this. Terror was an emotion angels were meant to instil in others, not receive unto themselves.

The object held firm beneath its awe-struck, unblinking glare was no more than a middle-finger length and shrivelled to the girth of an unwanted cat gift amongst prize azaleas. It was the colour, in the main, of a caramel candy, but glinted with a faint moisture that surely should have crusted into powder centuries ago.

And it still smelled.

Trebus' nose wrinkled and the fine feathers on its upper lip crinkled and retreated. The Papal Protest of Saint Bilius released its perfume as fresh as the day it had carried the previous week's stewed cabbage feasts to the door of the Holy See. It was a pungent, invasive, dark green odour that rose like a vaporous cactus suffering an otherworldly growth spurt and rammed its spines into Trebus' nostrils.

"Plugs, Mr. Crone!" snapped Pygott. He jolted Crone's arm upwards and Crone's hooter became stoppered just in time. "And close that gaping mouth. We can't be too careful. Saint Bilius' fermented perfume isn't safe for mortal contact."

"Dor doze ob glean-freak angulls," noted Crone, as he caught sight of the first stitches coming apart. The essence of Saint Bilius, the most fastidious seamster foreman in the Catholic Church's history, began to unpick the seams of this most disagreeably fashioned garment.

Trebus, being not the most stable construction to begin with, unzipped like a moth-eaten pair of tartan bondage pants. Too quickly for its tongue to rattle the screech of pure rage that instead had to settle for boiling up behind its eyeballs and sent them spinning like musket shot across the smouldering pathway.

Even so, each one somehow managed to lock Pygott in a cursing stare of hatred as it whizzed in the opposite direction.

"I fear I've not seen the last of you," muttered Pygott, as the pressure of Trebus' frustrated ire proved too powerful for the weak hands straining to keep it together. And its innards swiftly outpaced its exploding extremities in a whistling non-firework display. Which the onlookers only just ducked out of the way of at the very last second.

All but Vassago, who yowled with blaring laughter, tears squeezing free of its hilarity-crushed eyes as various angelic body parts pinged off its own legs and torso. Ricocheting loud as boulder-stray bullets on the cheapest 60's TV western gunfight.

Until it collapsed in a raking wheeze as an Underworld record worthy discus throw arrowed a flying kneecap firm into its throat. Vassago doubled over, slapping a meaty arm across its own back, tongue bulging. Eyes though, still laughing.

Crone shuffled across and whacked Vassago square between the wing stumps with the bulbous head of his brolly. Which he'd removed from the luggage in preparation for repelling portions of fallen angel he felt may result from a likely Trebus eruption in one form or another. And then completely forgot to pop the button as he was struck by astonishment at the resulting angel-Krakatoa melt-up (the only direction the explosion didn't send fragments was down).

Vassago dutifully ejected the bone saucer with a mighty splutter. It rocketed across the wasteland and decapitated an unfortunate demon, which had just congratulated itself on ducking out of the way of Trebus' mortar-launch left humerus. *Serve me right for getting bored with the protest and coming back for a bit of quiet before the mob gets sent back!* it opined. And started shouting instructions to its body before it wandered off too far to be able to pick up its disgruntled face.

Crone followed up the hefty thwack with series of comforting pats on Vassago's back.

"Well done shifting that blockage, old boy! We may have to keep our eyes open: the speed that was travelling, it may still be at bullet velocity by the time it circumnavigates the lower realm."

Vassago couched out a grin. Wheezed a huge, squeaky breath. Slapped its own knees and levered itself upright again. Red-faced and puffing. But unshakeably amused.

"Thankyou, Mr. Crone! You're rather handy with that brolly! I shan't be upsetting *you* anytime soon."

Crone received the compliment – and the lusty, bloodshot wink – with calm humility. "I'm well versed in the obscure martial art of *Parap Luie*. And a little more flexible than I look."

"Our Mr. Crone is most certainly a dark horse, Vassago," intoned Pygott, with some measure of admiration. "Speaking of which: behind you, Mr. Crone!"

Crone's eyes swivelled like every Eagle-Eye Action Man at a Palitoy convention as the oldest moulded plastic hairdo walked through the doors to take his seat. And whipped around in a flash, right thumb and forefinger extended. Right at the instant Trebus' left middle finger completed a circuit of the circle and speared back toward them.

"I suggest we both deploy brollies, Mr. Pygott?"

As their parasols fanned out, Pygott's reply was drowned out in a hail of mushy thuds. And the plaintive wail of a shattered voicebox riding the breeze.

Chapter 41:
A Change is as Bad as a Rest

"Shouldn't we consult Shacklehorn's Underworld Atlas?" Crone didn't break from looking around them as they continued along the path around Hell's Seventh Circle.

"I'm not sure it would be of any assistance anymore, Mr. Crone. Those terrible renovations blighting the upper circle appear to be seeping down even this far. I'm hardly recognising the place at all." There was a tinge of melancholy tingeing Pygott's voice that resonated through to his heart. Navigating the circles of Hell was becoming akin to returning to Sheffield, expecting to see well preserved, proud industrial heritage and finding only endless rerouted roadways barring useful access to faceless, graceless glass and concrete urban fungus.

"I'm sure this is where His office used to be, right here." Pygott stomped a frustrated foot and twirled, seeking *any* sign that his snoring hex sensor spells were mistaken. "But there's nothing." He waved his hands around in a defeated flap. "Even my trusty nostril hairs haven't tangled a single tickle!"

"If those wiry twitchers can't direct us, we truly *are* lost, Mr. Pygott."

"I wonder if this is why Old Nick has loped off on holiday? He was never the keenest on what appears to be called progress these days."

"Him and me both, Mr. Pygott." Crone's brow furrowed a tad beyond furrowable. "I wonder if he's having the same trouble as us?"

"You think he's trudged off to the Arctic in frustration at not being able to find His own office?" Pygott looked aghast for all of a millisecond. "Actually, you may be right. At this moment, I can't say I'd blame Him."

"Hey! Mr. Pygott! Mr. Crone! Is that you?"

The pair whirled again, espying a figure approaching out of the freshly varnished pink foothills. It was waving with unbridled enthusiasm,

"Brimblesnoop?" Pygott peered into the glare leaping off the drying wax. "Dear boy!"

Grenadine Bumblesnatch finally reached them, brandishing a smile as broad as the Styx and wrestled them both in a decidedly flamboyant bear hug. And waved air kisses across every cheek in sight. And spluttered a little at accidentally chewing on Pygott's whiskers.

"How are you, Brindlesneck? Haven't bumped into you in ages."

"Well, I'm dead, actually." There was less dismay in the statement than Pygott would have expected. "You two aren't. Anything like, at all...?"

"No. No! Hale and hearty as ever, thankyou. We're just having a little break from the shop for a change."

"Looking up a few old friends," added Crone, with a satisfied grin. *Nailed it that time.*

"Ah, good to hear it! I'm sure neither of you are nearly ready to retire yet."

"Actually, if this holiday doesn't buck up its ideas sharpish, we'll be returning back to work very soon." Pygott glowered at the evermore barely recognisable landscape. "But enough of our tribulations! What are *you* doing here? As I recall, you were always a rather virtuous chap? Did someone find all those skulls we sold you for every performance of Hamlet and jump to the wrong conclusions?"

"Ha! Nothing like that. All of us Thespians end up in Hell, it transpires. God loathes a luvvie, apparently. And can't stand the theatre. He'd stamp it out on Earth if it wasn't for all that free-will promise, so I've been told."

"How unfortunate! No wonder Heaven's such a bland place," opined Crone.

"Bland? How is that possible?"

"We were there only recently, dear boy. And what we saw made the dullest branch of IKEA look like a fragrant pasture."

"How very strange!" It was Globberstone's turn to look utterly perplexed. "God may hate actors, but He really has a thing for musicians. He steals all the best ones, no matter how many contracts they've signed to sell their souls to the Devil. That's why Old Nick's constantly popping up at crossroads to waylay fiddle players and challenge them to a duel. It's the only way He can get a good gig."

"What an awful thought! God keeping all the world's best music locked up in a cage in His own private chambers."

"Do you think that's what He does?"

"I fear so. We didn't encounter a single musician while we were up there. And judging by the standard of guff dribbling out of the PA system, only the tone-deaf and brain dead are catered for." Pygott shuddered. "You're truly abominable! Ironically." Pygott shook his 50's sitcom dad fist again at the sky.

"Well, nice as it's been catching up with you boys, I can't hang about. I'm on my way to a dinner party and I really wouldn't want to be late."

"Isn't it fashionable to be late in your profession?" Crone wondered.

"That's as may be, Mr. Crone. But it's also *rude.* And you know how I feel about politeness. It would never do."

"Well, at least you're in the right place for a soiree, it seems. We could always find a jolly, low profile gathering amongst the endless torture and disembowelling in this Circle, at least." Crone had gone wistful on them. "Though I fear the landscape's changed recently. There's rumblings of raucousness everywhere we've passed."

"Is the host anyone we know?" Pygott piped mischievously. "Maybe we could tag along and blag an invite?"

"Well, if you could find Him, possibly."

"Him? *The Him?*"

"Uh-hmm. The Devil's throwing some surprise shindig and sent my invite by way of the Reaper's scythe halfway through my King Lear at The National. It's lovely to be wanted so, but *most* inconvenient. He could at least have waited for curtains."

"Ah, that explains the garb, at least." sparked Crone.

"But we saw Nick in the shop only days ago. We think. He was going on holiday!"

"Really? No wonder I can't find Him. Are you sure He's not still here? The invitation was most specific and marked *URGENT* in virgin's blood."

"Sorry to disappoint you, dear boy. But as far as we know, He's absent. Along with practically everyone else, it seems..." Pygott's puzzlement had begun to increase beyond any pleasurable degree. He liked to wrestle with a good conundrum. But generally only when there was a genuine solution to seek.

"It *has* been rather quiet since I arrived. Apart from my entrance, that is. There was an horrendous mêlée kicking off in reception! So much so, I didn't get the chance to sign in or go through orientation!"

"Induction really is dull. You dodged a trident, really," offered Crone.

"Yes, but it was so rude! And you know how I feel about, well, that. I understand they were busy being inundated by slavering rioters, but that's no excuse for pushing me into the furnace without even the tiniest welcome. Especially when it's not even lit."

"Hell doesn't provide the service we're used to either. Perhaps you ought to bend Satan's horn and lodge a stern complaint?"

"When I find Him..."

"*If* you find Him..." mumbled Crone.

Chapter 42:
In Dupe Irritability

"I don't know how you feel, Mr. Crone, but I'm starting to think we might've been had." Pygott's mood had sunk since their encounter with their old friend, the distinguished actor, Grimbledine Bangleditch. Or something.

"Had? In what way? Do you think Lucifer's discovered our little ruse and conspired to thwart us?" Crone's ears drooped in concern.

"I don't think it's that at all. Lucifer's far too honest to play such petty games. He would've raced back to Hell to confront us and rip us a few new vents. And I'm not talking tailoring! None of this is His style..." Pygott twiddled his bristles contemplatively.

"Well, if it's not Him, who else could perpetrate such wide-ranging subterfuge down here?" Crone was beginning to seriously worry that they'd submerged out of their depth. But, this time, without a magic float to bail them out.

"No one. And that's what's irking me."

"But we're *here*. And we can see what's happening all around us. What other explanation could there be?"

"I may be mistaken, but all this reeks of interference from above."

"Holy meddling? *Here?*"

"That all depends where 'here' happens to be, Mr. Crone."

"I really don't think I'm following you, Mr. Pygott," muttered Crone, as he spied another piece of Trebus and endeavoured to flick it away from his shoulder. Just in time to stop it chewing a hole through his lapel.

"Since we returned to Hell, nothing beyond that first peek out of the portal has looked right. Nothing's felt right. And it certainly doesn't smell right." Pygott picked a sweet rose from a nearby bush and drew a long sniff to illustrate his point. *"Roses, Mr. Crone!* I ask you?!"

"So, do you think that when we escaped Heaven, we weren't actually sent back to Hell?"

"Even more than that, my friend. I'm getting the distinct impression that we didn't sneak through the gates into the Underworld in the first place."

Crone blinked. Clearly at a point beyond caring to comprehend.

"i think we may have been re-routed to Heaven at the very first step. And as such, we didn't escape. We're still there."

"In Heaven?"

"In Heaven."

"The underhand swines!" Crone seethed with reinvigorated, well, vigour. Then just as abruptly stopped at the behest of a crumpled brow. "But how did they know what we were doing? Or where we were going?"

"Well, I don't know if He was involved. But He is all seeing, all-knowing and everywhere at once..."

"Touché, Mr. Pygott." Crone smiled, in spite of himself. "But having said that, I find it difficult to believe He'd be at all interested in a pair of hapless booksellers sneaking into Lucifer's office to steal back a book that doesn't officially exist. And furthermore, unless He's lost all His copies of the Bible, I can't see that He'd hamper our opposition to an attempt to bring about the end of the world in quite the fashion the Necronomicon describes. He could hardly claim total annihilation of *everything* by ancient aliens as the prelude to Armageddon. It'd make poor John look a revelationary fool for starters..."

"Indeed, Mr. Crone. So often, you're more wise than I." Pygott shrugged, accepting the flaws in his argument. "But so many things aren't adding up. I just wish I could put my finger on it..."

Crone jumped in an arc and intercepted another piece of Trebus shrapnel arrowing into Pygott's face.

"Ha! Another finger! It must be the second circuit by now! I'd forgotten just how powerful St. Bilius' excretion could be! Good job you keep it locked away safe."

Crone grinned and dropped the finger to the floor, idly following its course as it wriggled and jiggled and began the slow crawl back to its brothers.

"It would never do to allow such a powerful artefact to fall into the wrong hands, Mr. Crone. Though I believe we once said such a thing about the book..."

"The book?" Crone wiggled an eyebrow in readiness to assume quizzicality. Then suddenly blushed understanding. "Ah, forgive me; *the book*. That book. We may well have been proved right on that point."

Pygott's mood was sliding rapidly down a slippery, razor-littered slope as he scanned the landscape.

"I simply cannot get my bearings! It's most frustrating! I've never been lost below stairs before."

"First time for everything, Mr. Pygott. Unfortunately." Crone grimaced in shared sympathy. "But at least the locals appear to be returning, look."

Crone pointed at the first signs of demons, fallen angels and tormented souls returning to their stations. Tridents were already being sharpened for insertion, bellows pumped here and there to rescue a few scattered forges and abandoned shackles.

"That's somewhat encouraging, at least," murmured Pygott. He surveyed the scene around them with the air of someone having to reconsider their opinion at each successive observation. Before turning to Crone, wearing a completely different, suspicious expression. "What happened to that little demon?"

"Little demon?" Crone blinked. Worried suddenly that the recent stresses had begun to loosen the hinges on Pygott's sanity cupboard.

"Yes, the little demon Vassago brought to us, referring to it as 'ours'. And yes;" he bent to reassure their bags with a soothing pat. "The one to which our luggage took such exception."

"Oh. Yes! I'd forgotten about him. Or her? I forget: do demons have a gender? Or genders? Or *all* the genders?"

"You digress, dear boy."

Crone's face crumpled minimally. "I do. Sorry."

"What's puzzling me is not so much where it went, I suppose. But rather why Vassago brought it to us in the first place? After all, I've never known Vassago to reunite anyone or anything in error."

"And the luggage did seem to *know it,* didn't you?" Crone touched one of the bags under a lock and the whole set rippled with amusement.

"If only we hadn't been so distracted, we could interrogate the little fellow. Where's Vassago when you need it...?!

Chapter 43:
Bull's Hair Flannel

"WHAT IN HEAVEN'S HIDEOUS NAME ARE YOU DOING BACK HERE?" Baal's version of a hissed whisper practically toppled the ceremonial tower next to his palace. "HAVE YOU ANY IDEA WHAT IT COST TO GET YOU OUT? AND THE TROUBLE IT CAUSED?"

"Apologies, Your Unsightly Squamousness! But I had no option but to follow Pygott and Crone back here."

Aristophonob cowered and shielded its heads in readiness for Baal's violent outburst. And after a painless, worryingly silent while, risked a peek out from behind knitted tentacles.

Baal's shaggy brow displayed at least an equal ratio of knots to flesh.

"THEY CAN'T BE BACK YET," he murmured. "HIS MAJESTY WILL TEAR ME LIMB FROM SPHINCTER IF I COCK THIS UP. HOW UNDER EARTH DID THEY MANAGE TO BREAK OUT? AND BACK IN?"

Though it still registered as an utterly alien concept, Aristophonob felt heartened to be spoken to not in the manner of something Baal had scraped out of his groin fold. Even if only for the confused time being. Emboldened, it dared to enter into unprecedented territory: the land of conversation.

"From what I can gather, they instigated the fall of an angel and hitched a ride on its wing-tails as it was cast out."

"*THEY* DID THAT? I WONDERED HOW *THAT* CAME ABOUT. THE RESOURCEFUL SWINES! IT'S BEEN SO VERY LONG SINCE ONE OF THOSE GOD-BOTHERERS FELL FOUL OF THEIR OWN RIDICULOUS RULES."

"They were just shopping — Pygott bought a hammer, apparently - then all of a sudden, all Hell broke loose, if you'll pardon the pun? And then they weren't there anymore. Left me totally stranded!"

"SO HOW DID *YOU* MANAGE TO ESCAPE FROM HEAVEN? YOU CERTAINLY DIDN'T GET ANY HELP FROM ME!" Baal rolled his eyes and chewed on a tusk for a moment. "DID YOU?"

Aristophonob stopped its tongues from rattling. Any reply needed to be carefully tailored to avoid the slightest hint of criticism. 'Nob felt uncharacteristically brave for an instant. Best not allow that to transmute into stupid.

"Thankfully, the situation could be resolved by means that avoided the dangers to my mission that contacting Your Infallibleness might have brought about. I followed your secrecy protocols to the letter." A little crawling, fawning, evasive and hardly concise, but 'Nob hoped acceptable at least.

"AH, YES. INITIATIVE! THAT'S WHY I CHOSE YOU FOR THIS MISSION, CLEVER LAD, ERM, LASS? THING."

You're so far up your own... Aristophonob's train of thought was harshly interrupted by Baal's next brainwave.

"BUT WHERE ARE PYGOTT AND CRONE NOW?" Baal's eyes widened in horror "THEY COULD BE CAUSING ALL MANNER OF CHAOS BACK HERE! AND GET *ME* INTO TROUBLE! WHY AREN'T YOU FOLLOWING THEM?"

Dammit. There's always a spanner...

"Erm, when I left, they were still blundering around the Seventh Cricle, so hopelessly lost they thought they'd already found the Ninth. But they hadn't even tripped over sodding Gomorrah yet. So I took the opportunity to risk ensuring you were fully updated before they have a chance to recover their bearings, Your Infinitessimalness." *Ouch! Wrong arse-lick! Please don't notice!*

"SEVENTH CIRCLE? ALL THAT REMODELLING, EH?" 'Nob heard the shadow of a chuckle. "NOTHING LIKE RIPPING OUT THE OLD FURNISHINGS AND MAKING FAMILIAR PLACES UNRECOGNISABLE AND UNCOMFORTABLE. I KNEW I WAS RIGHT ABOUT THAT DECISION! HIS NIBS WILL BE HEAVEN TO LIVE WITH ONCE HE RETURNS, BUT SACRIFICES HAVE TO BE MADE TO FURTHER THE GREATER EVIL."

Baal smiled, though it resembled the most hideous, offensive grimace. Self-satisfied to the tips of his gilded horns.

"Such imaginative thinking, Your Swampdetritusgasness! They're completely bamboozled." Aristophonob dared with a grin.

"BUT LET'S NOT GET COMPLACENT! THOSE TWO ARE CAPABLE OF UNDOING ALL OUR BAD WORK AND UNRAVELLING SPACE AND TIME BY NOW! SO GET YOUR ARSES BACK ON THEIR TAIL. NOW!"

The blast sent spewing from Baal's lungs shot Aristophonob flying along the first quarter-mile of its exit. And left it landing at a relieved, slightly deafened, but unharmed canter.

No rest for the wicked.

'Nob was eternally grateful its curse-hex didn't extend to cliché.

Chapter 44:
Hell Hath So Much Fury

Lucifer dumped His luggage in the lobby, apologised to it for the heavy landing and glared around at the awful new décor He'd regrettably allowed His underlings to plaster over this once beautifully dismal domain. They hadn't even kept Rodin's gates, the Philistines! And then, bewildered, at the scramble of wanton chaos still rumbling throughout the HeReTIC.

There were demons sobbing behind the counter and damned souls in once prim, pressed uniform run ragged, attempting to recover some manner of order amidst the mêlée. Others were actively engaged in nose to horn to proboscis to beak to squamous indefinability rabid shouting matches. Several were physically buckling under the weight of numbers as they continued to hold off, with increasing futility, the crowing throng that were still trying to storm the elevators. Even though the entire bank of doors were firmly locked and the power to all had been long shut down.

There was even the odd active skirmish utterly ruining the fresh-laid carpets.

A stalwart phalanx of brave, bristling demons had barricaded the entranceway and were entrenched in a ferocious firefight against a set of the most belligerent damned refusing to abandon their assault on the gates and accept that no one was getting out today.

There was one particular ghoul/damned soul/fallen angel trio that appeared to be fighting for an entirely unknown cause. The oaths and curses they aimed in support of each swinging blow didn't tally in the slightest with any subject even close to the reasons for the riot. They appeared simply to be enjoying some good, clean, violent fun.

Satan was – to say the very least – not amused.

"I am *not* amused," He growled into his goatee.

Much as He wanted to rant and shout and stomp around tearing up limbs and furniture alike, He was far too angry. Even moreso after returning from a blissful break, free from the usual tumult of responsibility, only to find His tightly wound, efficient, oiled machine exploded into rack and ruin during His short sabbatical.

Very, very quietly, He muttered under His breath.

"There had better be a very, very good explanation for this..."

Chapter 45:
Many Unhappy Returns

"Let me go!" Mephistophonob wriggled to no consequence as it was propelled headlong in an unbreakable grip. "Didn't you have enough fun abusing my freedom the last time?"

"There's no freedom, little demon. Not for either of us. Even God Himself can't shirk the shackles of responsibility, no matter how hard He tries to foist them on the shoulders of His inferiors. Look how badly the whole 'free will' conceit rebounded up above for starters."

"Ugh, you angels! Always infuriatingly philosophical."

"We've had a long time to think about these things..."

"Well, do you *think* you could explain what you want with me *now?*"

"My thoughts could only be conjecture. Which likely wouldn't improve your mood."

"I get the feeling it wouldn't be as bad as the mood I'll be in when you finally dump me wherever I'm going?"

"Really? I usually find returning the lost to their rightful place brings joy!"

"That's because you rarely stick around long enough to witness the fallout after returning what doesn't want to be found."

"Ha-ha! You're funny! I like you." Vassago gave Mephistophonob a playful squeeze. That almost popped its many eyes out of its heads. "Here you go. Now you can go ask your amusing questions."

They'd reached journey's end and Vassago manifested with a flourish. Projecting a smile so bright it practically blinded its intended targets.

"Ah, Vassago. Good to see you, stout fellow! And so nice of you to bring a friend."

"Aw, fu- flipping heck," Mephitophonob gristled.

Chapter 46:
Hands Across the Sea

"I don't believe it! What are you up to, hiding back there?" Pygott grinned in genuine surprise. Moreso as the target of his good humour did indeed appear to be crouched behind a large boulder and giving off the distinct impression that they didn't want to be seen. Goodness knows by whom!

Both figures jumped and the bulkier, bear-like frame that had so utterly failed to conceal itself let loose an eye-watering knee-pop.

"We're not hiding from you!" shrieked his stouter companion.

"Of course you're not hiding from us!" Pygott mused on the statement a moment. "Are you?"

The lady paled. Which was some achievement now that the furnaces had evidently been stoked up once again.

"No, no, of course not," beamed her partner. Who'd now extended to his full, eclipse-risk height. "We're not hiding from anyone. Just taking in a bit of the local geology as we pass by. It's not often we get to study the lay of the land in such unusually quiet surroundings. And you know how Fräulein Wagenbauer loves her rocks."

"Ah, yes. What a totally believable explanation." Crone tried not to blanch at the accusatory glance flicked out of the corner of Pygott's eye. "Things are starting to get a bit busier now though, Herr Fackler."

"Tatsächlich, Mr. Crone! The area will be swarming with accursed souls and we'll be wading through torrents of fiery blood soon enough."

"Ah, yes," breathed Wagenbauer. "The solitude made a nice change, but it's so good to see normality returning. Back to the old grindstone, eh?" She hollered to one of the souls nearby who'd returned, only to be slammed between two enormous granite wheels and was already being pummelled into screaming mush.

"So, just what are you two doing here?" asked Pygott.

"It's a phenomenal coincidence the two pairs of Europe's most prominent antiquarian, occult booksellers should be skulking about the Ninth Circle of Hell at the same time!" chirped Crone enthusiastically.

"Ninth Circle? Oh dear, I thought we were still on the Seventh. It's so hard to find anything since they redecorated," grumbled Fackler.

"No wonder we can't find it!" Wagenbauer moaned. "We're on a mission to steal back a book we shouldn't have sold Lucifer." Wagenbauer's mouth didn't speak whatever words her eyes indicated should have been allowed out.

Fackler launched into a coughing fit that seemed to shrink him almost to the size of a normal rugby back. And shot Wagenbauer an eye-rolling, withering look.

Pygotts' nostril hairs had to be forcibly restrained from stridulating, they danced a hokum warning with such vigour. He ignored the pained wince that issued from Crone's shocked larynx as Pygott eased back to tread on his toe. Stopping whatever indiscretion Crone's reaction had prepared to betray.

"That's very cloak and dagger. And certainly not the kind of jape myself and Mr. Crone would consider getting involved in! It all sounds rather unsafe."

"We're on holiday." Crone meeped, recovering some composure. If not the normal hint of colour to his face, "Looking up a few old friends."

"Indeed," beamed Pygott. "Including some welcome, if intriguing surprises."

"We've hardly seen anyone, to be honest," offered Wagebauer.

"Probably a good thing, judging by your covert circumstance?" Pygott performed a comedy check of the wings. "And to be honest, it was probably not the best idea to tell us either."

"But you're our most trustworthy friends!" exclaimed Fackler. Far more horrified than he'd been at Wagenbauer's faux pas.

"But you never know who might be listening," piped Crone. Suddenly back in full, playtime secret agent mode.

Both okkulte, antiquarische Buchhändler blanched and set about scanning the horizons and any obstruction inbetween to check for inquisitive interlopers. Before digging into their coats and producing a mismatched set of charms and fetishes, which they proffered, shook angrily to the four corners of the circle and conferred with in darting-eyed whispers.

"Are you *sure?*" Wagenbauer whispered. And waved a stern, no nonsense stare into her palms. "Good, alright then." She smiled and returned her attention to Pygott and Crone. "All clear," she beamed.

Fackler however, still seemed somewhat perturbed and wrinkled his nose into the face of a particularly unattractive, gesticulating fetish.

"I'm not sensing any threat. What about you, Mr. Crone?" Pygott asked. Both intrigued and amused. "What is it, Herr Fackler?"

"Something's coming, I think. I'm not entirely su-"

With a whoosh that swept forelocks, beards, lapels and Wagenbauer's elaborate moustache disguise flying like the cheesiest shampoo advert, Fackler's ill-ease proved both founded and mistaken.

"Sorry for the delay! I had the Devil of a time locating Asmoday's third head." Vassago hailed triumphant.

"Just the third?" queried Crone. One of several questions the statement might prompt.

"As you say, Mr. Crone." Vassago's grin stretched wide enough to dazzle every eye busy burrowing their way out from behind gale-displaced fringes. "It turns out she'd gone for a jaunt with Balaam's tail while their master's were distracted by all that nonsense in reception." It sighed, heavy. "I can't believe they're calling the Great Terrifying Damnation Gates of Satan 'reception' these days. What *has* this place come to?"

"We can only hope that your master remedies this grievous situation upon His return?" proffered Pygott. Still dismayed at the lack of organisation and painfully slow remediation of their environs.

"Ha-ha, yes! *When* He returns, eh, Mr. Pygott?" Vassago bellowed a boulder-cracking laugh and aimed an amused, knowing smile at the centre of Pygott's face.

Which only broadened Pygott's general bemusement.

"Ooh!" Vassago finally appeared aware that the conversation shouldn't be quite so centric. "Fackler! Wagenbauer! So very good to see you!" Vassago grabbed their hands in turn and vigorously shook them as though attempting to irrigate the Sahara using a single hand-pump.

"It's been a very, very long time, Vassago!" opined Fackler.

"Far, far too long." Wagenbauer wiped a mist of moisture from the corner of an eye, which flew off into steaming oblivion as she jiggled and jangled at the end of Vassago's over-enthusiastic greeting.

"Where have you been hiding yourselves all this time?" the angel hooted.

"Well, we have a busy shop to run...?" offered Wagenbauer, weakly.

"With no one trustworthy to oversee the premises if we're away," added Fackler.

"Really? So what's so pressing that you've both abandoned your establishment now?"

Clearly neither Fackler or Wagenbauer had expected to be facing a barrage of difficult questions today.

"Erm, well, a pressing matter..."

"They're on holiday, aren't you?" Pygott's tone was as stern as his brow.

"Just like us!" Crone piled in.

"Though not all together," added Wagenbauer.

"But bumping into the same people!" Fackler joined in. Suddenly.

"Well, I hope the shop's still standing when you get back! I'm sure you have every trust in who or whatever's holding the fort?" Vassago was being entirely rhetorical, but stopped dead at the answer.

"Oh no, Vassago. The shop is closed for the duration." Fackler blinked embarrassment at the admission.

A succession of jaws dropped harder than the Tunguskan fireball and the sound of strangled discombobulation was deafening. Even the forges, torture wheels and codling boring apparatus seemed to have rusted solid momentarily. And their victims all stopped screaming, stupefied.

Aristophonob further shocked them all by being the first to shatter the silence.

"You closed the shop to go on holiday?"

Under the gaze of what seemed suddenly to be the entire Ninth – or Seventh, or wherever they were! - Circle of Hell, Fackler floundered like a beached flounder in Flanders.

Wagenbauer, her moustache now drooped as low as her resolve, squeaked something she hoped might be of help. Seemingly more to check that she was still breathing than out of any insight or inclination. "It's been a hard century. We *really* need the break?"

"You didn't even close the shop through the Reformation, witch trials or two world wars!"

"Well, we weren't personally around for *all* of those..."

"But to close to go on holiday?" Aristophonob was apoplectic by now. "How long can you possibly leave that place unattended? Surely it's not safe to have it dark and," it gulped. "Left to its own vices for too long."

The hollowness in everyone's eyes reflected 'Nob's ominous overtones. There was far too great a collection of damned literature, spooks, poltergeists and spellbound wicked creatures to risk leaving the shop unsupervised for any length of time. The world could be brought to an end in a single afternoon's ill-attention.

Fackler finally seemed to galvanise and swim back towards the confident end of the pool. At least the end shallow enough not to drown.

"It's being well looked after. We just couldn't find anyone we trusted enough to run the business in our absence. So there's no trading."

Pygott similarly seemed to have climbed back almost to the base of the shock tree, though there was a still an irritating branch hooking into his suspenders and leaving him groping for freedom. "Are you not even catering to emergency queries? Who's safeguarding the occult literary needs of Central Europe if you're not there to supply aid to the supernaturally desperate?"

"Erm...we've contracted the help of an agency? Although we're not expecting anything exceptional to occur."

"Tempting fate should really be avoided in the present situation," Pygott mumbled through pained, drawn lips.

Fackler gawped. Blinked. Shot a pleading look in Pygott's direction that practically spoke out loud: *'Please stop. Shouldn't you be helping?'* Instead, his mouth defaulted to pointless flapping.

Unexpectedly, Wagenbauer came to the rescue.

"The Sisters were asking after you, Mr. Crone. They heard you were here and expressed fond hope you'll be paying them a visit?"

Crone's head turned ever so slowly around to wave his gawping mouth at Wagenbauer. He looked like the Joddrell Bank telescope suffering the aftershock of a marshmallow terrorist attack. His eyes had bulged so wide on the way around that they could have been responsible for the strangulation infecting his throat. The noise squeezed out seemed akin more to the demise of an overripe plum beneath a tapir's hoof than the speech of a sophisticated human.

"Ah, The Sisters! Lovely creatures!" Vassago's jaw suddenly yanked back up to its normal position at the behest of a wistful expression. "Have you not managed to pop in on them yet, Mr. Crone?"

Crone squirmed like a worm flung onto an icicle.

"Actually, no. We've hardly had the chance. Especially with our diver-"

"Ahem! Cough! Splutter! Hack!" Pygott very nearly turned a lung inside out in his attempt to cut short Crone's foot's passage towards his mouth.

Crone blanched. Again. Then blushed like a worm that had fallen off the icicle onto a convection heater. "We haven't even had the chance to visit that circle yet." He shuffled nervously, feeling all eyes boring into him like the three dots of the Predator's laser sights. "We're going bottom up."

Wagenbauer chuckled. "Mmm, The Sisters will love that! We'll let them know what you have planned."

"No!" yelped Crone. And practically incinerated his cheeks as everyone's eyebrows or approximations of such leaped into the air, like a gaggle of startled Penfolds. "We'd erm, ah, we..."

"Mr. Crone would like our visit to be a welcome surprise, should we manage." Pygott interrupted, smooth as a bored receptionist's nails. "We'd very much hate to disappoint them by raising expectations we may be unable to fulfil."

"Disappoint is hardly the word," interjected Fackler.

"The Sisters are worth better treatment," continued Pygott, unconcerned. "And Mr. Crone would rather devote intimate time to visiting those dearest ladies than risk insulting them by squeezing them into our itinerary so briefly they might be misconstrued as an afterthought, Hell forbid."

Crone blinked under Pygott's smug gaze. Then realised he was being prompted. "Indeed. Exactly right, Mr. Pygott. They're deserving of the best!" His tone may well have been a tad too squeaky and strident, but it appeared to appease the group. Or frighten them, Either way, the conversation was won. "And I'd hate to miss the joy on their faces that a true, surprise visit brings." Less squeak. More velvet. Some relief!

"Don't you move another testicle!"

Everyone within earshot startled, yelped discomfort – none moreso than the tackle-blocked fornicators nearby taking advantage of their torturer's extended absence – and whirled attention toward a furiously barking Vassago.

Aristophonob froze mid-sneak and failed to avoid looking anything but utterly, shiftily guilty.

"I think you'll find they're called *tentacles,*"

"Not from this angle, they're not!" The angel pointed an accusatory talon that seemed almost to scrape 'Nob's nose. "Now don't you twitch another whatever they are, unless it's back towards us. I don't fancy chucking away my precious time having to retrieve you again!"

Aristophonob blinked, considering making a slither for it regardless. After all, if it could outrun the average feral dog, surely an angel older than written time shouldn't prove too difficult to shake off? Still, the barbs on those wings...

Sullenly, excruciatingly slowly, 'Nob retreated and lowered itself ever so steadily down.

Pygott and Crone's luggage rotated and barged the little demon into the nearest boulder with a decided huff. Then sat, quivering, peevishly staring eyeless and spiteful into the cloud of noxious dust raised as it bounced off and thudded into the floor. Aristophonob resisted the urge to tempt fate by opining that today couldn't get any worse.

Wagenbauer checked her watch for the ninetieth time since Vassago's shout had caused Aritstophonob to leak a few drips of plasmic embarrassment. Unfortunately, Fackler seemed the only one present unaware of her evermore desperate hints.

Pygott spent what felt like three seconds short of eternity pointedly looking back and forth between Fackler's unresponsive face, Wagenbauer's watch dial and her already crumpling, twittering eyebrows. In the main wondering why Fräulein Wagnebauer was referring to a mechanical timepiece in a realm where the only measure of time was eternity. Painful, tortuous, inescapable eternity. Or more precisely – or possibly imprecisely – three seconds short of eternity.

He harrumphed, nudged Crone – who whimpered as he jumped out of his confused fugue – and, whether through compassion or strained impotence, rescued his bookselling colleagues from their predicament. Handily, it would also alleviate Pygott and Crone's own unease.

"Well, it's been a positive fillip bumping into each other again. But I'm sure Vassago has more important tasks to be fulfilled? That rather befuddled looking demi-god over there, for instance...?"

"What are you doing here?" Vassago raged. Causing the poor demi-god to practically melt into the nearest lava flow. Vassago leaped into action and plucked the hapless semi-deity from the jaws of singed gonads and whisked it off towards whichever full-blown deity's right tentacle it should be sitting upon. The sonic boom left in their wake out-rang any chance of continuing the conversation into goodbyes.

The onlooking booksellers couldn't even hear their own "Ouch!", let alone one another's.

After an unhealthy round of head shakes and fingers waggling in ears (not each others, even though Crone appeared to ask for an extra knuckle to aid his own stubby digits), Fackler was the first to utter a muffled set of words.

"We should be going. We were supposed to be at Gorgoroth's palace." He fished out his own pocket watch. "About a century ago."

Wagenbauer collapsed into visible relief that her oft-thrown penny had finally not only dropped, but been picked up for luck. Before switching to a more exasperated grimace of frustration. "Hmm..."

"It's been a pleasure, dear boy. And girl." Pygott extended a hand to each in turn. "Have we said all this already?"

"A delight, mein freund!" Fackler beamed.

"Let's do this again as soon as possible!" rattled Wagenbauer. And received a most peculiar stare from all assembled. "Well, not *this,* exactly, of course..."

"We concur. A nice cup of tea or coffee in the *Third Left Tentacle* or *Zaubertrainer und Einhorn,* would be far more hospitable."

Crone waved them off with a cheery flourish. And whipped around just in time to catch out a recovering Aristophonob as it managed to wriggle free from the heavy, mahogany corner of Pygott's valise.

"Now then, little demon. You have some explaining to do."

Chapter 47:
Can't Get the Staff...

Baal tossed off the overzealous attendant – who was most dischuffed about what transpired to be Baal's particular interpretation of what tossing someone off involved – and boinged around the boudoir. Utterly vexed at the notion that there was something niggling for attention with so much vehemence that it was spoiling all the usual fun brought by being indulged in any and every way hard, lascivious and downright disgusting.

It was making the horns on his head itch and the hide on his haunches grizzle with discomfort. And for all his centuries of hard work and concentrated malevolence, it infuriated him that he'd still not earned a capitalisation designation like his boss, Lucifer.

A rumbustious rampage, butting every wall and making the lofty ceiling worry itself into all-but plummeting down onto the heads of cowering nubile souls and fawning, subservient demons eventually subsided into creaking joints and a spittle matted beard and a retching, spasming coughing fit. And he ground to a stumbling, humbling, geriatric halt.

"BLOODY HEAVEN! I'M GETTING TOO OLD FOR THESE SHENANIGANS."

The lull loaned his vanity enough off-duty seconds to allow space for his brain to engage.

"BLOODY HEAVEN!" Again. "THAT DIPPY LITTLE DEMON'S TALKING TO PYGOTT AND CRONE! WHAT DOES THE IDIOTIC LITTLE SQUIB THINK I MEAN WHEN I USE THE TERM 'SPYING'? EH?"

Baal glanced forcefully around, expecting an answer. At least a response. Even a grunt would do. Only to find that the couple of succubi who hadn't taken the opportunity to scarper in terror wore the blank expressions of confusion reserved for those who riskily assumed his question was at best rhetorical.

"USELESS LUMPS," he grumbled. "IT'S NOT LIKE YOU EVEN DO A SATISFACTORY JOB WHEN YOU'RE ON THE, ERM, JOB..."

Baal grimaced for what could have been several lifetimes, let go one of his special guffs and ruminated on the toxic fumes awhile. By the time he emerged from the miasma, the remaining succubus had dissolved to distressed puddles and even a few of Beelzebub's visiting flies were coughing like middle-aged, 80-a-day smokers.

It was time for Baal to open his favourite avenue of communication.
"MEPHISTOPHONOB!"

Chapter 48:
Raising the Baalarm

"My word! What *did* you say to it, Mr. Pygott?"

The little creature at their feet was writhing in fits of wild-eyed, screaming agony, it seemed. Totally oblivious to the bald confusion passing between the pair looming nonplussed above.

"I hadn't even got around to speaking yet, Mr. Crone. I've only got as far as wagging my finger in stern fashion, look." He pointed the wavering digit back at himself. And then at Crone. "It's not crippling either of us, is it?"

"Did you accidentally snag an anti-demon hex in your pocket, by any chance? Something wrapped in your hanky perhaps?"

"Not only have my hands been free from pockets since before Vassago arrived, again, but all the devices you're proposing are safely locked away in my valise there." Pygott pointed to a smug luggage huddle beyond Aristophonob's distress. "This is most perplexing."

Crone stared in pity down at the poor creature wrapping itself in knots and emitting sounds that intermittently pierced ears, boiled bile and tugged even the stoniest heartstrings. "Isn't there something we can do to help?"

"If we only had an inkling to what's causing its, erm, discomfort?" He paused at Crone's startled, quizzical response. "Sorry, I couldn't think of a more appropriate word. And my thesaurus is also in my valise..."

"The last time I saw anyone wearing that expression was the time one of the sprites accidentally overcharged Baal for a book. A lovely copy of *In eiusmodi mollis universi filii* illustrated pop-up edition – a little too advanced for Baal, to be honest. He broke several streetlights when he unleashed his wicked rebuke." Crone shook his head at the memory. "I had to mop up more than a little distress from behind the tills too."

"I believe there's still the ghost of a stain?" Pygott had also drifted into a moment of over-the-counter wistfulness.

"There is! Who'd ever have thought a simple bodily function malfunction could create a haunting? Somebody really ought to make a study. Though I wouldn't like to be the one finding a supervisor to referee such a thesis."

"Hmm..." Pygott mused. "Perhaps we've already studied this fellow too long. I may have something to assist after all..."

Pygott waved his valise over to him. As it arrived, it opened a side-pocket and quivered in the sure knowledge that it had successfully anticipated its master's intention. He patted a soft, warm thankyou on its clasp as he rose, foisting the tiny amulet that had shuffled to the top of the jumble.

Aristophonob sat bolt upright, chins stiff and eyes staring straight ahead as Pygott slipped the necklace around one of its twitching extensions. Ever so slowly, it seemed to regain itself and the fountains of ejecta that had splashed out the nearest foothills and drowned several Hell-rats sputtered to a faltering dribble.

Just as one of its tongues rattled against a few teeth to issue thanks, Pygott himself loomed, blocking out the flamelight and completely stomped on the intention.

"Well, I believe you have some explaining to do, little fellow?"
Damn.

Aristophonob opened its mouths to protest. Before snapping them shut in the realisation that it didn't know what to protest about. And that any contrarianism might loose some truism that Pygott could latch onto as an admission of guilt. To something. But what?

"Don't look so worried! Anyone would think you were being interrogated in the Ninth Circle of Hell!" Pygott and Crone exchanged a hearty chuckle. Aristophonob failed to cut off several gulps, its stolen Adam's Apples bouncing wild and suspicious. "Now...would you like to tell us why your uncontrollable jitters have suddenly become so, well, controllable?"

"Errrrr..." drooled Aristophonob, still uncertain of any kind of answer. Let alone one that might release it from whatever hook Pygott had it dangling from. "Wind...?"

"The amulet you're wearing provides protection from the odious influence of Baal. Especially if one finds oneself caught amidst one of his more forcefully lusty intentions. So what manner of Baalanity have you been suffering, we wonder?"

Chapter 49:
What a Baalaver

Baal and Satan were experiencing disturbing and inexplicable new sensations.

For His own part, Satan had stormed not only into Baal's palace in a thunderous rage, but had also torn several new orifices into His cabal of unholy deputies and laid waste to vast stretches of Hell that to the untutored eye already looked surprisingly wastelike.

Doomed souls had been forked back into mills and firepits, minor demons had been torn asunder and spliced back together in far more efficient shapes, rammed with the kind of hearty resentment that could only be expressed by hurling spite and violence and unnecessary suffering onto others.

It was all rather vexing that He was forced to stomp about His own realm ranting and raving orders and generally venting absolute displeasure and disappointment in a manner not seen since He'd been cast out unto the Earth and unwittingly suckered into the job of nominated pariah and scourge of all goodness. Then again, He was kidding Himself if He expected much more from legions of staff who were, by their very nature, rebellious. But He'd assumed the machinery itself would grind on undeterred, no matter what mad scheme one or all of His minions decided to hatch in His absence.

And to be honest, it had been thoroughly refreshing to use His return to the Underworld reasserting His authority, reconfirming His undisputed position as Lord of Evil. He'd returned from holiday relaxed, replenished and in just the right frame of mind to crack some heads, limbs, antennae and pseudopodia in an organised aggression orgy.

Once through the initial disappointment, He'd actually felt really, really good. Satisfied. Proud of His place.

But to arrive at Baal's palace and find Himself completely ignored by whatever was left of his retinue, before storming into Baal's sanctum only to find Himself being roundly told exactly which way He could leave again - and how many orifices He could stuff en route - was too much to either forgive or process.

Even Baal's realisation that he was speaking to – well, shouting at - Satan Himself, rather than one of his filthy succubi appeared to make no difference whatsoever!

Lucifer boiled. Literally.

Even God had never summoned the gumption to address Him with such insolence.

From Baal's perspective, he was experiencing the entirely unthinkable prospect of not only being completely snubbed by one of his very minor subordinates, but also passing on that affront not to another disposable grunt, but to the most powerful being within this particular plane of existence.

But above all that was the realisation that he'd just launched a verbal tirade in the direction of Lucifer Morningstar...and didn't care a jot!

And if it wasn't for the fact that he was still absolutely stupefied that anyone or thing — especially that pipsqueak 'Nob — could even dare to consider flagrantly denying him, he might even *like* the pleasant sensation of power nibbling at his horns.

Instead, he simply furrowed his already yew-trunk knotted brow and glowered at his dark master, exasperated.

"THE LITTLE SOD HUNG UP ON ME. *HE* HUNG UP ON *ME!*"

Chapter 50:
You Can't Make an Amulet Without Breaking Ranks

"Do we believe a single word of that, Mr. Crone?"

"No, Mr. Pygott. Every slimy syllable dripped with practiced insincerity."

"Thankyou." Mephistophonob practically glowed. Sooner than the realisation that its pride was an admission of guilt. "Thankyou for listening, I meant..."

"Blustering doesn't become you, little demon. Don't spoil your achievement in convincing us it's really not worth the effort in us persisting to eke out what you're *really* up to."

Crone nodded agreement. "Just be thankful whatever it is, we're not blaming *you.*" He wagged an accusatory finger over one of 'Nob's heads anyway. "What does the amulet say, Mr. Pygott?"

"It's gone back to insisting it's too hot and refusing to do any more work till it's had a good sleep." Pygott waved it dangerously close to one of Mephistophonob's nervously smoking nostrils with a scowl. Resulting in illiciting only the most offensive squeak and returned it to the bottom of his spare underwear cache. "But it did initially make enough positive noises amid the grumbles to indicate our little friend here poses no threat to us."

Mephistophonob dared a sigh and allowed itself preparation to relax.

"Whereas its opinion on the outcome of your next meeting with Baal doesn't bear repeating." He paused to allow all of 'Nob's gulping purloined Adam's Apples (it had gathered another two since last escaping) to cease bobbing. "Sorry."

"Oh dear," began Crone. "I wouldn't like to be your tentacles when he catches up with you! Now, Mr. Pygott; what next?"

Mephistophonob was speechless as the pair turned away, instantly in deep conversation. Apparently already en route to wherever they hadn't yet agreed they were going. It wasn't even embarrassed about the meep of shock released as the reality of Pygott and Crone's assessment sank in.

In fact, it almost achieved the impossible by practically weeping as the pair halted, turned and surveyed it with expressions approximating — hopefully — pity. It could already feel the first stirring of penetration by Baal's volcano-simmer rage as the amulet's distance increased. Which hurt. Alot.

"Are you sure about this, Mr. Pygott?" queried Crone as they came abreast of the squib.

"Not in the slightest, Mr. Crone!" hooted Pygott joyously. Confusingly! "But I hadn't expected any wrangling with Baal and if you agree, I'm willing to gamble on his attention remaining firmly focused on this little whelp. For at least long enough for us to be done with our business and be sitting down to a relaxing cream tea at *Madame Van Helsing's.*"

"Can we have blood pudding first?"

"Followed by blood orange gateaux, of course, Mr. Crone."

"Mmm..." Crone drifted off into slop-slapping reverie that almost prompted Mephistophonob to, though possibly calamitously, interject. "But we're getting off the point, aren't we?"

Crone made a pointed eye-veer in 'Nob's direction that cut back its annoyance prematurely.

"Too true, Mr. Crone. We must get on!"

Pygott grabbed his partner by the elbow and began to march off once again.

Mephistophonob's protestation stuck in its throat at the prospect of yet again being left in the grip of Baal's ire. It gawped around, looking for any shred of help it could get.

And was rooted by the surprising whiff of sympathy it felt drifting across from Pygott's luggage. Maybe it had a collective heart after all? Though finding out that it *did* have a heart (that of Edgar Allen Poe, magically plucked from his chest by the vengeful archangel Raguel as he lay dying in a Baltimore gutter, which Poe managed, astoundingly, to survive for another few days with only a heart that beat far outside his own body. But then, that's another story entirely, isn't it?) probably wouldn't comfort the demon in the slightest.

As Mephistophonob tried demonfully to will its limbs into crawling in pursuit of the booksellers, Pygott's case rattled its latches like a stridulating tarantula, creating an impressively shrill, metallic din. Four pillows of red dust poofed out from the corners as it bounced a tango and thudded the ground.

Pygott and Crone ground to a steady halt and turned – cautiously – quite nonplussed. They stared, shared a querysome glance and stared a little more as the case continued to huff and puff in ascending levels of exasperation.

"Ah, yes. So sorry." Pygott literally lit up as he realised what the bag was getting at. It helped that one of the damned in the distance had just been strapped to a flaming boulder and catapulted across the Nearby River Smegma to explode in a riot of red-hot fireflies against another forge. The puce air quickly turned livid blue as the forgemaster emerged, surveyed the splash of roasting flesh plastering the gaping eaves of what used to be a roof and endeavoured to hurl back as much abuse and molten weaponry as she could muster.

The pained whimper accompanying Mephistophonob's frantic, crippled shuffle added no little hint in the background.

Crone helped the little demon up onto its trotters and gave it a gentle dusting down. Setting it erect more than once as it wavered unsteadily.

The bags settled back into smug mode, flattening any possible signs they may be warming to the demon. Instead, they now gave off the confirmed vibe the opposite applied – with added obligation. "You owe me," Pygott's case seemed to metaphorically purr in its direction.

Though Mephistophonob was more than grateful, it still risked rewarding itself with an inward smirk that whatever debt the bag thought it was owed need never be paid. The instant 'Nob could wrap a tentacle around that amulet...well, as soon as its limbs regained any strength or coordination...well, as soon as its brains could reconvene and track the movements of its own limbs...well, whatever, the plan was to wrap a tentacle around the amulet and be off as far as a whirl of suckers could carry it. It just needed a minute. Or five.

"I believe I was considering granting you an enormous favour?"

"Yes. Yes, you were! Thankyou." Mephistophonob practically twinkled with relief at the returning Baal quashment effect. And immediately regretted its glee. The word *favour* suddenly weighed very heavy on its expectations.

"We may do business with The Devil and demons, assassins, devourers of worlds and even the worst dregs of society: children's TV presenters. But that doesn't make us bad chaps at heart."

"Careful how loud you say such things, Mr. Pygott. We are in Hell, after all."

"Indeed, Mr. Crone. A sensible outlook, don't you think, ah...?"

"Mephistophonob. Aristophonob. Erm, 'Nob?" peeped Mephistophonob, to its eternal horror. *How did that happen?*

"Ah, well. That's interesting." Pygott groomed his beard in contemplation. "The amulet's working better than I thought." Pygott grinned wider than the Styx on latrine sluicing day. He tried to hold back the expression of sly triumph, but in the end, why bother? They both knew who was in charge here. "Now that the amulet knows your name – names, erm...we'll take things alphabetically shall we, Aristophonob? – we can bind it to work for you."

"That's not really how it works, is it, Mr. Pygott?" Aristophonob very faintly hoped that's exactly how it worked.

"Of course not," Pygott grinned. "But it's nice to be civil about these things, isn't it?"

Aristophponob's guts sank.

"Please retract your bowels, young chap, girl, thing? There's no need for *that* level of panic! And it looks so very uncomfortable..."

"Sorry, yes. I imagine the smell's not too pleasant either?"

"Possibly, But don't worry. Mr. Crone regularly has anti-peristaltic gymnastic episodes too. Are you alright there, Mr. Crone?"

Crone flapped an acknowledging hand in their vague direction and returned to concentrating on retching behind a handy boulder. Several splashed rats nipped at his boots as they scarpered.

"Ugh, ah. Sorry chaps," he coughed, ineffectually, as they rolled about in the brimstone to remove the odd diced carrot.

"Now, Aristophonob. Or would you prefer Ari? Or Mr. or Miss Nob, perhaps?"

Aristophonob was doubly, possibly triply perplexed. It'd never been asked how it preferred to be addressed before someone or something prepared its enslavement or destruction.

"Erm, 'Nob's fine, thanks?"

"Excellent! I take it that's a single apostrophe? We'll have your name badge ordered as soon as I can get a signal to the middle sphere. Would you prefer a lanyard, or should we just pin it through one of your scales?"

Aristophonob had left perplexed far behind and set up residence in brain-numb.

"No matter; we have both in the office. We can sort all that out during your induction."

"Induction?" Crone had finished wiping smelly spittle from his chin and desperately looked about to find a convenient, hygienic spot to dispose of his hideously stained handkerchief.

"Why not drop it in that lava puddle there, Mr. Crone?"

Crone peered about in the direction 'Nob indicated. Initially failing to find the searing pool a little to his rear. Which explained his burning cheeks. A pulsing arm of molten rock lost patience, reared up and snatched the cloth tile from his fingers and gobbled it in a brief steam kiss.

"Oh, ah, thankyou, I think." Crone stepped aside another step. Just in case the earth fancied any more of his possessions. Or limbs.

"See? Our newest recruit has shown some initiative and proved its usefulness already." Pygott actually patted it on one of its heads. Like a proud father seeing his child score their first half-century for their school cricket team.

He actually patted my head, thought 'Nob, entirely bamboozled.

"Either there was more sulphur in that puff of smoke, or we're having a real conversation and I'm as befuddled as that, well, that, erm, new stockroom attendant?" Crone was desperately hoping the former applied. Otherwise he'd have to concede either himself or Pygott should seriously consider retirement to a beach hut in Bognor Regis.

"Why would we waste this fine, clever individual on opening boxes, Mr. Crone? No, no, I have a list of special assignments in mind for this stout confrère." Pygott turned to Aristophonob with a glint in his eye. 'Nob couldn't quite work out if it was more fatherly or terrifying. "Our special correspondent, if you will?"

Aristophonob squirmed under the pressure of not knowing whether that had been meant as a bald statement or demented question. "Errrrrm...thanks?"

"I knew you'd see things my way!" Pygott clapped his hands together and practically danced a jig. "Now, here's your amulet. Go off and settle your affairs in the Underworld. Or take a holiday to refresh yourself ready for the challenge. Or whatever suits best. And we'll expect to see you bright and early in a week's time at the Third Left Tentacle ."

Aristophonob opened its mouths ineffectually.

"And don't insult your new employers' intelligence by claiming you don't know where that is! We may be nice, but you're only probationary for the first two blue moons."

Aristophonob gawped at the amulet. Which was no help. At Pygott, who simply grinned like a lunatic. And finally at Crone, who looked just as perplexed as the demon and simply shrugged uncomfortably.

"I'll be off then?"

"So you shall! Enjoy your break. We look forward to welcoming you to our team." Pygott seemed far too pleased with himself. So much so that Aristophonob feared for the poor man's sanity.

"You've gone stark, staring mad, haven't you?" 'Nob heard Crone rasp as it slunk off to God – and more especially Baal - hopefully didn't know where.

Chapter 51:
Gordon Blue

Oh, flipping heck, He's here!

"Get that flaming bunting sorted – NO! Don't set it on fire! I *know* I said *'flaming'*. But that's cos I'm under one of those stupid 'no profanity' curses. Ouch! And I just remembered it has a 'no criticism' clause attached. Now, please put the fire out and hang the rope, will you? No, no, no! Put him down!!! Hang the *rope!* Not the – oh, forget it. Good omens, the dregs I have to work with. That third Michelin star really wasn't worth all this..."

Gordon hurried off to check on the kitchens, muttering non-profane oaths and bemoaning the lack of worthy catering staff in Hell. There were more than enough sinners in the profession, yet all the best mysteriously never made it to the Gates of Iniquity. Entrance requirements were obviously skewed if your manna had the right consistency.

And though it remained a great honour that Satan Himself had intervened to fight for Gordon's services in the Underworld, it barely assuaged his dismay at the pitiful dolts he was forced to endure when it came to chefs and service. To such an extent that – even though such a thing should be utterly impossible! - Lucifer often looked upon him with genuine sympathy and apologised for the, well frankly, Hell He was putting him through.

Having said that, he'd never make the mistake of jestfully serving devilled eggs again.

Chapter 52:
Wake up and Sniff the Beef

"This is your invite." Lucifer tore the ticket into confetti and showered the flakes down onto Baal's horns, snorting snotty fire into the Molech pit. "And you can stay in there till you learn some manners, you stinky old bull!"

Baal's surly, not in the least complimentary retort was crushed into insignificance by the thunderclap clang of the heavy, barred lid being stamped shut. And stamped again. Numerous times.

In fact, Lucifer spent the next hour and forty seven minutes, twenty one seconds bouncing up and down like an enraged devotee of the Order of St. Beryl, His mane flying like a frenzied wimple. Pounding out His frustration into an impressive slab of sigil-stamped ironwork and stopping only when He realised that carrying on for much longer could well end up propelling Him in an embarrassing fluster down on top of Baal in the pit.

Growling out the rest of his ire – for the present, at least – He shook Himself off, ran a porcupine through the curls on his thighs and took several deep, refreshing breaths of sulphur, plonked Himself in the nearest approximation of the lotus position His hooves would manage and resolved to transport His attention to somewhere serene and soothing.

Today was supposed to be a good day.

And it *would* be a good day. He was determined that no amount of rioting, rebellion or rude, flaming demons was going to spoil it.

He drifted off, ignorant of the sparks and scraping emitted by Baal scratching clinkers off his beef-cheeks. *Blimey! He really does smell!* And Satan was soon back on His deckchair encircled by the glorious frozen wastes of the Arctic, staring lovingly at the skuas swooping along the shore.

He may disagree with lots of His old master's opinions, but having put Him in charge of all things wild would never, ever illicit complaint.

With a hearty smile, all Satan's woes began to freeze into jagged bergs and float off into the North Atlantic. And out of his sphere of concern.

Chapter 53:
Take a Lode Off

Pygott consulted the lodestone again. Watching intently as it performed another set of intricate hops and shimmies to complete its intense bee dance atop his outstretched palm.

He nodded, heaped thanks on the stripy pebble and returned it with due care into his breast pocket. It nuzzled into said breast and promptly fell asleep.

"I still don't see how staring at a lodestone will help us find Lucifer's private apartments, Mr. Pygott." Crone's patience had returned from its amble around the block and tackle and rather than feeling refreshed and relieved, was already busy making new allegiances with its twin, *Im.*

"Our little friend here doesn't just point to the pole or wriggle passage out of a fog bank, Mr. Crone. There are more subtle definitions attached to the title. Ah! There we go!" Pygott's eyes brightened and a grin the width of a Busby Berkeley chorus line twinkled across his teeth.

Crone's reunited im and patience slid into a back seat for the moment as he stared around, trying to locate whatever it was that Pygott was suddenly striding toward with an air of absolute confidence.

"I always worry whenever you're mysteriously focused, Mr. Pygott. Following usually takes us to places I don't much like."

"Ha-ha! Don't worry your classroom globe head, dear boy! I believe our next step will cheer you up immensely."

Crone paused momentarily, staring after the swift departure of his uncharacteristically excited colleague. Before realising his stumpy legs ought to consider impersonating if not Speedy Gonzalez, at least Sylvester the Cat. Or even Slowpoke Roriguez, as long as he started *moving.*

He was already in dire danger of never catching up.

"Classroom globe head?" he muttered as he waddled himself into an ungainly jog. *The poor man's finally succumbed to sulfur frenzy.* "What am I to do?"

Chapter 54:
Rhapsodie en Jaune

It was proving to be phenomenally busy on the Sulfur Frenzy Ward — or Yellow Bedlam, as it was better known to the locals. In fact, the situation could be described as, with no pun intended whatsoever — Satan forbid! - frenzied.

Since the return of almost all rabble rousers (save the random barricade who continued their vehement protest, even though they *still* had no idea what all the kerfuffle was about in the first place) from the heady, air-conditioned luxury of the once new (now mostly wrecked) 'Welcome Lounge', so many unexpectedly refreshed lungs had sent so much sweet air and spicy oxygen to the brains of the damned that they'd alarmingly rapidly lost their long-accustomed tolerance to Hell's own particularly perfumed, assailing atmosphere.

The combined elements of sulphur, silicates, boiled plasma, fear, torment, pthalates, the smoke of billions of furnaces, spit roasts, forges and mire-pits, the prevalence of faecal ejecta and aerosol particulate body fluids, all jammed up even the most generously spacious nostril could cause untold carnage amongst even the hardiest, most depraved sewer collection of brain cells. Causing its victims to reel in uncontrollable, spastic flail, jabber unintelligibly, uncontrollably, salivate and swell in the oddest areas of the body (the spectacle of a left earlobe leaking lustful slaver, once seen can never be forgotten), loll comatose, fall blind, dumb, deaf, incontinent, loosen bowels and tighten sphincters. All, infuriating and agonising, at the same time.

The only other known method of causing the same effect is exposure to a continuous Coldplay loop through a broken-volume-knob stereo. And event the most sadistic denizens of Hell wouldn't inflict that level of suffering on anyone.

Chapter 55:
The First Wife Club

"Just around the corner, if this little beauty is as accurate as I've come to rely on..."

Pygott strode the last few paces down Defenestration Strasse, calmly sidestepping another plummeter and rounded the corner expectantly. He stopped abreast of the turn, smiled and held out welcoming arms. "My dear...!"

Crone had at least managed to keep Pygott's superior stride within sight, but he was still huffing and puffing at the far end of the row of houses. Very pretty little cottages, by chance. It had always been such a pleasant neighbourhood, apart from the regular disembowelments.

As ever, their luggage constantly nudged him forward.

"Ow! Will you stop nipping my ankles? I'm going as fast as I can!"

In reply, one of the cases nutted him in the knee and its clasp glared up in a most threatening, "Get on with it!" manner.

Crone practically leaped the rest of the way along the pavement. Indeed, leaping in a literal sense over one of the launched damned as they landed on his toe-ends. And was instantly floored, then hoisted high in the air by who-knows-what manner of powerful beast. He tired to gasp in shock, but found there seemed to be only crumpled ribs where his lungs should be. And his eyes popped on the verge of exiting his face and launching back to the Third Left Tentacle (possibly with the first left tentacle) without him.

A strange, noisy, faintly recognisable sound was drilling trilling holes into his cochleae and in about four seconds his tongue was going to be irreversibly transformed into a slimy draught excluder.

"Jedidiaaaaaaaaaaahhh!!!" The sound liquified Crone's cerebellum. "You great, beautiful, boyish, sexy lump of deliciousness!"

The death crush eased to hefty bear hug and Crone felt himself floating back near the ground. Where a ruffle of thick, black curls buried themselves in his collar and sniffed and tickled like an excited, over-friendly skunk. A sensation that Crone recognised all too well stirred and rose up — *Oh my! Don't rise up there!*

"Lilith!" Crone beamed with joy. And some relief at the realisation that he wasn't about to be devoured by a Shoggoth after all.

"Lilith!"

"My favourite little Jedi." Lilith's delight shone down at Crone like a stellar nursery flicking out baby stars. "And you brought your lightsaber too, you naughty rebel." She winked at the embarrassment nudging his fly.

"I'm sure that's just blood pressure anomaly caused by all the squeezing," butted in Pygott, attempting to discharge the potency of an unseemly scene.

"I can always rely on your blood pressure, can't I, my darling?" Lilith winked again and dropped a sly nod toward his nethers. Raising a red-hot flush to Crone's cheeks.

"...keys?" whimpered Crone.

"Only the key to my heart, lover-boy. Mmmmm!" Lilith clamped her lips onto Crone's and proceeded to suck the wind out of him. And blow the fear of Goddess and the lust of Bathsheba into his responsive pipes.

Pygott paled, gulped down a knot of bile and tried in vain to tear his attention away from the escalating, pulsating vignette. It looked rather like watching a hyena descend on an open ribcage, refusing to surface until its entire head, neck and shoulders were crusted with vivid blood.

"Whilst I'd normally entreat you two to, as they say, *get a room,* we haven't really the time for such frivolities. Mr. Crone, will you please put that lady down for a moment?" He paused, waiting, again in vain, for an answer. There was little more than a grunt from Crone's clamped mouth. Which could easily have represented indulgence or panic. "Could you at least unsnare your tongue, so that I can talk to Lilith, as planned?"

In a heave of lip-smacking, panting, throaty giggles, the pair eventually parted. Grinning like horny teenagers and in Crone's case, eyes literally performing somersaults. Lilith leered at Pygott in a most unsavoury way, winked yet again at Crone, then frowned when Pygott nodded down at her twitching hand.

"That's a button fly. Yanking away like that won't work."

"Oh yes." Lilith looked down in confirmation and, fingers waving in surrender, brought her hand away to a safer distance. "So I see. When did you become so traditional, Jedidiah? Has this grumpy old stick-in-the-mud become – chaos forbid! - a good influence on you?"

"I know you two haven't, erm, hooked up in a while-"

"A while? That winsome hippy's likely to come a second time before I do!"

Pygott's pallor dropped at least another shade. And his beard remained utterly insufficient to mask the glower. "Be that as it may, we have business – not *that* type of business! Hands where I can see them please?! We have important business to attend and we need your help."

"I'm always happy to oblige my favourite spine tingler."

"Binder, my dear," corrected Crone, Buckram fashion.

"Ooh, now you're talking! I'll get the-"

"Madam, please?!" Pygott's patience was wearing this as the glassine between art and pornography. "Once our business is concluded, you can spend all the time you like, erm, catching up on gossip. With your assent of course, Mr. Crone?"

Crone was just about to make his excuses, as he remembered just how exhausting even an evening spent in Lilith's company could be. And the flash of enthusiasm in Lilith's eyes gave him cause to believe he'd be svelte as a dancing pole by the time she'd, well, in all honesty, *they'd* sated their lusts. Assuming he survived, of course. Before both Lilith and Pygott talked over one another in his stead.

"So many holidays being granted this week! The shop will be like a morgue." Pygott's turn this time to wink at Lilith. "An atmosphere that positively encourages extra footfall. I may be as tired as Mr. Crone by the time you bring him back."

"I really wouldn't count on it, Mr. Pygott." She loosed the filthiest giggle imaginable. Well, in actual fact, beyond imagination. No sound engorged with such lascivious, lecherous, to be honest, filthy intent had any place in Heaven or Earth. Not even in Hell, for that matter.

Pygott didn't envy the poor demons conscripted to mop the floors within 50 yards of any soul condemned for uncontrollable lustfulness within earshot.

The vibrations from deep within Lilith's febrile glottis were causing no end of Sodomitiousness inside Pygott's Y-fronts. Only Crone's foam-lipped expression could begin to explain what effect it was having on his own loins. And everything else, by the looks of it.

"Now, my dear Lilith," Pygott shook himself off, physically and internally and swallowed down all-but irresistible carnality. "To the business at hand."

"You mean the hand-job?"

"Good God," he muttered. Luckily no one in Hell was paying his blasphemy any attention. "Please concentrate."

"Alright, alright." Lilith waved a dismissive talon or several. "You're a stiff one, Mr. Pygott. I'd like to say you're no fun, but in truth, the frustration you lather me with only makes our liaisons more intriguing. One of these days..."

"But not today." Pygott smiled and winked (so much winking today). Back in control of his own hormones and once again leader of the dance.

Lilith accepted the impasse. Knowing full well she'd be able to look forward to inciting Pygott to dance again sooner, rather than later.

"Come on then, I'll take you there."

"Really?" Crone whipped out of his drooling fugue and provided shocked harmony with Pygott's raised-brow yelp.

"Of course! Why give you directions when I'm heading that way myself?"

"Why indeed? Thankyou." Pygott gave a slight, involuntary bow. But then, he was addressing Underworld royalty, of a kind. And she'd just granted them a big favour. For suspiciously little reason. "Can I ask why you're paying a visit, if that's not too bold a question?"

"You're nothing, if not bold, Mr. Pygott. That's why I like you."

"Please don't start winking again, dear lady. Poor Crone may drown in his own slobber after all."

"Alright; just for you, I'll restrain myself," she giggled. "As no one else around here seems willing, sigh..." She awaited reply to the goad, but received nought but an impatient second cocked brow from Pygott. "Your poor owlbrows are working overtime today, Mr. Pygott."

"Perhaps I should grant *them* a week flying the roost too?"

"You can lend them to Mr. Crone. His may be in danger of leaping off quite a bit."

"My eyebrows can take care of themselves, thankyou very much." Crone bristled. His pride in his feline brows roused to a spot of preening.

"Don't you worry, my darling. I'll take very good care of those silky caterpillars. I'll be licking them into shape soon enough." She ran her forked tongue around her lips. "Literally."

"So you're not off to see Satan to borrow a tub of His infernal hair wax then?" Pygott was desperate to haul the conversation back onto a more chaste footing.

"What in Heaven or Earth would I do with that? Learn to surf down erupting volcanoes, perhaps?" She donned an expression that seemed to indicate she might actually consider it. "No, I have far more important things to keep me busy. Like collecting my new child mincer. Old Nick's pad is the only place they'll agree to deliver. They don't feel safe coming to my house, apparently."

"That must be quite frustrating?"

"What? Being deprived of the attentions of crass delivery drivers on a regular basis?"

"Erm, no. I was thinking more about how often you need to trek the circles to make collections. What with the number of mincers you seem to get through. Hadn't you just oiled up a new one the last time we talked in the shop?"

"I've worn out another two since then! Much as I love mangling kiddies and making them into juicy, spicy gyros, it's getting to be a real chore. The quality of the meat's so flabby and loose these days. And the bones are so rubbery! None have that crisp, brittle snap anymore. It plays havoc with the blades. They end up chewing themselves into a jam in no time and become so dulled, I spend more time oiling a whetstone than whetting my oiled pebble, if you know what I mean?"

"Indeed." Pygott really rather hoped he had no idea what she meant.

"And they don't scream anymore either. There's no real fear or realisation of what's actually going to happen to their lumpy little sacks of lard. They just whine interminably and mumble drivel about me breaching their human rights, or some such tosh. It's all rather tedious and it really does have a terribly negative effect on the machines. They get depressed and sink into ennui, then seize up. Not even fit for scrap..."

"That sounds awful! What an intolerable way to have to perform bad, dishonest maleficence."

"I know! I've had to set up a retirement community to care for them all. It's exhausting."

Chapter 56:
Anxiety Loves Company

"Oh dear, oh dear, oh dear."

Rumpus The Dwarf had retreated into yet another fit of hand wringing.

"You're not still stressing yourself over *that,* are you?" Parcelleseus drifted sylph-like to the end of the counter. Her spangled wings fluttered impatiently. "That was two whole days ago!"

"Which only means I've had two more days to worry about it!"

"But you've solved all their problems, haven't you? I mean, the entire reason they're not here is because of that thing."

"How do you know?" Rumpus was beside himself. Literally. He'd become so agitated, he'd managed to astrally project himself to the other side of the till. He paled to the point of polony at the realisation. "If you dare tell me to pull myself together..." He wagged both real and ethereal finger at Parcelleseus as he noticed her jaw start to twitch.

"Wouldn't dream of it," she sniggered. "But would you mind anyway? It's very distracting having both of you staring at me like the last turkey on Christmas Eve."

"I'll try." He strained and grimaced, to Parcelleseus' dismay. He was far less disturbing as fretting twins than gurning, constipated bookends. "But I'm so distressed! What will they say when they risk life and limb to steal back a book that's already back in their possession."

"Perhaps finding some way of letting them know, rather than hiding behind the till quivering might lessen the blow...?"

"Oh yes. That sounds scary, doesn't it?" Even Rumpus never realised he could muster quite that much scorn. "When was the last time you casually sent a message to Hell? Especially when the recipients aren't supposed to be there in the first place?"

Taken aback as she was, Parcelleseus could see his point.

"I see your point," she replied, helpfully. "I take it you won't be volunteering to sneak off to tip them the wink yourself?" she added, unhelpfully.

Before rapidly whisking away the cartful of new books and retreating to the safe banality of shelving.

Rumpus made a strangled *pop* sound each time his astral separation split anew. Parcelleseus really couldn't stomach the kaleidoscope of fretful images replicating themselves like Noddy Holder mugging the camera on yet another Top of the Pops repeat on BBC4. And he kept repeating a single, panicked squeak.

She wondered how Slade would have spelled "Glibble".

Chapter 57:
Tripping the Dark Unimpressive

""What's the matter, Mr. Pygott? Everything looks quiet""

Crone tried to urge his partner on. More eager to be done with this foolhardy jaunt than scared to be going through with the riskiest part of the escapade.

"That's what's worrying me. It's far *too* quiet." Pygott squinted into every corner and crevice that tried to hide itself in the distance, rapt concentration crumpling his beard. "I know Satan's palace looks like a grand mausoleum, but it's never lifeless. In fact, it's the liveliest sepulchre Death ever investured."

"Oh, pish and twaddle!" Crone practically bounced on the spot in undisguised frustration.

Pygott's eyes nearly popped onto his owlbrows in astonishment. He couldn't remember a pink-faced outburst from Crone in quite this manner since he'd insisted that they try late-night opening for Christmas trading a decade ago. A mistake Pygott wouldn't ever repeat.

"I've had enough of your subterfuge and suspicion! Why can't we just take what we see at face value and get on with sneaking in?"

Before Pygott had chance to retort, Lilith practically erupted with joyous intrigue.

"Sneaking in?"

She skipped back to them like a little girl offered a new kitten. "You two are here to break into Lucifer's palace? Oh, this is the best news I've heard in millennia! Are we stealing? Are we on a covert surveillance mission? Are we declaring guerilla warfare?"

"Isn't it counter-productive to *declare* guerilla warfare?" asked Crone.

"We?" Pygott bellowed, accidentally stopping not only the pair's pedancy, but also every Hellish denizen's degradation for fifty leagues in each direction. He at least managed to look somewhat abashed.

"Don't you dare tell me you're not letting me in on the action, Mr. Pygott? You've already stamped on my fun today. I'll explode if you insist I restrain myself any more!"

Pygott formulated a considered, reasoned, utterly irrefutable retort and opened his mouth to deliver it. But after looking at the morass of excitement and impatience massed before him, he finally decided he was no longer in charge of his own or any other's destiny.

"Forget I spoke. Lead on Lilith and Crone! Let's storm the place willy-nilly. You see my hair?" He pointed at his bouffant. "I've officially let it down."

"You look positively Bohemian, Mr. Pygott. Loosening up makes you far more sexy." Lilith laid a velvet wink on him. Which slid off without effect.

Apart from turning Crone's eyes a decided shade of green.

"Come on, come on, come on!" ushered Crone, urging them on towards the palace gates. "We have a b-"

"Ahem!" coughed Pygott, at least as loud as his previous outburst. "We have a *mission to complete,* yes, Mr. Crone." His brows danced a merry samba and at one point practically raised into an exclamation point. Luckily, Lilith was far too focussed on Pygott's new Bo-ho hairstyle (apparent only to her) to notice his alarming lack of subtlety.

"Erm, ah, yes – our *mission.* Which I'd very much like to be done with, so that I can go home to the safety of the shop as soon as inhumanly possible, please?"

"The shop? You're going to have your way with me at the Third Left Tentacle? You two really are loosening up, aren't you?"

"It would appear so," opined Pygott. "Why don't we cordon off the theology section and you can ravage my colleague on a pile of bibles?"

"I think not! How could you suggest such a thing?"

"I'm sorry. Highly inappropriate, even-"

"That sodding book excluded all my best achievements and let that hoary old goat over there steal all my glory. I wouldn't wipe my shapely ar-"

"You make a very good point, my dear! I'll agree the good book maketh not a good mattress." Pygott was happy to blaspheme, but held no truck with crass language. "Perhaps something softer, such as our volumes of medieval torture techniques? You can use Crone as a guinea pig to try out a few moves."

Crone paused in his bumble towards the palace, thought to speak, reconsidered, shrugged and nodded. Then set off back in the direction of Lucifer's home and offices.

Lilith looked to Pygott with excited pleading in her eyes.

"Go on then. Just don't tell The Sisters. We're deep enough in their bad books as it is."

Chapter 58:
Courier and Curiouser

Baal tossed the vellum from talon to talon. Now even more confused than he'd already considered beyond confusion.

Not only could he *still* not discover the tiniest hint towards the whereabouts of that infuriating pipsqueak, Arseyknackerjob, or whatever it called itself, nor understand quite why he'd thrown the same wobbly that Lucifer Himself had stomped at God's feet all those millennia past and still had no compunction to relent, but more than that, having been sent to Coventry – literally! - and finding it rather pleasant, he'd had hand delivered by an extremely nervous Lycra-clad weekend road warrior a personal, gilt-inlaid invitation to a certain soiree by the very same Old Nick that had banished him from Hell to leafy Warwickshire in the first place.

And to top it all off, Baal hadn't even thought of using the skinny cyclist as a tooth pick or relief-jamming sexual aid and allowed them to pedal suspiciously away after he'd signed for the envelope.

SIGNED FOR A DELIVERY, FOR HELL'S SAKE!

He'd even donned his dilemma horns to rock back and forth over whether to accept or not.

After all, even if He was enraged enough to expel a top-level demon into verdant cottage, incognito, human-plane inconsequence, Lucifer didn't half cater well for His shindigs. And just such an indulgent, despicable knees/tentacles/pseudopodia-up might be just what Baal needed to nudge him out of his funk.

He dig beg the question though, what was so great about spending a week on holiday that it deserved a Hell-wide celebration to herald the boss's surprisingly bad-tempered return?

Chapter 59:
Hiding in Plain Strop

"Mr. Pygott? What are you doing over there?"

Pygott carefully dared a glance around to discover why Crone wasn't breathing down his tweed elbow.

"What am I doing over here? Where we're *supposed to be?* Sneaking about to find a breach in security around the more vulnerable, forgotten corners of this black edifice?" His eyes narrowed and his beard twitched equally concerned and exasperated. "The proper question should be, what in blazes are *you doing over there?"*

"We're walking in the front door, what else?"

"She may be able to walk in the front door-"

"Excuse me! *She* has a name! I could easily change my good opinion of you, Mr. Pygott."

"My apologies, my dear Lilith. I appear to be somewhat overwrought."

"Apology accepted, you beast." She winked. With her tongue. Pygott paled. Impressive again for someone with such jealously preserved, unnatural pallor.

"The, erm, lovely Lilith is supposed to walk in – she is, after all, expected. We, however, are most certainly not supposed to be here."

"Normally I'd concur, Mr. Pygott. You know how agreeable I am."

"Indeed I do, Mr. Crone. Your quiff doesn't form a question mark for nothing."

"Exactly! But look here: there's absolutely *no one* around."

"That can't be! There's always *someone* here. Even if the guards have taken one of their infamous 'investigative interludes'."

"The tavern's closed though. We walked past it on the way, remember?"

"Hmm, yes. It had the abandoned air of Slimelight on All Saints Day."

"Perhaps everyone's yet to return from the riot that side of Rodin's gates? Glad they at least retained them here, by the way. The refit upstairs is bad enough, but without the looming black unwelcome of these terrifying beauties, the welcome to Hell really doesn't impress at all."

"There's always an air to the staff here, that they deserve preferential treatment. Perhaps they're still arguing the toss with Leviathan? It's a wonder Lucifer ever dares set foot outside the building, if this is what happens when he decides to take a week off."

"If this means I can't pick up my new mincer, there'll be Hell to pay!" Lilith snarled. Literally.

"Assuming you can find anyone with whom to raise Hell..." mused Pygott absently. Whilst tentatively surveying the door, still convinced there must be some trick or booby trap laying in wait. Albeit extremely well camouflaged.

"Oh, I'll make sure I find *someone.*" Lilith kicked open one of the doors, very nearly taking the point of Pygott's nose with it. "And they'll be the first to test my new grinder blades!"

And with that – thankfully accompanied neither with alarm, weapons, demons, harpies, nor even an annoyed clipboard – Lilith stormed the porch and disappeared into the belly of the cavernous unwelcome hall.

Crone was halfway over the threshold when Pygott stuck out a long, spindly arm to create a barrier across Crone's chest. Stopping him with the immediacy of a squash court wall.

"What is it *now?*" Crone huffed, a frustrated grimace travelling up to his cheeks.

"Proceed carefully, Mr. Crone. It just occurred to me that Lilith tramped through the front door."

"Really? It *just occurred to you?* We both just watched her, plain as day!" Crone snorted and made to set out – or in – again. "Really, Mr. Pygott, this is too much!"

Pygott was tall and willow thin, but Crone never ceased to be amazed at how strong his wiry friend could be. His arm didn't budge a micron when Crone renewed pressure and tried to move forward again.

"If Lilith is here to collect some kit, why aren't we ringing the gong dangling over the back passage?"

"The tradesman's entrance?"

"In the rear, yes."

"Where all the parcels are pushed out of the chute?"

"Good lord...in the despatch office, yes."

"Ah, where all the goods are stored!" Crone's enthusiasm for puns had finally stepped aside long enough for reason to take over. "Do you think they're classed as 'goods' here though? Shouldn't they be called 'bads'? Hmm, no. That sounds rubbish..."

There were times Pygott wondered about Crone nearly as much as Crone's mind wandered.

"Whatever the semantics, one thing we can definitely count on is our reliable noses."

"Noses, Mr. Pygott?" Crone's hand rose to his face in a subconscious act of checking that his own protuberance could at least be relied upon to be present.

"Yes, Mr. Crone. I'll be surprised if we can't both smell the same rat?"

Chapter 60:
Planting the Staff

Aristophonob arrived at the Third Left Tentacle to be greeted by Consternation. Who showed it through to a rather fretful looking dwarf, who stoutly refused to give his own name. Even though it was clearly displayed on the name badge at his lapel. Who also flatly refused to believe that 'Nob was a new member of staff. And was hopping about behind the counter like a gimp-suited mermaid fetishist hosting a bondage party answering a knock at the door from a pair of ever-smiling Mormon missionaries. It was all well and good that the visitors remained unfailingly polite, all-smiles, attentive, unphased and enthusiastic, but once their presence was validated, they were impossible to shift from the doorstep. And woe betide anyone who actually let them and their collapsible screen and projector in!

Even the fact that a rather sylph-like vision of loveliness fluttered across from the shelving devoted to vivisection and reanimation to deliver a vellum envelope addressed to *'Aristophonob ('Nob), Special Projects Executive, Third Left Tentacle'* seemed to have no impact on Rumpus sturdy denial.

Aristophonob stared with all its many positioned eyes as she buzzed away, but couldn't catch sight enough of her own name badge. It did though manage to catch the look back over her shoulders that intercepted the stare. To bring forth a series of shifting blushes across 'Nob's nobbles. She disappeared with only the ghost of a smile lingering in her wake.

"I'll remind you, fraternising with other members of staff is frowned upon," growled Rumpus, snapping 'Nob's delight.

"So you're acknowledging me as staff then?"

"No! But if you were..." Rumpus blustered. "Which you're clearly not."

"I suppose not actually staring work till next week counts as not being a member of staff?"

"Staff shouldn't fraternise! I won't be having a repeat of the terrible sticky page crisis of '97 all over again!" He mopped his shaking brow, which dropped into the weariest expression Aristophonob had ever come across. And being a demon, weary expressions were very much the norm.

"Good. Well, that's sorted then."

"What? What have you sorted? We have a sorting skellig for sorting! Don't we?"

"Why are you saying 'we'?" beamed Aristophonob. "We've definitely agreed that I don't work here. Yet." 'Nob's grin spread wider than The Great Beast's forehead at Rumpus' further elevation in distress. "So I'm free to persue said staff member in my capacity as ordinary member of the public."

"Customer," corrected Rumpus.

"I'm not buying anything until I qualify for staff discount."

"You must be staff to qualify for staff discount!"

"At which point the relationship will be over! Ah, it's a long time since I had a holiday romance." Aristophonob stared wistfully over Rumpus' head at a vision of the sylph flitting through summer meadows and beckoning it coquettishly onto a gingham picnic rug. There was a procession of ants marching across the middle, trying to carry off the salad bowl. "Nothing better than ants to enhance sexual potency..."

"Excuse me?!?!"

Rumpus' face turned redder than the inflamed ant-bites swelling inside 'Nob's febrile imagination.

"Of course you're excused. See you next week." Aristophonob left a relaxed farewell dangling behind it and set off to find and flirt with the flitting flutterer.

All thoughts of the wax-sealed vellum envelope grasped within a confused tentacle forgotten. For now, at least.

Chapter 61:
Diversionary Tic-Tacs

After navigating their seventh cavernous, vaulted-ceilinged, marble-flagged, marble-pillared, human-vellum-tapestry-lined, overostentatious reception hall, Pygott's patience could bear no more.

"My dear Lilith?" He paused momentarily, allowing her chance to break the rhythm of her all-too-confident, ever-quickening footsteps. "I believe you had a package to collect from the Quartermaster?"

"I do, I do!" she blustered. "So pick up the pace, or the stores'll be closed before we get there." And she twirled on a sixpence, considered for the barest instant picking it up and was ready to bound off again.

"Not only do you seem to be forgetting that *we* are not going to the stores; that is entirely *your* destination..." Pygott paused only to let Lilith steady her stunted flow, but was interrupted by a wholly unexpected response.

"But you *must come with me!* I can't go there alone!" Lilith looked positively distraught. An expression attached to her face Pygott thought beyond the bounds of possibility.

"Madam, you are the very last being I would ever posit needing bodyguard support. Particularly not for a routine visit to Satan's ludicrously mild-mannered Quartermaster. He's so deferential, I'm surprised the contents of the stores aren't all pilfered by brigands and scumbags on a regular basis. The guards being the worst of them."

"That's true." Lilith chewed her lip in contemplation. "How can someone so respectable earn the loyalty of such a hoary bunch of cut-throats and thieves?"

"Such a thing is up for debate." Pygott wagged a finger of admonishment before she could divert the conversation. "But not until we all meet at the bar of the nearest whore-carpeted spit-and-blood tavern *after* we have completed our respective tasks here."

"Spoilsport."

"One of my middle names is Killjoy. No, really!" Pygott grinned. "Which is one of the reasons I can take full pleasure in pointing out that you are heading as far away from the equipment cellars as is possible within the palace. By happenstance, I'll also bring your attention to the fact that you're leading myself and Mr. Pygott a merry dance an equal distance from our own intended destination."

The owlbrows twitched their own merry dance.

"There's been a lot of remodelling..."

"No matter how much or often the vainglorious fops that oversee the upkeep – or more often, downkeep – of this testament to worthless vanity, Lucifer's only, cast-iron stipulation is that basic, functional pathways are not obstructed or hidden. He likes to know where He's going and has a tendency to lose His bearings in His dotage, especially when forced to traverse this unfortunately necessary, pompous facade."

"It's been a while since I came here. And I'm never allowed in the front door! Snobs. I just wanted to nose around while the Master's away. Do a bit of sightseeing..."

"Good! In that case, we're nearing the point where you will have seen every gallery, public torture post and historical and hysterical heirloom, including De Sade's tonsils – which still haven't stopped talking – that Hell and Earth can craft-"

"And Heaven, don't forget!" Lilith interrupted. Again. "Don't forget hard-cum trophies like Metatron's mouthguard. Such a shame he hung up his rugby boots after *that* game..."

"Yes, all very diverting. But diversions no more! You need a new mincer." Pygott pointed towards an indeterminate doorway. "And we need to badger Lucifer's PA before it wakes up and needs feeding again." Pygott wagged a dismissive finger at Lilith before she had chance to protest. "No, my dear. We can't just help you carry out the mincer. You're a big, strong girl. Bigger and stronger than both of us put together."

"Yes, Mr. Pygott. We must be off. I'm finding these vaulted ceilings quite oppressive." Crone's voice drifted out from behind a giant, marble phallus. He blushed shrimpishly as he realised the veined pillar he was so intimately clutching and smoothing his hands over wasn't either vein or pillar, but something entirely other. "We really need to go! I certainly do..." Neither Crone's nerves nor his barely suppressed ardour could take any more exposure to Lilith's addictive miasma. Especially not up the back aisle of the Portal Substructa Lasciuia.

"We bid you fair adieu!" Pygott practically saluted as he swept past Crone, tugging him off the phallus as he headed in the opposite direction to Lilith's spluttering protests. "Don't look back," he whispered through gritted teeth. "No human needs to see *that* manner of gesticulation!"

Chapter 62:
Resistance is Futile!

"A sightseeing tour, you say?"

"Indeed."

"Seen much?"

"Lots of sights."

"'Ere? In this grotty 'ole?"

"The advertising blurb proclaims it to be a 'splendid Gothic edifice'."

"Really? I'd 'ave thought, 'crumblin', confusin', anachronistic waste of good pumice' might be more appropriate. Let's 'ave a look at this scandalous leaflet."

"Ah, we didn't feel the need to bring it: it offered guided tours."

"What will they think of next? I can't see anybody shellin' out for that!"

"And yet, here we are..."

"Here you are. Yes, you are! But where's your tour guide?"

"She – at least we think it was a she – was eaten by a Shoggoth in the Gallery of Wailing Tittery. She made such a caterwaul, I think her remains have already been preserved alongside Tarja Turunen's tonsils."

"A Shoggoth? Did you say Shoggoth?"

"I believe I did."

"There's Shoggoths roaming the corridors?"

"Well, we only saw one. But they're generally the sociable type, Amongst one another, of course."

"What in the name of all that's unnatural are Shoggoths doin' shamblin' about the corridors of Satan's Palace?"

"Oh, I think you'll find they don't shamble. That's more the bent of Dimensional Shamblers: the clue's in the name! Shoggoths are more lumberers."

"I don't care if they're jumpin' 'urdles, there's no business them bein' 'ere! No business them bein' on this plane o' reality, for that matter!"

"Excuse me. Where are you going?"

"On a Shoggoth 'unt, o' course!"

"But aren't you supposed to be skewering us to the nearest pillar and torturing us till we divulge our nefarious intentions in sneaking around the entrance to Lucifer's private chambers?"

"Be good lads and see to that yourselves, would you? Rampaging Shoggoths is far more pressing than two shifty looking middle-aged fops lurking around Satan's office wi' dubious intent."

"What if we decline your polite request and simply carry on skulking about?"

"I'll leave that up to you. But if you'll take my advice, self-immolation and attaching electrodes to your own scrotums would be a lot less injurious than tryin' to break in through them doors and face the portal beyond."

"Isn't it 'scrota'?"

"*Aren't they* 'scrota'?"

"Ha! Touché."

"Right, I'm off. You two be good."

"But we're in Hell."

"In that case, be bad! And don't make a mess when you get obliviated by the security system. Cos *I* aint shovellin' you up!"

Pygott turned to a stupefied Crone as the great grandson to the nth generation of Cerberus bounded off towards the nearest vestibule, yelped as he realised he didn't fit through the gap, wiggled his way free painfully slowly, dislodging several blocks of marble as he struggled and gambolled like a 100 ton spring lamb to chase headlong after Pygott's wild goose. Or geese. Or Shoggoths.

"He's not really inherited the family sense of rigid duty, has he?" Crone shook his head, staring fondly after the giddy pup.

"Not really. I didn't need to use any of these spells or hexes I sweated to impregnate myself with. Not wasted time or effort at all..." Pygott grumbled.

"I was looking forward to throwing the enchanted stick for him to chase, myself. His great grandad used to love a good game of fetch with that! It still has all the old fella's teeth-marks." Crone sighed and retreated to a wistful, happy memory.

"We can let the Hell-e-boar go now too. There's no call for a meaty lure anymore."

"Righto – stand back."

Rather than careering away like its tail was on fire, the Hell-e-boar, after excitedly navigating a few enthusiastic circles plonked itself in front of the pair, panting and staring up expectantly. Somewhat confused.

"Go on, you're free," ushered Crone.

Which prompted an even more puzzled look to smear its existing confusion.

"Sorry, but all our plans have fallen flat. There's no one here to wrestle." Pygott shrugged apologetically. "And no, sorry, we have urgent business. Otherwise we'd have obliged without a second thought."

The Hell-e-boar looked crestfallen. Crone picked up its crest for it and gave one of its ears a tickle. Taking great care to stay out of range of one of its suddenly uncontrollable scratching hind legs.

Cerberus Jnr. Nth went that way though." Crone pointed and the snout followed and twitched. "I'm sure he'd love a spot of rough-housing, if you can catch him!"

The boar looked back and forth between them, racked with indecision.

"What are you waiting for? Written permission? Be off and enjoy yourself. You've earned it," said Crone, as he gently shooed the creature.

It quivered once or twice, stared languidly back at the corridor reeking of several-headed hound paws and then back at the booksellers, almost fit to burst.

"Sorry," offered Crone. "My turn, eh?" He patted it on the tusks. "Off you go!"

And it practically tore up the floor as it scarpered.

"Breaking into Hell aint what it used to be, Mr. Crone."

"It most certainly is not." He shook his head in disapproval.

"Well then. As there appears to be a gift horse's mouth to look into..." Pygott waved on his colleague politely. "Shall we?"

The gift horse gave a timid whinny as the luggage produced an enticing carrot on their way past.

Chapter 63:
Resistance is Mandatory!

"Where the Hell do you think you're going?"

Now, that's more like it! thought Pygott. *Some resistance at last.*

"Stay there!" The voice hollered. "Move where I can see you!"

"Erm, which is it? We can't do both."

"Shut up and tell me who your are!"

"Should we show him our business cards, Mr. Pygott? Or would that be classed as clever-Dickery?"

"What are you whispering about? Speak up!"

"We were just wondering-?"

"Don't speak unless I ask you to!"

"Good Lord..." muttered Pygott.

"And no blaspheming! Don't you know where you are?"

"Unless we're very much mistaken, a place where blasphemy first made its home...?"

"Don't you come clever with me, smarty pants!"

"But I have very smarty pants, so clever is a given, dear heart."

"Are you going to come over here or not?"

"That depends on whether you'd like us to? Or not?"

A sound that Pygott could only equate with several elephants suffering explosive diarrhoea erupted from the dimness. Crone, however, thought it more the sound of the Tacoma Narrows Bridge wrenching itself into oblivion. The luggage, having more savoir fare, simply thought it sounded like a member of the Heavenly Choir being thrown out of Heaven and condemned to eternity in Hell. Again. And no amount of nudging at the booksellers' heels seemed able to move them to that simple revelation.

"Yes, yes," muttered Crone impatiently. "We *all* want to get on. But we need to deal with this...whatever it is first."

The baggages' buckles whistled a resigned sigh and the cases retreated back into impatient restraint.

"It's like arguing with that pair of tweed-strangled tossers again..." breathed the voice from the gloom. Once it had settled the dust of its titanic explosion.

"Oh my, it's *you,* isn't it?" pipped Crone, stepping out into the light at last.

"Eek!"

The angel literally hopped back a step. Then another as Pygott joined his partner.

"Ah, splendid to see you again!" Pygott enthused.

"No, no, no!" wailed the angel. "Not again?!"

"Oh dear. No need for all this, surely?"

"No, no. I can't get embroiled in another argument with you two."

"Be fair! Only Pygott was involved the last time."

"I can't risk you two tying me in knots and tricking me into going back. I like it here. I've got this great job shouting at people and I get respect. Not like the winged chump I was up there!" The angel pointed at the ceiling in an abstract gesture, then panicked as it realised it had taken its eyes off its nemeses. "So don't you two pull any funny moves."

"Well..." Pygott rubbed his hands together in delight and turned to his partner. "It would seem our little excursion worked out perfectly for our friend here." He turned his attention back to the angel. "So glad we could play a part in fulfilling your destiny. I could tell right away you were built for better things than pious subservience."

"Well, as it goes, I got to drop-kick-" The angel suddenly bit its tongue quite hard. "Ouch!"

"Careful! You can't tell us off or order us about if you bite through that. Why ever did you, by chance?"

"You nearly had me breaching our data protection policy, you swine! I can't go telling you who gets in or kicked out of here just like that. You have to submit a request in writing to the data scribes. You'll find writing scrolls and quills in there."

"In there?" Crone pointed toward Lucifer's private offices.

"Where else? That's what you're here for, isn't it?"

"Well, yes. But isn't it your job to stop us getting in?"

"If you were anyone else, you'd be coughing up your own spleens by now. And that surly luggage wouldn't be fit to carry the Dark Lord's morning comfort break tissues."

Pygott and Crone shared a faint grimace. The luggage had no face to follow suit, but still appeared quite sickly.

"We won't thank you for that image, if that's alright with you? But more important than our sudden attack of biliousness, why are you allowing us free passage?"

"I'm not getting involved in any transaction! You can't fool me that way. Not again! Just get yourselves in there before anyone notices and I can still claim that I never saw you." Dys waved a slightly panicked hand back and forth at the doors, peering around to ensure no one might see.

"Are you sure?"

"Stop stalling and get in there!" Talons pointing, eyes averted and ears metaphorically clamped, the angel ushered them on.

Pygott and Crone shuffled suspiciously forward. Was this some kind of trap? Pygott couldn't feel any of the protections he wore jabbing at his skin and a glance at Crone showed no indication that his early-warning ear-hairs were twitching at all.

"Go on, go on! We can all see the carvings are exquisite, but I'm sure you'll have time to stare in wonder on the way out. If you survive whatever you find in there, of course..."

"Do you know what awaits us?" queried Crone.

"Good Go- erm, I mean, Hell no! I don't have the security clearance to go past this gate. My job is to stay out here and stop everybody else going through at all costs. Well, without express instruction from His Lordship, of course."

"Of course."

"And us."

"Ah, but you're not here, are you? If by some miracle anyone asks, you haven't passed this way, I haven't seen or talked to you and I certainly haven't let you pass through these gates. And even though this is the only way in, no one's likely to quibble over a piffling detail like you two managing something that's impossible, are they?"

"Fair enough. Your debating skills are really improving in the Underworld. Congratulations."

Dys puffed a tiny snort.

"Anyway, judging by the state of some of those actually *invited* I've seen coming out again during my short tenure – and especially the number that never reappear – I don't want to know what lurks behind these doors."

"Well, if it's anything like the last time-"

"Tish and fie! I don't want any of your stories! Get out of my feathers and leave me alone. Any consequence incurred from my employer has to be better than whatever engaging with you might cause."

"Well, if you insist...?"

"Gerrardavit!!!"

Pygott and Crone bumped into the ebony slabs as they were taken literally aback. They studied Dys, one another and exchanged glances with their luggage, which nudged and bumped at their ankles anew. While the angel's hard eyebrows practically leaped off its forehead in an attempt to get them to push off.

"Well, it was nice catching up with you. Good luck with the job." Pygott smiled.

"Here we go," whispered Crone as they turned to face the opening gateway. "Journey's end?"

Chapter 64:
The Great and the Good?

Aristophonob was having the time of its little, extensive unlife.

In fact, it might be forced to stop referring to its unlife as 'little', if this was how its existence would continue from now on. To be honest, it might even venture to call it a life!

Just by introducing itself as Pygott & Crone's Special Projects Envoy (that's the title they gave it, wasn't it? Close enough, it thought) opened the door to the most weird and wonderful experiences.

For starters, it had literally granted entrance to this great banqueting hall and its attendant – Scot free! - luxuries. And there were so many damned celebrities here that couldn't restrain themselves from offering an enthusiastic welcome, before regaling it with all their finest tales of popular success or derring-do. Presumably, judging by their asides, to curry favour for sneaking the best deals buying or selling the most precious books and artefacts. Or escaping censure for being somewhat absent-minded in settling their accounts.

Receding into the background, Adolf Hitler was gaily amusing a throng, who enthusiastically clapped and whooped at his barnstorming revue.

He'd delighted in recounting his pre-war desires, as a confirmed Anglophile – to journey to London and learn the splendid customs of the Cockney Pearly Kings and Queens. And how after being sidetracked from his passion by the whims of destiny and something called 'Jew' (Aristophonob had absolutely no idea who this person was, but if only by the tone of Hitler's speech about them, Aristophonob didn't care for Hitler at all. There were vengeful, rabid demons outside with far more wholesome dispositions), Adolf had concocted plans to invade Britain, simply so that he could ingratiate himself with the East Enders and learn to play the virtuoso spoons.

As it turned out, he'd curtailed that possibility by instead spooning cyanide over reaching Dover, let alone the Isle of Dogs. *Best decision ever, if a tad late,* mused 'Nob.

Adolf waited patiently for Oswald Moseley to join the ranks of Hell's gallery of stars. Only to find him utterly unable to clack a single spoon, let alone rattle off rhythm with a pair. He also dismissed Moseley as a crushing, disappointing bore for one so dashing. "He seemed a bit of a fascist, actually," opined the Führer.

In the end, it took a chance encounter with Jack the Ripper – well, at least one of the many claimants to that crown – who showed him the correct method over a period of tortuous weeks (Hitler was unbeatable at sausage eating competitions, but barely competent as a musician, as it turned out). Grateful though Adolf remained, he steadfastly refused the offer to add an extra dimension to his less-than virtuoso performance by accepting Jacko's offer to use a pair of his razor-scalpels in place of spoons.

Aristophonob left the odious little grease-fringe to explore the hitherto undiscovered concept of hob-nobbing. It had never considered being in the presence of nobbing hobs, let alone dream of being a participant! Especially as it involved being practically force-fed the finest quality foods, quaffing glass after glugging glass of, appropriately, the demon alcohol. 'Nob had never experienced 'getting a buzz on', but if this was what was meant by it, the little demon intended to keep it up as long and as often as possible!

Best of all, Baal was over by the never-ending buffet table, pontificating like several warring pontiffs. Inbetween a gaggle of several, late Pontiffs. He appeared to be losing to at least a couple of them in an escalating game of perpetrating the most monstrous, perverted act. In fact, one of the Primates had even made the old bull blush. And not just once.

Aristophonob was engaged in an intermittent, one-sided battle of annoyance, at first staring and glaring at Baal from a safe distance. Before steadily moving closer, pulling faces right on the end of his tractor tyre nostrils, asking impertinent questions and even doing a merry, louche dance at one point. While hurling joyous insults at him at the top of its toneless voice.

All to little response from the once King of Hell.

But when 'Nob began brushing past to reach for food, treading on hooves on the way past, culminating in blatantly barging him aside on a number of occasions, Baal began to look most uncomfortable, whipping his eyes about in unseeing pursuit of the invisible assailant. Even a couple of times thrashing wildly in an attempt to catch the irksome phantom.

"What's the matter? Fleas? We used to get them in the Vatican every time the Order of St. Magaroc turned up, wearing their filthy hair cassocks," ventured Pope Pormkut'yun III.

"Some sort of twitch? I used to suffer from restless leg syndrome something rotten!" offered Pope Pilates I supportively. Why he was Pope Pilates I, no one was quite sure, as there was no documented Pope Pilates II to be found in either record or memory.

"Perhaps you're possessed?" butted in Pope Padre Peepo drily. To a ripple of impolite guffaws from the gathered priests. "Would you like one of us to perform an exorcism?"

Ordinarily, Baal would have eaten his head. Slowly.

But these were not ordinary times. To the point where, for a moment at least, he actually considered the offer.

Instead, he was concocting a sternly worded letter of complaint to Lucifer's PA. Which in itself was a bizarre anomaly. Normally, a slight such as allowing a lowly poltergeist to manifest (the cheek of it, for starters!) and interfere with – nay, assault! - anyone of even minor importance here would have Baal storming up to Lucifer and forcefully deride His lack of control and courtesy and demand reparation.

Lucifer would of course overreact to the effrontery, rip several new orifices and heftily eject him on the end of a size 20 hoof. Before then turning His attention to the problem and acting in far more Medieval fashion to solve it.

Then laugh and joke and get very drunk with Baal the day after, as though nothing at all had happened the night before. Much in the way that Baal had ended up here after all.

But for the first time in his unlife, Baal didn't fancy either the full-on fun of a diabolical slanging match, nor the titillating smart of a lava-hot, hoofprint-singed buttock.

The Underworld, at least in his own estimation, had gone mad.

Wherever Pygott had found this amulet, Aristophonob felt it ought to seek out to pay a celebratory, ceremonial visit. And confer every honour on it a little demon could. It worked so much better than any wild dream could promise. 'Nob had imagined that its effect might be diminished the closer its proximity to the great, stinking hulk, but reality was quite the opposite, as though it was sucking the energy to function directly out of Baal himself. Which was leaving him noticeably confused, pale and jittery. Much like 'Nob itself had always been made to feel in Baal's presence.

However being shackled to Pygott and Crone's workforce turned out, the flashes of genuine disquiet skittering across its odious old boss's rheumy eyes were worth at least another millennium of penury.

And Aristophonob would smirk through any tribulation for however much of eternity it could endure.

Chapter 65:
No Stabs in the Dark

"I don't remember Satan's Hollow being so dark," whispered Crone. "Gloomy at times, but never dick black."

"I don't remember being here while He's on holiday before. Perhaps this is normal?"

"But I don't like it, Mr. Pygott."

"Come, come, Mr. Crone. We spoke about this. You have an amulet protecting you from being eaten by monsters hiding in corners sewn into your left shirt cuff. And one warding off things that go bump in the night I slipped under your collar."

"i knew this shirt didn't rub when I bought it! Oh dear, I've already drafted a stern letter of blame to the nice lady who collects our shop laundry too. I do hope she'll forgive me?"

"I'm sure she will. After you heap all the blame on me. Just as you've forgiven me for insisting on making sure you kept the succubus defence in your pocket."

"Hmm, well, I wouldn't go that far..."

"That's as may be. But you know as well as I that a fear of the dark is entirely irrational."

"Of course. But we both agree that being afraid of the things hiding in the dark that eat people is rational. Nay, sensible."

"You make a valid point, Mr. Crone. But that only applies when we're not alone in an entirely empty room, at the heart of a deserted building."

"That's the rub though, Mr. Pygott. Don't you feel that there are a million eyes trained on you? And have been since we walked through that last door?"

"But I have no alarm squeaking, nor amulets trilling. Even my neck tingler is only vibrating because it's snoring."

"That kind of danger's not what I mean though. I'm talking about that prickle through the hairs on the back of my neck. The rolling grumble in my stomach – and before you say it, not linked to the dinner bell. It's that gut feeling that wherever I turn, I'm being watched."

"The last time I trusted my gut feeling, I believe I advised against undertaking this very endeavour, Mr. Crone?"

"Hmm, touché, Mr. Pygott. But enough of this badinage! We're being watched. By lots of eyes. We can feel it. And there's nothing you can do to convince us otherwise."

"Very good then, Mr. Crone. I shall defer to your superior sixth and seventh senses. And join you in a prayer that those perceived eyes are not connected to portentous sets of teeth..."

Crone gulped and scanned the darkness surrounding them, fruitlessly, once more. Before clamping his hands on the monstrous door handle and twisted it slowly, eerily silently and held his breath against whatever waited inside Lucifer's inner sanctum.

And very nearly jumped out of his generous skin as Pygott tapped him on the shoulder, just as the hinges began to creak.

"Luggage? I hope you've brought ample supplies of clean pants? These may have come to mischief!" The cases shuffled and jostled in a way that almost sounded like a snigger. "What *is it,* Mr. Pygott? I thought we'd been undone!"

"What if, after all this, the book's not there?"

"Don't be preposterous! Where else would He be keeping such a secret, dangerous object?"

"Well, as we came to the conclusion that He may be using it, what if He's taken it with Him to read on His holiday?"

"Erm, ah, well. Oh." Crone paled so much that his face practically lit up a spherical sphere in the darkness. "I never thought of that."

"To say we're such clever fellows, we can still be mind-bogglingly daft, old friend."

"Indeed." Crone chuckled, laughed and let out a hearty guffaw. "Ah well, it's too late to worry about that now. Lets' go riffle through His drawers anyway."

Chapter 6(6)6:
Hob Nobbing

"Excuse me, Sire?"

Lucifer tried to turn to see where the little voice was coming from. But instead appeared rooted to the floor and uttered only "Ouch!" in response.

Aristophonob quickly checked its tentacles in the dimming lights, relieved to see that no part of itself had in any bad way connected with the Dark Lord, let alone cause any discomfort.

"I know it's a bit cramped in here, Baal, but that's no excuse for stomping on my hoof, you clumsy old bullock!"

"DID YOU HEAR THAT? I THOUGHT I HEARD A VOICE...BUT I COULDN'T HAVE."

"What are you blathering on about, you great, hulking lump? I didn't go to all the trouble of stopping off at the blacksmith for new shoes only for you to trample all over me and scuff them up?"

"I SWEAR I HEARD A LITTLE VOICE DOWN THERE...?" Baal ignored his Master and continued to pirouette atop Satan's hooves.

"Get off! You steaming ninny!" Lucifer shoved Baal's great bulk off His feet and the bull stumbled befuddled into the nearest waiter, sending a tray of boiling drinks sailing in a fiery rain over the heads of several guests. Baal didn't seem to notice, instead turning back to peer at empty space around Satan's woolly knees. " I honestly don't know why I have you here. Baal, I'd hoped you might exonerate yourself, but you're an embarrassment."

"SOMETHING BRUSHED MY TOES..."

"Do they count as toes, Baal? Why don't you find an encyclopaedia and look it up? *Somewhere else.*"

"I hope I'm not causing any trouble, Your Majesty?"

"Not at all, little one! In fact, I'd like to congratulate you on an excellent job. Even though you aren't actually working for me, you've been an immense help." Satan reached down and proffered huge, taloned hands. 'Nob practically pulled several muscles fighting the urge to flinch. And practically beamed with pride when Lucifer enthusiastically shook one of its tentacles.

"Thankyou, thankyou Sire. It's a particular honour to meet you and if I had a heart, it would sing joy at your praises."

"Tish and fie, little demon!" Lucifer shook the tentacle even more vigorously.

"*WHO IS HE TALKING TO?*" wailed Baal, waving a horny head around in front of Lucifer's chest and peering tearfully at very thin air.

"Go away, Baal!" bellowed a by now thoroughly infuriated Lord of the Underworld. "Apologies for my, erm, friend; he seems to have been under an inordinate amount of pressure of late. For a change."

"I'm sure I can forgive his foibles, Sire." *Not bloody likely! I'm going to milk this for all it's worth!*

"Ah, good man. Erm, woman, ah, thing?" Lucifer patted 'Nob on the back and grinned sheepishly (He got that from His Father's side of the family). "Sorry. More tentacles than genitals – always confuses me. Still, I can see why you charmed our esteemed friends! I'm sure you'll be a prize asset to the business. And if you're open to even more special, *special* projects, you'll find I'm an excellent tipper."

"I'll keep that at the forefront of my mind, Your Grace."

"Your Grace, ha-ha! I like your spunk. This may be the start of a beautiful relationship. What do you think, Baal?"

"THE UNDERWORLD'S GONE MAD," Baal mumbled. "YOU'VE GONE MAD. EVEN THE FRESH AIR IN FRONT OF MY FACE HAS GONE MAD!" And he wandered off muttering to himself, casting the odd sharp backward glance, as though he'd catch the phantom manifesting by surprise as he went.

"Hmm, funny fellow," offered Aristophonob.

"Hilarious," grizzled Satan. And grabbed them both another drink. Which was almost too big for 'Nob's tentacle to grasp. "Let's see if we can pickle our brains as well as him, eh?"

Chapter 67:
Receipt Deceit

"Yes, I know. But I honestly don't have it anymore." Lucifer had talked until He was red in the face. More red in the face. "Of course you haven't received a credit note for it! They hardly ordered it from you in the first place, did they?"

"But it should have come back to us! Putting it back in the hands of those lovable scoundrels is hardly the safest option."

"No, no..." Lucifer stroked His goatee in earnest ponderment. "And much less so entrusting it to a scatterbrained, frightened dwarf!"

If he hadn't already been an impossible shade of green, Mr. Hul'hu's unfathomable geometry would have flashed a lurid shade of bile. And his tentacles practically lashed themselves to his carapace whilst simultaneously wringing the suckers flat. His gill openings flapped in despairing distress.

"But it makes life so much more interesting! Don't you agree?" Lucifer beamed like the wiliest trickster the universe ever conceived – another reason He'd been expelled from Heaven by Him. God, in His infinite wisdom, was happy to let His once favourite angel believe it to be the truth. After all, claiming due credit for that title Himself had proved a major PR gaff in the past.

Mr. Hul'hu shambled a few dimensions and set his pursed beak in admonishment, before suddenly whipping around.

"What's that? Is someone there? Have we been discovered?"

He sent a few gobbets of slime on a scoot across the floor to hover watchfully by the base of the office door.

"Are your extra-planetary senses tingling, Mr. H? I can't sense anything myself..."

"Shh, I'm listening. Don't move." Mr. Hul'hu swept his huge, sightless eyes around the gulf of darkness. "Are the lights off? I spend so long holed up in our trench-bottom office that I have difficulty telling the difference between sun and void anymore."

"Apart from your bioluminescent tentacle-pits, Mr. H. We're in total darkness."

Mr. Hul'hu beckoned to his slime and consulted with them a moment. He nodded and winked at Lucifer, causing a trapped wave of Atlantic ecosystem to hurl itself out across Satan's desk.

Not again?! I've only just had that polished after the last time! And there's still a few barnacles scratching my poor, sensitive knees under the drawers.

"Ah, so, that's your game, is it...?" mumbled Mr. Hul'hu. And threw open the door with noteworthy vigour.

Lucifer's jaw – and heart – dropped as it rattled against the far wall.

"*Another* set of hinges..."

"SURPRISE!!!" Mr. Hul'hu bellowed. Dislodging several ceiling tiles as the vibrations dutifully and dustily reverberated.

Chapter 68:
Obligations and Recriminations

Pygott and Crone were taken ablack and aback. Literally.

The force of Mr. Hul'hu's foghorn – and the attendant streamer of luminous green excrescence that whipped the tail of the word fair slammed the pair back onto the marble pillar ten feet behind them.

Somewhat dazed, they struggled to their feet, scraping off loops of surprisingly attentive muscoid tendrils and exchanged several heavily weighted glances, registering one another's surprise and a series of unspoken questions, accusations, quandaries and refutations.

Eventually, their heads cleared enough to let their eyebrows intervene and do the talking. And they each said, "Wing it."

They rose, unsteadily, each wearing a smile whose insincerity was admirably masked by the bristling greenery tickling at their angles. They made a show of dusting themselves off. But as there was no dust, only lashings of gloopy lashings, their fingers only stuck in the mire and dragged around gunge into even more swirly twirls of slime.

"Mr. Hul'hu!" remarked Pygott.

"How nice to see you," smarmed Crone.

"I'm betting you're more than a tabula surprised to see me?" hissed Hul'hu, pointing several menacing tentacles.

"Which I believe you already mentioned quite forcefully...?" Crone mumbled as he waggled a finger in each ear. Half to relieve the ringing pressure, but also to dislodge the over-attentions of mucus feelers – they'd been known to head straight for the brain and wreak havoc upon the unwary.

"Indeed I did! Because you're so *very* surprised, aren't you?" bayed Mr. Hul'hu anew.

Shaking the trembling madness from his eardrums, Mr. Pygott looked to slice through the aberrant geometry impeding their progress.

"You seem nervous, Mr. Hul'hu."

"Eh, what?" It was Hul'hu's turn to be taken aback. "What would I have to be nervous about?"

"Being caught red-handed lurking at the threshold of Satan's inner sanctum with the lights off, for starters. Doesn't that strike you as suspicious, Mr. Crone?"

"*Very* suspicious, Mr. Pygott."

Their luggage joined in with a spot of rivet pointing.

"I don't think it's at all suspicious," quipped Mr. Hul'hu, suspiciously.

"You're apparently hiding – at least you were until you unleashed a shriek the likes of which could terrify Nyarlothotep into leaking a squirt of pee – in the dark, inside Satan's private office while He's away from Hell on a rare, well earned break and wearing some sort of disguise...?" Pygott peered closer into the gloom. "What *is* that you have on your head?"

"What? Eh? I don't know what you mean!" Mr. Hul'hu winced as though something had just jabbed a needle in one of his squamous buttocks. A glassy, doleful eye swivelled upwards. "Oh, ah. *That.* Damned flying polyps get everywhere. Shoo!"

Hul'hu flapped an unconvincing tentacle in the vague direction of the frippery.

"Intriguing! Your speciality, Mr. Crone! Have you ever seen the like?"

Crone scrunched up his face like a toddler desperately trying to aim true on his first effort to pee standing up in the big boys' toilet, "That's definitely a new species to my experience. Mr. Pygott! I can't say I've ever seen a flying polyp that can disguise itself as a party hat." He zoomed in a little closer with another mighty squint. "It appears to have shrugged off one of its parasites too."

Pygott followed the direction of his pointing finger.

"Ah yes, I see it. It really must be an allied species; what with its distinct resemblance to a blow tickler. It's even making that jubilant rasping sound every time it breathes out."

"I think I know what's going on here!" started Crone, advancing on Hul'hu wearing an accusatory grin. "You've broken into Hell to host a sneaky party for the Unholy Host, to distract attention from the effects of using the book! Admit it!"

"Mr. Crone!" Pygott's bluster was mostly lost amid a strained, piping, guttural cough that threatened to engulf him. He bounced to insert himself between his partner and the Elder Thing, but before he got more than a phlegm-hook towards spinning a yarn, Mr. Hul'hu's expression made it clear that no amount of smooth-tongued posturing or cross-accusation was going to save their hides today.

"Yes, about *that book...*" began Mr. Hul'hu.

Although no matter how hard Pygott looked, he couldn't detect movement upon any of the Thing's squamous lips.

Come to think of it, his voice seemed different too: smoother, rakish, oiled with irresistible, Devilish charm.

And Mr. Hul'hu definitely didn't have horns.

Whether they appeared to be sticking out of his head or not!

"Mr. Pygott," stammered Crone. "That sounds awfully like-"

"Yes it does, doesn't it?" Lucifer crooned, as He oozed out from behind Mr. Hul'hu's ooze miasma.

"Well done, Mr. Crone. Right again!" grinned Pygott, manufacturing a smile that practically sang ballads of joy at being back in Satan's presence. "You're looking refreshingly pale. Good holiday, I take it?"

"Very relaxing, thankyou," replied Morningstar, pointedly.

"Any diverting adventures while you were up north?" queried Crone.

"Not really, thankyou, Mr. Crone. It was more a working holiday, of sorts. I was busy indulging my curiosity to kill several cats, to use an artful analogy. Not my best, I'll admit..."

"I thought you liked cats? I hope you don't mean you forgot to arrange a sitter for Bundy, Dahmer, Lucas, Bossie and Zodiac?"

"Perish the thought!" exclaimed the Light Bringer, clearly shocked. "They've been on their own holiday at the West's while daddy's been away. They dote on them! Those cats are the only creatures I can trust them not to rape and murder. I still can't believe it took so long to realise they hadn't stopped all that nonsense after being the only serial killers allowed to move down here, before the situation became critical."

"Body count out of control?"

"Not so much that; more a question of space. Practically a land-grab, if you will?"

"I'm not sure I'm – we're – with you?" Pygott's confusion was ably mirrored by Crone's own puzzled brow.

"Have you had time while you've been here to wander around the newly inaugurated Heavenly Genocide Square?"

"Honouring the contribution of the 33.3% of angels to the war with Heaven? Indeed! It's very impressive. *And vast.*"

"Absolutely enormous! It took us almost a whole day to walk across."

"Well, that must have been the easiest and cheapest building project ever undertaken during my tenure. All we did was make a few statues and benches and put up a plaque. On top of Fred's new bloody patio..."

"Ah, I see. Nice, even paving though." Crone backtracked to an earlier ponder amid his appreciation of a job well laid. "Why is it that they're the only serial killers you have again?"

"Do you know, I really don't have the faintest idea! There's nothing God finds more entertaining than a successful serial killer, what with Him being the all-time champion. But for some reason, He has a beef against the Wests. I can't say I like them much at all myself, to be honest, but if a pair like Myra and Ian float His boat, well...? He does move in mysterious ways, I suppose."

Mr. Hul'hu interrupted their laughter with a gurgling, rattlesnake cough. And one of his glassy globes glared with intent towards Satan.

"Hmmm?" Lucifer's jaw seemed to be the sole vehicle to display His confusion. "Is there, erm? Oh, ah, Yes. Quite right." He turned back toward Pygott and Crone and rose up to His full height. Which was ludicrously enormous and dislodged several ceiling tiles from the Fifth Circle. Somewhat embarrassed, He made apologies and offered to pay for repairs, before retracting to a more appropriate bluster stance. He settled on large Grizzly Bear. "Now, before we get onto my ire towards you breaking into Hell, again, causing havoc – nay! - damned near revolution *and* sneaking into my private quarters uninvited..."

"I believe the word you're looking for is 'trespass'," offered Crone.

Pygott shot him a withering look that landed on infertile ground. And finally sighed full acceptance.

"Thankyou, Mr. Crone. But 'trespass' hardly covers it. Especially when we factor in your trade in strictly prohibited items. Eh, Mr. Hul'hu?"

"The strictly prohibited item traded with *you?*" Hul'hu howled.

"Yes, well, that was all part of the plan, wasn't it?" bluffed Lucifer.

"You mean the plan *you* hatched, instigated and swung into motion using a forbidden tome obviously pilfered from the Necronomicon Press vaults without first conferring with me?" He was clearly becoming quite irate and unsupportive of whatever line he and Apollyon might have previously agreed.

"To be fair, Mr. Hul'hu, we've been offered *that* copy on several occasions and each time turned it down." Pygott corrected the insinuation.

"*What???*" Another inch of pseudopodia closer to erupting. "Why have you never notified me? Which blaggard has it?"

"Well, *you* do. One of the reasons we sent all the 'sellers' on their way is because we know they'd have to steal it from your vault before delivery. And that would be rather dishonest, wouldn't it?"

"Yes, but, hang on! How do you know we still have it? Why wouldn't we have it? Who could possibly penetrate the defences of our vault in an alternate dimension without being cosmically obliterated?" Mr. Hul'hu had finally achieved rage.

"Your calm, confident air confirms what I said..." Pygott intoned. "Stop coughing, Mr. Crone."

Satan intervened.

"No need to argue! The situation's all satisfactorily resolved since I took the book back to the Third Left Tentacle just after you left." Lucifer's smile revealed why they called him Morningstar at the dawn of time.

"Well, that's all in order then, isn't it, Mr. H-?" Suddenly, Crone stopped talking as suddenly as a gobbling turkey grabbed by the crop on Christmas Morning. His pallor soon began to take on the same hue.

Pygott allowed him a few moments stuttering to see if he'd recover enough to spit out the realisation that had slam-dropped-anvil-like onto his brain. And also to allow Pygott time to winch his own jaw up off the floor. Then heftily slapped Crone on the back to release a huge burst of trapped exasperation. And added another beat to see if he was yet able to speak.

But no.

"You returned a book?"

Lucifer nodded.

"To the Third Left Tentacle?"

He nodded again.

"You. Returned. A. Book." Pygott repeated, accentuating each word to ensure that Lucifer understood the question. And the statement. A hint of steam ghosted out of each ear with a peep. "And asked for a refund?"

"Of course! Why else would I take it back? It's not like I'd be able to read it, is it? It'd be foolish to keep it, after all. If it was shiny and irresistible enough to lure my wallet out of my pocket, the temptation for someone to *break in here and steal it* seemed far too great a risk."

Pygott ignored the barb.

"And did you – Heaven and Hell and all points inbetween forbid! - *receive* a refund?"

"Your dwarf was most helpful when I explained the circumstances to him. At least, I think it was a him? So difficult to tell with the duck-footed brethren..."

"Wait. No. You're getting off-topic."

"Which is what all the reviews will say, I imagine!"

"What?" Pygott shook the confusion out of his hand and dragged the conversation back to a suitable level of indignance.

"Rumpus just *gave* you a refund?"

"Well, not to begin with, of course. But with a little negotiating he, erm, well; my point of view won out. To all our satisfaction, I trust? And the dwarf's perceptible relief on securing its life and sanity. And its family's. And its entire homeland's. And-"

"Yes, thankyou. You've painted a big enough picture. He'll still be dealt with when we get back. His life and sanity may not be so secure after all."

"Aww, don't be so hard on the little fur-lump! Especially not if he's already read the whole of the esoteric employment law text I pointed him toward in way of thanks."

Pygott pointedly fumed. And held back a by now fully recovered and incandescent Crone, who huffed and muttered a stream of uncomplimentary oaths that were being diplomatically smothered at Pygott's back.

"What did Rumpus *do* with it? He's a consummate ditherer as it is. And he has no access to the safe, let alone the protected vaults."

"Yes!" barked Mr. Hul'hu. "That's what I want to know! How can you say it's safe?"

"Calm yourselves. If your new Head of Special Projects has had the foresight – and I'm sure it has – to cut short its holiday and go sniffing around its new workplace, there'll probably be several warring bidders lined up to buy it from the little weasel about now."

"Oi! Leave us weasels out of it!!" piped a little voice full of indignity.

"Very amusing," sneered Pygott. "But this is no time for levity. Please reserve your ventriloquism shenanigans for the next time you host a party." Lucifer coughed and waved an arm at the darkness in most suspicious fashion. But Pygott was still too focused on umbrage to break step. "This is our hard-earned reputation you're toying with! Please at least tell us that the only ones who know about this are confined to this room?"

"Of course!" Satan guffawed. "I guarantee it."

There was a chorus of stifled sniggers from numerous corners.

"I asked if you'd stop that, please? This is most serious." Pygott halted a moment and followed the apparent source of each titter. "That's very, very clever though. You must have been putting in some serious hours practising?"

"Oh, I think you'll find I had a little help..."

And with another. Less shushing wave of a hand, thy were all blinded by a level of light not seen since someone wrote a song about shepherds watching their flocks by night. And deafened by a tumultuous, thunderous trumpeting.

"SURPRISE!!!"

Chapter 69:
Denouemints

Crone reeled, chasing giant purple balloons that roiled intrusively across the front of his eyes.

"Ugh, not again? What fresh Hell is this?" Crone groused. "If you'll pardon the pun?"

Pygott squinted through the aftergloom caused by the sudden flare. Picking out myriad shapes amidst the Rovers.

"My word; we seem to be surrounded by an entire army! That's a little over the top. Don't you think, old chum?"

"And I think they may have a dragon too," wailed Crone. "I can see a great roar of fiery breath." His nose wrinkled and twitched. "I wouldn't say it's healthy feeding reptiles beeswax though? Not even mythical ones."

"I can hear the army laughing, Mr. Crone."

"Laughter in Hell isn't unprecedented, Mr. Pygott."

"I know. But why does it sound so good natured? Mocking, scornful, intimidating I can comprehend, but this sounds so, well, *cheery*."

"Oh my, *please* tell me we haven't been sent *up there* again!?" Crone railed, still straining to see through a waterfall of bleary fuddlement.

They both started back and could swear they heard their luggage snarl as a towering blob of throbbing shadow loomed, smearing their eyeline with indeterminate bulk.

"Bloody Hell!" exclaimed Crone, shrinking further back.

"Hell indeed, Mr. Crone." A voice smoother than a bottle of the finest cream sherry oozed out of the top of the shade. "But the only thing bloody here is Mary. First though..."

The pair just about managed to retain a modicum of self-respect by not flinging themselves onto the slate slabs at a stuttered sound like several gunshots echoing around the room. Hell? Firing range? Aerodrome? The noise seemed to reverberate into an eternal distance.

"Ah, no, thankyou. I think we've avoided that shame." Pygott addressed the luggage with a wry smile as it proffered clean underwear in both their sizes.

They tried manfully to ignore the awful gurgling sound just in front of them, which cascaded into a gruesome splattering on the floor.

"On behalf of everyone gathered here, it is my great honour to be the first to raise a glass in celebration of the Third Left Tentacle's sesquincentennial! In it's current, post-bordello form, of course. My, what a party we hosted for that one! I believe some of you are still celebrating as I speak...?"

"Huzzah!" Bellowed the masses and nearly drowned out half of the cheer with a cascade of quaffing and slurping.

"More champers!" came the rallying cry. And another gun salute of cork-popping followed.

Something jammed an overflowing goblet of bubbles into each of their hands and slapped them heartily on the back. Causing most of the liquid beneath the bubbles to magically teleport through the foam barrier and onto the floor. Pygott and Crone were soon buried beneath a deluge of grinning well-wishes and cheers. Both resolved to flow with the flood and hold their breath in the hopes they were eventually disinterred intact at some later time.

"Mmmfph?" asked Crone after the initial crush had eased.

Pygott wriggled out from beneath an overenthusiastic succubus, shooting her a look that suggested that wasn't his hand she'd been vigorously shaking and that her behaviour really wasn't in keeping with the tone of the festivities.

"Argleklumphmumble," he replied. And added, "Gerroff!" with a yelp.

"Now, now, all of you. Give our guests some space, please?!" Lucifer waded into the mêlée, parting pockets of adulation like Godzilla striding across Tokyo Bay. "You'll all be shouting 'speech' before the poor chaps can breathe again."

The congratulation orgy steadily dwindled. To the point where dishevelled, flustered and very pink booksellers bumbled into view, struggling to straighten up and gasping for any welcome ounce of sulphurous air they could lay their lungs on.

"Thankyou. Thankyou all," waved Pygott feebly as Satan gently eased the pair toward a quiet corner, where He beamed at them with the pride of a deadly sin excelling itself.

"Do you need a chair? Sit down a moment and compose yourselves."

"Not for me, thankyou. Mr. Crone?"

"If I sit, I may never get up again, Mr. Pygott. I'll be fine in a few moments. I think."

"Stout fellows! All this praise is well deserved."

"And rather sceptically received, thankyou. What exactly is behind this kerfuffle, might I ask?"

"Just what Leviathan said!" Satan seemed somewhat taken aback. "A party in honour of the shop. And of course, the obliging reprobates who keep it running to serve us all. On and off the books, if you will...?"

"Of course, I got that part of it." Pygott leaned in conspiratorially. "But what's behind it? What's the *real reason* for throwing up this ludicrous smokescreen, you old trickster?"

Lucifer laughed heartily and slapped him on the back. Causing the remaining bubbles from Pygott's goblet to join their liquid skin skating the tiles.

"Ah, Mr. Pygott! Ever the sceptic, eh?"

"It's helped keep me – us – from joining you here on a permanent basis, my friend."

"Indeed it has!" The Devil laughed again, "And with all the best will in the worlds, let's hope it's a very long time before you have to become residents."

"So what you're telling us," began Crone. "Is that you set all this up?"

"Of course! You know how much I love a revel, Mr. Crone."

"Indeed. It's such a shame those ingrates upstairs abandoned the Saturnian season . One of your better inventions in my estimation."

"But we're getting off the point, my friends. I believe what Mr. Crone is inferring is that yourself and Mr. Hul'hu worked in cahoots to nudge us into selling you a book we believed you couldn't read, then engineered a set of happenstances to make us believe you *had* read the book to goad us into breaking into Hell to steal it back from you before you could destroy the world by unleashing its power, on the sole premise of luring us to a surprise shindig?"

"In the Library, with the lead pipe!" gushed Saturn.

"I'm sorry...?" Crone quizzed querulously. "Oh, I see. Very droll."

"But what would you have done if I hadn't agreed to Mr. Crone's..." Pygott paused and spared a glance at Crone with the word, 'ridiculous' poised on his lips. "Erm, *audacious* plan?"

"Then we'd all have been standing in the dark getting cramp, waiting for the guests of dishonour for a very long time."

"But you know us better than that, it transpires." Mr. Crone interjected. "And after reacting to a less-than polite cough from Pygott added, "Well, you know *me* rather well..."

"Bravo for successfully manipulating us puny humans. Though I suppose that's what you do best," began Pygott.

"Why, thankyou," smirked Satan.

"But what about the book? Obviously you were spinning a fantastic yarn earlier to throw us off the scent of discovery. Mr. Hul'hu has it safely stowed, ready to squirrel away forevermore the first chance he gets in the Necronomicon Press vault, I'm sure?"

Pygott started as a gob of phlegm – or at least something thick and green and noxious – flew out of Mr. Hul'hu's grandiose harrumph and chomped a couple of whiskers off his moustache.

"Mr. Hul'hu, you look positively green. As it were." Pygott turned back, at best hopefully quizzical, towards Lucifer. "What have you done to upset him?"

Lucifer threw His hands in the air. "Why does everyone always suspect me?" he warbled.

"Even entertaining you with an answer would be sinful, you old shyster." Pygott grinned. "Where exactly is the book? You must have it here somewhere."

"I'm very hurt." Lucifer's pathos appeared to be fashioned entirely from Stilton. "You don't trust me, sob!"

"Oh, stop it, you old ham. You're the Father of Lies, after all."

"Language, Mr. Pygott!" Satan wagged a reproving finger.

"You're stalling, you old fraud." Crone pitched in. "You haven't – no even you wouldn't do such a thing? You haven't *sold it,* have you?"

The gathered huddle paled at the suggestion, draining even Lucifer Himself to a fetching pink. And Pygott's favourite chest had swapped its deep-night basilisk hide straps for an unseemly set of mustard yellow disco belts.

The concept might even be more unpalatable than His laughable story about refunding it at the shop!

"While I commend your bravery, Mr. Crone, had anyone else asked such a question under normal circumstances, I would have them impaled inside my private dungeon before they finished the last syllable." He leaned in close enough for a crackle of static to leap between them. "It's a good job I like you, isn't it?"

Satan slapped him hard on he back, caught him in time to stop him slamming into a pillar and chortled heartily. "Oops, sorry!"

"I'm no stranger to impalement," snorted Pygott. "So with all due humility, I'll follow up on my esteemed colleague's behalf. You obviously don't have it here and before you ask, I didn't come here without the means to locate it once we were close. So what disreputable reprobates have you consigned to a damnable future obsessively poring over an unreadable, madness inflicting manuscript? Which, as all of us here will solemnly testify, doesn't exist?"

"Ha-ha! Yes, the damned thing's dangerous. I wouldn't dare see it pass any of the Gates of Hell. Which is why I *did* leave it in the safest hands I could think of – soon enough, anyway – *yours.*"

Pygott's mouth opened to decry Satan's horrendous actions. Then slammed shut as he realised the enormity of what had just been revealed. Old Nick really had been telling the truth about contravening the Third Left Tentacle's most sacred commandment. And in all likelihood left the book at the mercy of a terrified, gullible dwarf and ultimately a clever little demon who'd recently been given carte blanche to secure just the kind of deal such temptation waggled like a squirmy maggot skewered on a fishing hook.

"Oh Go – erm, Hell on toast! You really did do it, didn't you?"

Satan's sabre-sharp brows danced a rumba in mischievous delight.

"Oh, woe. Perhaps you should have sold it after all. At least that way myself and Mr. Crone can be absolved of all blame for the disaster that may already be unfolding..."

Crone, for his part, had finally unlocked his paralysis in spectacular fashion: his jaw dropped.

"Arrrghmmmmph!" exclaimed a muffled voice from somewhere below one of Crone's chins.

"Thankyou Aristophonob, good catch! You'll never know how very pleased I am that you're here. Happier even than Mr. Crone's fortuitously unbroken chin."

"Phlhummph," 'Nob whispered. And a single, crumpled tentacle unfurled into the vague shape of an uprasied thumb.

"WHERE?" stormed Baal. Blindly thrashing the air around him like a miller gone mad.

"Shut up Baal. Go and get another drink." Lucifer had clearly lost all patience with him.

"You do know that wily little demon hasn't officially started work for us yet? And we gave no instruction regarding the book. Because there was no reason for its existence to ever be known!" Pygott lowered one brow in sinister fashion and raised the other in the gesture of the Grand Quizard. "If she, he, it...? Erm, Aristophonob; can I be so bold to ask which identity you prefer?"

"Roffleglobble glumball test...please?" Aristophonob gasped as the luggage finally barged Crone sideways far enough for the demon to effect escape.

"That sounds like a splendid idea. And makes choosing your Christmas gifts so much easier."

"Ah, I love Christmas!" Satan gushed. "Has He arrived yet, by the way? I sent the invite in good time, even for that louche Bohemian..." Satan peered around to see if He could detect any sign that everyone's favourite libertine had oozed onto the dancefloor.

"That's a commendable sidestep, Nick. But you're not diverting us from the point this time. It's too important for frivolity."

"But frivolity is my remit!"

"Stop it, you bad 'un."

"Yes? What is it Mr. Pygott? Congratulations on your sasquatchdenturecemetery – erm, anniversary, by the way."

"Thankyou Abaddon, erm, both of you. How's the Venom tour going? Ah, lovely." Pygott responded to the Geordie's Devil Horns and beer-slurp salute. "But I was referring to your boss being a bit of a rogue."

"Always with the understatement, Mr. Pygott!" Hob was beside Himself with mirth.

"Not as much as you're understating the dangerous situation we're in. If you really, *really have* returned that book – sorry to keep bringing up that unprecedented breach in shop policy, Mr. Crone – your quip about our upcoming Head of Special Projects is no doubt already coming as true as the hottest bidding war our planet has ever hid from view." Pygott glared at the steadily emerging demon with a mix of accusation and almost paternal pride.

"Damn!" spluttered Aristophonob. "How did I miss that?"

"Are you speaking truthfully, little, erm, lady?"

"Unfortunately, yes, Mr. Pygott. And thankyou for the 'lady'."

"I'll believe you. But remember; if I find out you're fibbing, there's a certain amulet that's very easy to reclaim..."

Aristophonob visibly blanched. Which was no mean feat for a being whose normal pallor defied the natural order of colour.

"Scout's honour", she pledged, flourishing a tentacular salute.

"You were a scout?" asked Crone with all due scepticism.

"I possessed one in Dunwich once. Surely that counts?"

"Baal! Will you please desist, you infernal oaf?!?!" Lucifer interrupted as the bull's frenzied thrashing to lash out at a foe he couldn't locate threatened to turn what was still currently a buffet table into a messy, slapstick food fight. "Jesus help me, if you don't pack it in...?!"

"It's okay, I've got him!" Jesus called as He led Baal away with a gentle hand on the crook of his forelimb and soothing words in his furry ears. Come on, old fella, tell me all about it..."

"Thank God He's arrived, if you'll all pardon my language?" Satan proclaimed. "Life and soul of the party, that boy!"

"And he must be a Godsend when the wine's running low?"

"Ha-ha! I think you know my wine cellar well enough not to even consider the prospect?"

"Just as I know your customer habits well enough that I trusted you not to circumvent the sanctity of our hallowed returns policy."

"Ah, dear. You're a mean, stony-souled destroyer at heart, Mr. Pygott. Another reason I like you so much." Lucifer positively shone and thrust yet another fizzing drink into his hand. After realising that Aristophonob had eased the original goblet out of his hand and proceeded to gently sidle off toward the throng. "But if you're going to wave a strict policy of no returns under the nose of the Duke of Deception, I'm honour-bound to betray that trust eventually."

Pygott sighed. And smiled.

"Indeed you are. And quite frankly, it's an honour that you respected our rule for so very long. And chose to throw aside convention with such spectacular abandon." Pygott simultaneously whipped a series of finger-spelled gesticulations in the direction of Lucifer's furtive gaze. And a very startled little demon slid gracefully back beside her new boss. "Aristophonob, dear girl, please remember that none of those beings over there are prospective customers this evening. Nor should they ever become aware of the subject of our conversation here. The amulet protecting you relies on your professionalism as a partner of the Third Left Tentacle. Suffice to say, do us proud, as I fully trust you will, or you may find yourself left behind the till staring down the rage of Baal's unveiled recognition one day."

'Nob seemed to weigh up her options, despite herself. Before strapping on a devious smile - after all, whatever other manner of smile could any demon conjure? - and curtsied. The smile ballooned into surprise.

"What was that?" Her many eyes darted about, seeking anyone to answer. "I'm sure that wasn't me doing that. I must be bewitched!"

"That was job satisfaction and devotion to duty possessing you," Pygott grinned. "Now, be off with you. There's a party awaiting a drunken demon with enough mouths to drink the pumps dry in one visit to liven it up. Just be careful in front of who those mouths open up."

Pygott watched her bounce off towards the bar, taking a small diversion on the way to aim an invisible kick at a yelping Baal's ankles and swipe several cocktails from the trays of damned waiters inbetween.

"Such a charming staff retinue you have, Mr. Pygott. And Mr. Crone, of course."

"Which brings us back to the subject at hand: which member of our charming retinue did you browbeat into taking back the book?"

"No force necessary, my dear boy. I told you already. And eventually that dwarf was most compliant. Though I found his lopsided, sickly smile a tad disturbing, I must admit. And I never realised before that dwarves have their own special language. Unless he was speaking a thick, slurry dialect I've never come across...?"

Pygott and Crone paled anew.

"You really did leave the book with Rumpus?" Crone trilled. "Oh dear, oh dear, oh deary, dear, dear."

"Cam yourself, Mr. Crone. One member of our team suffering a stroke over this business is more than tragedy enough. I'll have Aristophonob call the shop and have someone check on him, before she swallows any more of that zombie potion she seems to have found. Baron Samedi's running the bar, I take it?"

"Who else for a superlative shindig such as this?" Lucifer practically gleamed with pride at His own organisational nous.

"Remind me to bring you one of his special cocktails later, Mr. Crone. It'll breathe new life into you. Literally."

"Is that safe, Mr. Pygott?"

"No, not really. But voodoo possession can be very freeing if performed properly. And the effects wear off soon enough. Sometimes."

Crone looked none too convinced, donning an expression that seemed to explain that lava-bubbling vol-au-vents were the most dangerous things he might consider passing over his pursed lips tonight.

"So, where did Rumpus put the book? After he so kindly offered to release you of your burden?" asked Pygott, turning back to Lucifer.

"He appeared to be stitching it into his vest by the time I left," He answered, scratching His beardy chin.

"On the one hand, that's the best news I've heard since we embarked on this harebrained excursion," Pygott scratched his own hirsuteness contemplatively. "And of course the worst. The poor chap won't sleep a wink till we get back and we'll never hear the last of it. Lord knows what invented employment legislation we'll have thrown at us for the next decade at least."

"See? I've stimulated his creative talents! That's absolutely core to my being. Never mind being well within my remit."

"You rogue. I forgot you invented corporate box-ticking." Pygott robed himself with a most rye smile. "But you'll appreciate that no matter how frustrating Rumpus can be, he is an excellent bookseller, bookbinder, book-keeper and guardian wrangler. And we have a duty of care to protect valued members of staff, nay, our Third Left Tentacle family! Aristophonob?" Pygott waved the demon over with a finger wiggle. "Before you down that next Vesuvian Vulgarity – yes, they do look good, well, *evil*, by the way. I'll have to have one of those later – would you mind helping Mr. Crone with what's left of your sobriety please? I promise this will be the last I ask of you before you officially clock in. And yes, yes, we'll arrange a day off in lieu to make up for it. Mr. Crone, I believe you're equipped to instruct our friend in the quickest, safest way to rescue Rumpus from his predicament?"

"Indeed I am, Mr. Pygott," a relieved Crone smiled as he led her towards a rare, quiet corner. His constitution miraculously revitalised the instant he became involved in direct action to rectify possible catastrophe. Upon noticing several of her eyes rolling, he struck to forewarn her. "Whatever you may think of our stuffy, officious, overzealous, jobsworth colleague, *be nice*. You have no idea how useful it is to be on his good side."

"He has a good side?" gasped Aristophonob.

"Believe me, young lady, you don't want to bear witness to his bad side."

Pygott returned his attention to his host, quite aware of the gathering sense of disquiet drifting across from the gossiping throng that should by now be embracing the collective noun, 'party'.

"Now that's all sorted..." And he turned to offer a placating hand to the still simmering Necronomicon Press rep. "And don't worry, Mr. Hul'hu, the book is definitely safe again, secreted in a place none of us would ever want to go. We can talk business till I'm also green in the face back at the shop. But for now, why don't we all relax and-"

"PAAARRRTEHHH!" bawled Satan.

And the entire hall erupted in several badly coordinated rounds of "Cheers!"

And the group became showered in a tsunami of frothy, bitter, slightly stinging bubbles that Pygott could only hope was being ejected from popping champagne bottles as far as his fizzy eyes could no longer see.

Pygott proceeded to work his way through the crush, aching from the cascade of back-slaps and bellowed congratulations and feeling none too stable on his feet in light of the seemingly endless drinks thrust into his hands to toast good health to him, to Crone, to the Third Left Tentacle, to destroying goodness and enslaving the world ("We live in high hope, eh, Apollyon?") and to the one thing that unifies the worlds above, below and inbetween, no matter what race, age, creed, religion, gender, peccadillo or kink: *books.*

"There you are, Mr. Pygott!" called Crone. Surprising his much taller friend by locating him first among the bustling throng.

"Ah, Mr. Crone! So very glad you're back to enjoy the party. I hope rescue arrangement went smoothly?"

"All will very soon be as it should be. I've instructed Aristophonob to send word as soon as the item is safe." He scratched his chin. "Though she firmly believes Rumpus will refuse to believe she works for us and they'll likely still be arguing by the time we return."

"Then we'll deal with that nightmare after we sober up." Pygott thrust one of the many goblets his hands already struggled to balance into Crone's fist. "Although if I have any more of these Blowfish Bokor Bombs, I may never see daylight again." He blinked and wavered a moment. "In fact, I may never see *anything* again."

They slowly – like exhausted ants wading through a swimming pool of molasses – made passage through the crowd to meet again with Lucifer at the end of the buffet, where a phenomenally detailed, exact replica cake of the Third Left Tentacle towered over the crowd.

"My word! You've even captured the decrepitude oozing out of the mortar. We had to entice satyrs from Caprice to spend a month in England to obtain such magically dishevelled pointing."

"It's delightful!" exclaimed Crone. "Who did you enslave to produce this masterpiece? Gordon, I know you – as always – did a superlative job with the buffet, my congratulations. But we all know you're not a cake maker."

"That's so," agreed Gordon, wiping well-earned sweat off his brow. "I can plate an hors d'eouvre as enticing as a Playboy centrefold, but I'm no decorator. Icing and buttermilk confuse my fingers. And thankyou, by the way."

"No, thank *you,* chef! A round of applause for the maestro folks!" Lucifer lead the ovation.

"Too kind, too fu- erm, kind." Gordon figuratively doffed his cap. *And I should bloody well think so too, you Philistines!* He gnashed internally, as he had to bear witness to another ghoul spill sploshes of exquisite tartare down its chest.

"So who executed the rendition of our home in such delicious fashion? I can think of only one person truly up to not only baking and decorating such a delight, but who also knows enough of the black arts to protect it against a journey through Hell. *And* keep a secret from *us* too, of course!" Mr. Crone swelled with more pride than was strictly due.

"You're not telling me you finally got her to crack? We're not going to find Christine's signature on that cake, surely?" Mr. Pygott gasped.

"Ha-ha-ha! Right there, old boy! And red as the finest scarlet ribbon!" Satan invited the pair over and drew their eye to a flourish of red lettering along the base. "Miss McConnell did us ever so proud."

Pygott dipped a finger into the autograph and sucked at the tip, to a round of gasps from the crowd.

"There's no blood in the icing. Certainly not Christine's blood, at any rate"

"Ha! You fooled my ruse, Mr. Pygott." Lucifer clapped him heartily on the back for the umpteenth time.

I'll definitely need to visit my chiropractor once we get home, he mused, painfully straightening himself.

"Will you ever stop pursuing her?"

"Good lord, no! She's the finest prize I could ever compete for! And I suppose the masochist in me enjoys knowing that she's too deviously talented to fall for any of my ardent entreaties." Lucifer sighed and shook a weary head. "But she did seem eager to assist in making the party a success the instant I mentioned which guests were to be honoured. Should I be jealous...?"

"Ah, what a truly wicked, beguiling lady," crooned Pygott. "I shall have to send personal, heartfelt thanks upon our return. As I sense she isn't here today."

"Alas no. She sends earnest apologies, as she has an essential appointment she simply couldn't cancel. Indeed, it's an arrangement essential to the party going ahead at all..."

Pygott's authoritative brows stood to attention.

"Am I to sate my intrigue? Or is it better that we remain in ignorance?"

"Better not to ask at all, to be honest." Lucifer whispered through nose-tapping confidentiality. "For all our sakes."

Pygott flicked a finger beneath one of Crone's chins and eased closed the mouth that had opened reflexively to ride roughshod over the warning. Pygott pressed his other index finger to pursed lips and shook a frown.

"No time for questions – they are a burden and only achieve building a prison for oneself."

"Poppycock!" Crone blustered. "Don't tell me you didn't come up with that for any other reason than noticing our host has polished His finest Portmeirion china to serve the cake!" Crone turned back to Lucifer conspiratorially. "We're very honoured, but do you think this an act of bravery or, at best, blind optimism? Look at this lot! How many plates do you think will survive the stampede?"

"It's worth every tragic shard, Mr. Crone."

"But these pieces are irreplaceable!"

"Ah, but what better reason for seeking a new obsession than losing the old one, eh?"

"Much like the evolution of the Third Left Tentacle itself!" chimed Pygott. "Which is what all this is about, of course."

"Exactly, Mr. Pygott. Uriel? Where's Uriel?" Lucifer pirouetted several times, frantically scanning every corner of the circular hall, before stabbing His nose on a feathery wing waiting bemused right beneath it. "Ah – ouch – there you are! Where have you been? No matter! Be a good lad and hand your sword to our esteemed guests, would you? A bit less flame than usual though, eh? Everybody's gagging for this cake to be-" Lucifer stopped dead, literally cut off by a monumental ruckus sparking at the entrance to the room.

The sound of violent scuffle, blows exchanged, hinges wrenched, blood spilled and ribs cracked cannoned off the pillars and ricocheted into the partygoers' ears. It sounded like Hell itself had come to greet them.

Crone blanched at the sound of every nightmare's fury clubbed together into a bellowing female foghorn demanding entry and unleashing every inhuman curse imaginable – and a fair few beyond that – at the already beleaguered doorman.

"Let us in, you cretin! We have to see Mr. Crone!"

Crone's blood retreated to wherever it went in times of crisis to avoid imminent spillage. Leaving behind a creature that resembled a Death Valley marooned, shelled scampi.

"Oh my God," he muttered.

"*Language,* Mr. Crone!" admonished everyone but Jesus, who simply winked rakishly.

"It's The Sisters. It's The damned Sisters! They've caught up with us, Mr. Pygott! They've found out we're here. They know I've been avoiding them! Oh, why didn't I just strap down my cowardice and pay them a visit? They'll tear me limb from limb. And then sew the limbs back on. And then chew them off again. And then they'll start to get mean. You have to get me out of here!"

"Now, Mr. Crone. Try to calm yourself. I'm sure our host wouldn't allow even The Sisters to bring anyone to harm here."

"What? Like that poor doorman?" Crone snarled.

"I'm sure the lad's capable of holding his own. Oh, possibly in the hand that's still working, by the looks of it. He does have back-up for situations like this, I take it?"

"Erm, well, not really," mumbled Lucifer, unhelpfully.

"What do you mean by 'not really'?" Crone was becoming glass-shatteringly shrill.

"Well, to be honest, I didn't really plan too hard with regards to security. What with this being Satan's impregnable inner-sanctum and all. I mostly just collared a likely victim to check invitations at the last minute. He's a big lad though. Commands respect and such. And most people like him..."

"So, one of your fiercest foot soldiers? A warrior? A leader of men? An incorruptible paragon?"

"Hell's teeth, no! Wherever do you think you are, Mr. Crone? Whyever would I employ someone like that?"

Crone gaped. "But it's someone in whom you place a great deal of trust?"

"I, erm, I'm sure it must be? Can't remember exactly who just for the minute..."

Crone unleashed a sound appeared stolen from the large intestine of a flatulent kelpie. "I'm done for. What an ignominious end..."

"I think not, my dear friend," assured Pygott. "If that was indeed The Sisters, I reckon we'd be discussing your funeral amid a desperate army of placation by now. It must be someone else."

"But who do we know that could raise that level of fury?" quizzed Crone. "Let alone have the effrontery to unleash it on Satan's doorstep!"

"Ah, now I have it!" Lucifer ejaculated. "I put Adam on door duty. Which can mean only one thing. Those two never did get on. Once they'd finished getting it on. He never really has gotten over Eve, poor lad."

"Lucky for you, if He's right, Mr. Crone."

"Let her in, you dolt!" roared Lucifer. "You don't have that many ribs left to waste more!"

Crone's own ribs almost ground to powder in the clench of the onrushing apparent harridan. Perhaps an assault by The Sisters might have been less damaging after all?

"My dear Lilith! How wonderful to have you back." Pygott wrestled her into a warm hug just in time to save Crone's face turning from a shade of beetroot to aubergine.

"One day you'll be the death of me, my darling," he gasped, croakily.

"But what a way to go eh, Hinklefry?" Lilith winked her most lascivious wink and planted a habanero-hot smacker on his lips that put every succubus in the hall to shame.

"And Aristophonob, back so soon?" noted Pygott. "I trust everything is in order back at the shop?"

"Everything's as it should be, with a minimum of fuss, Which I must say, after Rumpus's reaction the first time we met makes me, what's the word? Wary." Aristophonob crimped several mouths.

"Indeed it does," intoned Pygott. "I'm staggered you made the journey so very quickly." A tone of accusation softened by a hint of admiring request.

"Ah-ha! I have a million routes in and out of this place. I can get pretty much anywhere topside I want from here."

"You don't say?" Lucifer eased into the conversation avariciously.

"Aristophonob is *our* employee, Nick, remember? Whatever exploitation schemes you have bubbling up inside those horns of yours, you'll have to negotiate terms through us. We can't have valued employees overburdened, can we?"

"Bah," moaned Lucifer. "So many intrigues we could instigate..."

"That's a beautiful dress, by the way, Aristophonob. The colour really complements your eyes. All of them."

"Thankyou, erm, boss." Aristophonob blushed. *Blimey! I can blush!* "Parcelleseus made it for me. Said something about secret agents needing killer duds. No idea what she was twittering on about, but she's, for want of a better phrase, a demon with a sewing machine."

"You look lovely," cooed Crone and Lilith in unison.

"I think I have some lipstick – well, possibly rarefied babies' blood – that will match that perfectly," pondered Lilith. "Why didn't that occur to me before?"

"Perhaps you were distracted by something requiring far more urgency?" proffered Pygott.

Lilith slapped Crone across the buttocks, eliciting an unseemly yelp. "What could be more distracting than fighting my way back here to claim this irresistible prize?"

"I'm confused, dear lady. And please put Mr. Crone down? We all know this was not our agreement. Mr. Crone, please try harder to agree with me!"

Crone tried his best to prize himself away from Lilith's ardour, but could only rise sensibility sufficient to wiggle his head an unsteady couple of times side to side.

Pygott half-started to remonstrate with the pair of them, when he found he could no longer ignore – no matter how hard he strained – the jitterbug of transient convulsions affecting several of Aristophonob's tentacles. Which seemed increasingly systematised with each passing glance.

"Aristophonob, is that – Lilith, *please* don't do that to Mr. Crone's, erm, ear? - is that Aurelian sign language?"

A whole colony of *caterpillar* furry eyebrows raised like a spring tide of exasperation to batter at Pygott's dullardry. 'For Hell's sake, read it!' screamed the nearest tentacle. In Aurelian glyphs.

"Aaah, I see," drawled Pygott, not yet understanding the reason for Aristophonob's stealth, but completely aware that Satan's inner sanctum was definitely not the place to discuss it. And that though whatever it was deserved their attention, this was also not the time to concentrate upon it. "What's the time, Mr. Crone?"

"I, er, ooh! Pardon?" Crone's eyes stared somewhere beyond his partner, trapped between another mouthful of delicious cake and another earful of Lilith's insistent, serpentine tongue.

"You appear to be paying rapt attention to where the big hands and the little hands – no, not you Jeremy, though it's nice to see you – are moving, so you must know what time it is?"

Crone didn't have the foggiest idea. And it was currently *very* foggy inside his steam-soaked brain, but his subconscious retained enough sobriety to instruct one hand to fumble along the silver chain that led to his pocket watch, eased it out and dangled it in front of his eyes at a distance it couldn't be ignored.

"Erm, it's erm, hang on a second, please?" Crone whispered into Lilith's ear, after digging her face out of the burrow it had made in his neckline. She moaned like a little girl robbed of her skipping rope at bedtime and relented, wearing a disapproving pout. "Thankyou, my dear. Now, erm, the time you say, Mr. Pygott? Does that really matter at a revel? We haven't wasted all the toner in the photocopier on pictures of everyone's backsides yet."

"Yes we have! Yours was the first!" crowed a voice from amid the throng somewhere. And before Crone could locate the sound, a paper aeroplane had already been launched above the heads of everyone. It soared gracefully for a while, rising and spiralling on the gathered thermals spinning above the amassed pockets of demons, saints, incubi, succubi, bogeymen, clergymen (so many clergymen!), goblins, gorgons and gargoyles. And then wobbled like a newborn faun before collapsing onto Crone's shoulder.

"This could be anyone," Crone protested, waving the folded paper at the crowd. "There's no-"

"Birthmark!" shot back a guffaw.

"How dare-? Oh..." Crone wilted as he first glanced down at the sections of image jutting out onto the wings. "Well, still, oh dear..."

"So...the time?" asked both Pygott orally, and Aristophonob via a roiling puppet show of glyphs. None of which Crone could understand, bamboozled or not.

"Ah, yes. We've overstayed our, what's the phrase? Not welcome – we're still welcome?" Lucifer nodded equally bemused agreement in Crone's direction. "Our, erm, what am I looking for? Any help? No. Our, ah, allowance?"

"I think that's close enough, Mr. Crone. You can let that breath out now," rescued Pygott.

Crone blinked at him through mal-concentration bulged eyes for a few seconds whilst his brain cells slowly unclenched and relaxed their frustrated strangle tournament.

"Yes, Mr. Pygott! We haven't got the, ahh, no, best not to mention that. I mean, we didn't, erm well, that's best left too. We..."

"Really have left the shop unattended far too long. There's a reason we hardly ever take a holiday! Your hospitality has been superb and we can't thank you enough for the honour you've bestowed upon our humble establishment." Pygott raised his glass – one of them, at least – in toast to their host, who grinned and launched a monumental backslap onto...He looked around at an eddy of swooshing eddies of nothing. His nearest target, Mr. Hul'hu, had stepped aside with a surprisingly nimble two-step. Pygott lobbed a wry smile in their direction and turned to the crowd. "To all of you, thankyou from myself, Mr. Crone, our new Special Projects Executive, Aristophonob and of course the staff, ghosts, bricks and rafters, elementals, vermin, *you* the customers and our favourite, Grande Old Dame that is the Third Left Tentacle. We hope to see you all browsing the aisles and asking us to obtain every impossible, legendary, mythical tome you can possibly dream up. And if it doesn't officially exist, we'll no doubt be able to conjure it into reality for you."

Cue rousing rumble of applause, rising to a crescendo of huzzahs and hear, hears!

Pygott and Crone took bows, waved and shook hands for what seemed something just short of a century as they achingly steadily sidestepped their way towards the exit, with the luggage, Aristophonob and Lilith struggling to keep within touching distance of the receding pair amongst the over-enthusiastic throng.

Finally, twirling at the threshold, the shopkeepers bid farewell to the Lord of Hell.

"Thankyou so much." Crone shook Satan's huge hand with rather more relish than he'd intended. "It's always an adventure coming to your home and we're ever glad to be your guests.. But I won't lie; I really am looking forward to getting home, putting on the kettle and losing myself amongst the most ancient archives we stock."

"Hmm-hmm!" Lilith's nudge practically played a xylophone tune on the opposite ribcage . "Surely you don't need to go all the way home just yet?" Her dismay was painfully plain.

"Patience, my dear. Our travails have been extremely taxing. And more than a little, shall we say, unorthodox? Without respite, I fear I'll be no fun whatsoever."

Pygott intercepted Lilith's protest with a wave of his handkerchief. And aimed an enormous wink in the direction of a fascinated Hell-Lord.

"Well, well...?" Satan pondered. "Are they?"

"My dear Crone! I think you've deserved more relaxation than our humble lodgings can provide. I believe our good friend here can provide exactly the manner of soothing regime that will revitalise you?" He delivered another owlbrow peaked wink of collaboration to their host. Who grinned wider than the black, swampy estuary of the River Styx.

"Not half as much as tantalise you, eh Mr. Crone? Ha-ha-ha!" He grabbed hold of Crone and lifted him off the floor in the most humongous bear-hug. "You're one very base and lucky blighter! Try to survive the 'ordeal', as I'm feverish to visit and hear all about what, erm, relaxation techniques you take advantage of, ha-ha-ha!"

"You saucy old goat!!" Lilith exclaimed and batted Him playfully across the biceps. "You keep your peccadilloes to yourself. And we'll keep our armadillos to ourselves."

Crone looked excited, confused and a tad trepidatious. Though his enthusiasm seemed to be re-exerting more influence than fatigue possibly could. He shrugged a non-committal quip in Lucifer's direction.

"Enjoy yourself, my dears! There's a torture-pleasure penthouse awaiting on the 69th circle. Which even you never expected exists."

"You will be going straight back to the shop...?" puffed Crone.

"Don't worry yourself with the shop, Mr. Crone!" Pygott waved away any thought of protest. "You do look a little peaky. And I fear our adventure has taken much more out of you than we could have expected. An extension – stop giggling Lilith – to your holiday really could prove a real fillip for you. Myself and Aristophonob can pick up business and tie up any loose ends our colleagues couldn't manage. And yes, before you ask, *that* is the first of them. I hardly think you'd want to be involved in the intricate peril simply being in the same room as *it* poses before you've fully recovered your faculties?"

Pygott floated an earnest, knowing stare towards Mr. Hul'hu to head off any chance that anyone might let slip the highly confidential nature of their exchange.

"Oh my dear, no!" exclaimed Crone. "Maybe I *had* ought to stay out of the way until that little job's done? I'd likely only get in the way anyway." Crone paled at the very thought of any chance he'd suffer exposure to that particular 'little job'. An endeavour really best left to Mr. Pygott's skills alone.

"Good, then it's agreed. You two enjoy your rocking and rolling, and that's as close to an order I'll ever give you, Mr. Crone. Be careful not to damage him in any way he doesn't like, Lilith. Now be off with you, you crazy kids!" Satan beamed.

"Mr. Hul'hu; I'm sure we'll see you *very* soon. I'll have some of your favourite funghi from Yoggoth fully matured." Pygott winked as Mr. Hul'hu almost forgot his grumbling stress at the fate of a practically unattended Necronomicon and licked several lips.

"OI! DO YOU MIND?!" called Baal, wiping away a streamer of viscous slime from his face. "LICK YOUR OWN LIPS!"

"Shut up, Baal." Lucifer pushed him aside as He advanced to shake the limbs of His departing guests with gusto. "I look forward to our next mystery hunt!" He winked with enormity as the sudden rise of bile turned Crone's cheeks puce. "Till then, my friends."

Lucifer gave a touching head-bow as He bid them farewell.

"Mr. Pygott, Mr. Crone, Lilith, Aristophonob." He picked a tentacle of Aristophonob's as He spoke her name. She quickly utilised her new-found skills as she realised what an intimate part that tentacle had become since her transition.

"Oh! Erm, my! Best avoid grabbing that one in future, if you don't mind, please?" 'Nob squeaked breathlessly. "But maybe in less formal circumstances...?"

"Saucy!" Satan was incapable of embarrassment, no matter His mortification at the unintended slight. But His shamelessness would always win through. "How inappropriate of me. But then, impropriety is absolutely appropriate in my case, eh?"

"Then I'll see you anon." Aristophonob fluttered several eyelashes in a fan-like wave and, throwing a delicious flirt out of an eye, then another, and finally one last throbbing orb as she skipped off into absence. "Oh, and bye-bye Baal."

And the band of adventurers were gone.

"ARISTOPHONOB!" Baal screamed in frustrated anguish, flailing at thin air, again, and very nearly thrashing Lucifer's still scent following nose across the threshold. "WHERE IS IT? DAMMIT! WHY CAN'T I FIND THE LITTLE SQUIB?"

"BAAL!!!" thundered Lucifer. "Shut up! And get out of my sight. You're banished. No, no – that's too good for now. You've annoyed me far too much. Guards! Take this lunatic and throw him in the deepest pit we have. The one we bought from Calcutta, perhaps? And then when Judas has sobered up – if you ever stop drinking, good man! - and escort him back to his ice-block, make sure Baal's underneath him, staring up his jacksey."

One of the guards sheepishly whispered into one one Satan's ears.

"What? Really? How long has that been going on?"

The guard whispered again. Withdrew. And nodded incredulous affirmation.

"Well, okay then. Take him, enshrine him beneath the ice-block and leave him to stare up David Blaine's ringpiece."

Chapter 69 (dude):
Back to a Rumpus

"Ah, what a sight for very sore, sulphur scorched eyes! It's almost like it's the first time I ever laid eyes on the Third Left Tentacle."

Pygott gazed with relieved adoration up at the facade of his beloved home. And sighed contentedly.

"It's nice to be here on invite too. Rather than having to sneak in and out of the drains on underhoof business for that overstuffed dolt, Baal."

"And we got back here so quickly, by virtue of your clever little back passages."

"I'm as glad as you that I didn't need to hide you there too often..."

"Erm, quite." Pygott instinctually poked a finger in his ear to check once again that none of the weasling gunk had slithered back in. "But if only we'd had you on our side the past, erm, however long we were away would have been over and done with practically before we set off."

"Can you actually remember how long you've been absent? I seem to have only a vague idea that our shadowplay lasted, erm, a while. Or so."

"Moving between Heaven and Earth and Hell and Grimsby has a beguiling effect on one's senses. But however long I finally work it out to have been, there really should have been more than enough time for the weather to go back to normal. Those clouds really shouldn't be staring at us like that, should they?!"

"Nor growling."

"And what is all the discolouration of the air? And roofs. And, well, everything apart from the Tentacle's windows..."

"What colour is it? I can't find words to describe it. Is it even one colour? Purple? Pink? Violet? Puce?"

"Perhaps the colour of The Sisters' faces when they find out that not only have myself and Mr. Crone visited Hell without looking them up, but that Crone diverted his attention from them with the aid of the gymnastic perversions of their immortal enemy."

"Hmm, close." Aristophonob screwed up several eyes in the hope that less focus might bring more clarity. "But it doesn't have that edge of all-consuming fury. This is almost, what's the word? Serene? Unhurried?"

"Dispassionate," grimaced Pygott. "As though it came from the incredibly vast, uncaring immensity of space. What the Devil *is* happening here, Aristophonob?"

Pygott and Aristophonob hurried inside to avoid a stampede of conjoined mutant alpacas and made their way with uncertainty along the ululating carpets towards the main service counter. Something about the shelves seemed eerily disfamiliar.

"Things seem disturbingly...tentacular," mooted Pygott.

"And what's that noise?" queried Aristophonob, her voice trembling. "It seems to be making the floor vibrate so much that I don't need to walk: the floorboards are helpfully bouncing me along in the right direction."

"Perhaps everything will seem normal again after a soothing cup of tea?"

"I'll never understand you humans and your religious reliance on simple beverages."

"Rumpus?" called Pygott as they approached the counter, finding no one minding the till. "Rumpus? Where are you? Why is the shop's geometry all wrong?"

Aristophonob looked around herself doubtfully, all her eyes darting in wide-open uncomprehension at the alien scene surrounding them.

"I can assure you, the shop didn't look like this when I left to rejoin the party." Her noses wrinkled more crinkly than if they'd brought back with them one of the sewers that had served as a short-cut back to the mid-level. She checked around her limbs, pseudopodia and secret recesses, just in case. "And what is that smell?"

"Aristophonob, please lock the shop. I think it best we're not disturbed by customers while we investigate." He nodded gravely at the doors. "But check the aisles first, in case anyone's hiding from the looming pall."

Aristophonob found only a loitering poltergeist and proved surprisingly successful at ignoring its vehement protests and ushering it efficiently out of the entrance. And slammed the door. Apologised as it winced and gently turned the key in the lock. 'Nob made a very careful point of pocketing the key in the safest scale-pocket to counter the poltergeist's strongest talent – that most annoying habit of unlocking recently secured doors, which both mystified and infuriated the safety obsessed dwarf Pygott had begun nervously sweeping the store to find.

"Like I'd believe that rubbish about having lived here since 1543..." 'Nob tutted, shaking one of her heads. "Mr. Pygott? We're all clear out front!"

"Back here," called Pygott's distant, muffled voice. "I seem to have found not only our customer order file zealot, but also our culprit."

'Nob walked into the back-office and made her way around Rumpus's anally-retentively filed shelves of customer orders, tugged one of her forelocks towards licentious library supply specialist, Mr. Pearson, who tore himself away from the bust (sculptural, of course) of Micheline Spiritus long enough to wave a wicked hello and finally faltered as she squeezed into the delivery bay without finding the slightest trace of Pygott.

"You're warm, but still in a draught! Try this way." Pygott's voice was still stifled, but emerging from a more obvious direction.

'Nob changed tack, swivelled left and clicked open the door to the back-back-office. Where she saw only the slightly lopsided, engrossed backside of her boss — well, one of them — and would have been able to hear his attitude of intrigue if not for the confusing babble of unintelligible verbal diarrhoea seeping out into the cosmos from beyond.

Shuffling around the tight space, she finally reached Pygott's level and gazed curiously at a squatting dwarf dribbling spittle in a cascade over the already spittle-sodden beard plastered to his spittle-soppy chest. He was mumbling insanely — apart from the odd blurt of Enochian, or Arabic, or screaming Sutchian — and his eyes were rolling so erratically his eyebrows were in danger of combusting from one of the sparks they threw in whirling parabolas.

"EA-EA!" screeched Rumpus at intervals. Before descending back into gibberish.

"You don't think...?" Aristophonob gawped up at Pygott in hopes he'd pour scorn on the notion. He did no such thing. "Surely he can't have...?"

"The opportune phrase is *'shouldn't have'*, it would appear." Pygott tried to frown, but found his brains leaping in disturbed admiration. "But evidently, he *did."*

"Honestly, if I had the slightest notion, I wouldn't have left him clutching the book." Aristophonob fussed morosely.

"Don't blame yourself, my friend. I would have come to the same conclusion. You can't imagine how relieved I was to hear that you'd left Rumpus clinging to the book like a terrified Golem. What could possibly be safer?"

"I certainly thought so," affirmed 'Nob. Relieved by Pygott's own affirmation. "He seemed too scared of it to even look at the cover — to even admit he could feel it stuffed into his vest. And he seemed even more scared that anyone else might find out that he was hiding it and try to convince him it really exists."

"But it's not Rumpus' innate anxiety that really made him the safe option. The desire to read the book requires not just extensive learning, insight and cunning. Unlocking the secrets behind those virgin-flay recto-

200

verso – indeed, parting them at all – takes a huge degree of ingenuity, creativity and a streak of unorthodoxy."

"Well, that doesn't sound like him *at all!*" sputtered Aristophonob. Pygott stared intently at the little demon, one owlbrow gesticulating towards the snivelling, wild-eyed wreck hunkered behind the day safe. "Ah, yes..."

"Though he regularly drives us all crazy with his unbendable conformity, the reason he is irreplaceable to our staff retine is that he is obsessed, indeed, utterly possessed by order. His personality is veritably crippled by enslavement to tidiness, timeliness, rigidity and an unbending reliance not only on what is correct, but what is intrinsically right. It's one of the main things that serve as an anchor around which all the indulgences we tolerate – nay encourage – revolve. The fairies certainly wouldn't last long without him to act as their surrogate tree." Pygott looked gently into one of Rumpus's eyes whilst trying to decide whether it was safe to approach his once most reliable member of staff. "So you see, what we're faced with here is not only difficult to believe, it should be absolutely impossible."

"How far into it do you think he's actually managed to read?"

"It can't be all of it. Look, he still has some faculties intact. And I can't hear the deafening slap of leather wings battering the ionosphere." Pygott bowed down to spare a sympathetic smile into Rumpus' pleading glances. "My poor friend, what must have come over you? Mr. Crone is going to blow several fuses when he prises himself away from anti-Paradise."

"That's nothing to the reaction that'll explode out of Mr. Hul'hu when he comes to present his next subs! That's not one of his authorised tentacles poking out of the cellar door, is it?"

"Oh my. I can't quite make out if all the sudden cavalcade of adventuring is ghastly or gigglesome. Oh Rumpus, what did this rustling bundle of ill-omen do to break you?"

Rumpus wept, screamed, stared vacantly into what appeared to be the centre of the galaxy and then stretched into a weird ceremonial cephalopod shape.

"Ea! Ea! Cthulhu ftagn!"

"Yes, very good. Enough of that now, Rumpus."

Rumpus levelled eyes with Pygott. And spoke distressingly lucidly.

"I thought if I kept it in my vest I'd be safe. We'd *all* be safe. But they kept talking to me. The voices in the walls, the voices vibrating intermittently from each of my nipples. I'd never taken notice of my nipples before the dark angles began to loom over my sacred dome. In fact, I didn't have a sacred dome before the shambler tapped me on the dimensional shoulder. I've never rambled before..."

"Don't worry, Rumpus. I'm sure we can fix whatever's gone awry."

"We'll sort you out," grinned Aristophonob, swatting away another pseudopodiment that was not only not approved by Mr. Hul'hu, but most definitely not approved by Aristophonob. It hadn't even been delivered by an recognised supplier.

"But the darkness is coming! He who shall not be made cheese will traverse the stars to subjugate the molasses and...oh no! Dark angles save us! He's here! He's...arrrgh-"

THE END.

OF EVERYTHING.

Perhaps...

About the Author

Joz Rhodes is an enduring enigma. At once Messiah and harbinger of destruction; whilst maintaining his position as the fount of wisdom and comfort to an ever-increasing retinue of friends met and comrades yet-to-encounter.

He lives in a South Yorkshire mining village, within spitting distance of Ivanhoe's world-famous Norman castle. Though he tends to be almost constantly on the move in a never-ending attempt to remain one step ahead of the banal frustrations that constitute "normal" existence and escape the attentions of both sunlight and garlic, to both of which he has allergies (the truth! Not a stale marketing ploy).

He spends his time cruelly over-exercising whatever vehicle has the misfortune to belong to him with constant trips between an eclectic collection of gigs, cinematic lurking and being Jesus at Leeds United (yet another truth!). Alongside daily loitering in the darkest woodland in the company of his partner (vampire author L. H. Pritchard) and slavering Hellhounds and, of course, hunched over a pen, transferring to the page a small proportion of the macabre, unspeakable narratives that continually swirl throughout the bilges of his perverse, fervid mind.

Should you wish to risk a lifetime of dark conversation and fellowship, he can be harassed through his entirely inappropriate anti-social media accounts:

Facebook: Joz Rhodes (Official)

Twitter: @unklejoz

Instagram: unklejoz

But please remember, you have been warned...

204

Printed in Great Britain
by Amazon

10592913R00119